ALSO BY DARRYL BOLLINGER

Satan Shoal
The Care Card
The Pill Game
A Case of Revenge
The Medicine Game

THE CURE

A Medical Thriller

DARRYL BOLLINGER

JNB
PRESS

This book is a work of fiction. Names, characters, places, and incidents are the product of the author's imagination or are used fictitiously. Any resemblance to actual events, locales, or persons, living or dead, is coincidental.

JNB Press
Tallahassee, FL

www.jnbpress.com

Printed in the United States of America

First Trade Edition: December 2017

ISBN 978-0-9989975-0-6

For First Sergeant Clark Williams, USMC, Ret.
With many thanks

In 1918, the world saw one of the worst pandemics ever—The Spanish Flu. In one year, the virus killed fifty million people, more people than died in World War I. Spanish Flu was a Type A influenza, a subtype of avian H1N1. No one knows to this day where it came from and how it managed to spread so quickly.

"Even with modern antiviral and antibacterial drugs, vaccines, and prevention knowledge, the return of a pandemic virus equivalent in pathogenicity to the virus of 1918 would likely kill >100 million people worldwide. A pandemic virus with the (alleged) pathogenic potential of some recent H5N1 outbreaks could cause substantially more deaths."

Taubenberger JK, Morens DM.
1918 Influenza: the Mother of All Pandemics.
Emerg Infect Dis. 2006;12(1):15-22.
https://dx.doi.org/10.3201/eid1201.050979

Prologue

On a Wednesday morning in late October, Phillip Brown, Esq. stood at the gate in Terminal 5 at Los Angeles International Airport, waiting to board his flight home to Atlanta.

He was a Platinum Medallion level frequent flyer, which gave him early boarding privileges among other perks. Unfortunately, so were the other twenty people standing in the priority boarding line with him. He wanted to sit, but all the seats in the gate area were taken.

The gate agent announced that the flight was overbooked and she asked for volunteers to give up their seat and take a later flight.

No way, he thought. *Just start boarding so I can get to my seat.* He took a deep breath, feeling light-headed and feverish. Although it was cool this morning, he was sweating. He had loosened his tie, and his jacket hung over his shoulder.

Phillip was a senior partner with Brown & Fox LLP but no relation to the Brown in the letterhead, a detail he often failed to mention unless specifically asked. Brown & Fox was one of the larger law firms in Atlanta, and Phillip managed their international business division.

He had just flown to Los Angeles a few days before, where he had given a presentation to representatives of U.S. companies doing business in foreign countries. On the flight from Atlanta to Los Angeles, the man sitting next to him sneezed and sniffled the entire trip. Phillip chalked up his current malaise to some bug he'd caught on the plane, which he considered an incubator for disease.

"Are you feeling alright?" the petite brunette standing next to him said. "You don't look like you feel well."

Donna Ledford was an associate in a smaller law firm in Atlanta. Phillip had met her previously at another conference, and they discovered this morning that they were on the same flight home.

He shook his head. "Just coming down with a cold, I think. I took some Nyquil and will probably be asleep before the wheels are up."

They eventually boarded, where Phillip asked the passenger in the seat next to him if he would mind changing seats with Donna so they could sit together. He was glad to exchange his window seat for Donna's aisle seat, and everyone got comfortable for departure. Soon after takeoff, Phillip was asleep.

Three and a half hours later as they were making their approach to Atlanta, Donna woke him. "Phillip, you're burning up. Something's wrong." Without waiting for his response, she reached up and pushed the Call button.

Phillip heard the familiar "ding" and blinked. He felt worse now than he did when he was waiting to board at LAX.

He felt like he was in a sauna and he was suffocating. As he removed his tie, he noticed his collar was wet. His shirt was soaked and sticking to his chest. Breathing was difficult and his head throbbed.

"I don't feel so good, Donna." He reached up to open the vent and his hand felt disconnected from his body. The air was cool, but the vent was already open as far as possible. "God, it's hot in here. Aren't you hot?"

He turned to look at her and saw she was wearing a sweater. Phillip was confused, then felt something wet pouring out of his nose. He stuck his tongue out to lick his lip and recognized the metallic taste of blood.

As he took out his handkerchief to wipe his face, Donna's eyes opened wide, and she screamed.

1

Three months earlier.

After a few hours of restless sleep, Eric Carter awoke before sunrise. Rubbing his eyes, he saw Felix sitting beside him in bed. His face only inches away, the Maine Coon was studying him. Eric knew that within a few minutes, the large cat would reach over and gently touch his cheek, imploring him to get up. Felix wanted his morning treats.

"Okay," Eric said, as he reached over and stroked Felix's massive head. "Go on, I'm right behind you." He hoped the cat would take the bait, but Felix didn't buy it. He stayed put, waiting for Eric to lead the way to the kitchen.

Eric laid his head back on the pillow, trying to clear the cobwebs and regretting that last beer the previous evening. Last night, he'd taken his two senior scientists out to Frog Level Brewing to celebrate the forthcoming announcement from the FDA.

They were anticipating the approval of Fluzenta, a new antiviral flu drug. Fluzenta was the first universal flu vaccine. Before now, researchers had to develop a separate vaccine for each new strain of flu, a costly and time-consuming process. Fluzenta was a "smart" vaccine, engineered to adapt to fight comparable types of flu. It promised to revolutionize the immunization of humans against avian flu much as Jonas Salk's vaccine had done for polio.

Felix reached over and lightly touched Eric's cheek, the first warning. Slowly withdrawing the paw, Felix waited for a response.

"Alright, alright. I'm getting up," Eric said, throwing the covers back and then pulling on his sweats. He made his morning bathroom stop while Felix patiently waited in the doorway. Afterwards, the cat followed his owner to the promised land next to the kitchen island. Eric put a small handful of treats in the cat's bowl and then made coffee.

Before the pot finished brewing, he poured a cup and walked out on the deck overlooking the Jonathan Valley below. The morning light was peeking over the distant hilltop and just starting to creep down the mountains. He sat and took a sip of coffee, the warm elixir sliding down his throat.

He and Kate had built this house in the mountains of Western North Carolina ten years ago, on six acres of land next to his Aunt Gertrude and her husband, Harlan. Both properties were adjacent to the Great Smoky Mountains National Park.

In the beginning, he thought Kate shared his lifelong desire to live in the Appalachians, away from the vestiges of civilization. It was only two years later, after the house was finished and their daughter Alison was born, that he learned Kate's goal was to be a socialite instead. Mountain living wasn't in the cards for her.

He thought about Gertrude's sister, his aunt Ida, who raised him on a small farm in the mountains of North Georgia, only a few hours from here. She had died of pneumonia, at least that's what the family doctor had said. Eric had accepted that and vowed to go into medicine to help others.

After four years of medical school at Emory University in Atlanta, he realized that as a physician, he could help thousands, but as a researcher, he could help millions. Once he had fulfilled his military obligation, he opted to go into research instead of private practice.

The more he learned, the more he began to suspect that his aunt had died from bird flu instead. Raising chickens to feed her family, she had intimate contact with them her entire life.

Now that she was gone, there was no way to confirm it. But he had been determined to come up with a cure for avian flu. Fluzenta was the result.

As he watched the sunlight tiptoe down the ridge, he guessed it was close to seven-thirty. Eric went inside, refilled his cup, and toasted a bagel. He spread a little cream cheese on the still-warm bagel and went back out on the deck to eat breakfast before going to the lab. Early mornings were relaxing when your boss was on the West Coast with a three-hour time difference.

An hour later, Eric strode into his office, just in time for his nine o'clock conference call with Frank Liles, the CEO of Tera Pharmagenics. Before he could sit, the phone buzzed.

"Any news yet?" Frank asked as soon as Eric answered. As the listed contact on the new drug application, Eric would be the first to be notified of the FDA's decision.

Eric chuckled. "Frank, believe me, you'll know the minute after I do. You'll probably hear me screaming two thousand miles away. It's only the twenty-fifth, and they have until the end of the month."

"I wish they'd go ahead and make it official. We've been waiting for this moment a long time, my friend."

Eric had known Frank since they started the company a decade ago. Fluzenta had been their progeny and mutual goal. Eric handled the research and development while Frank raised money and dealt with the investors. Now, they were like expectant parents waiting for the birth of their first child. In addition to saving millions of lives, this child had the potential to make them both very wealthy.

He reassured Frank. "There's nothing left for us to do at this point. All we can do is wait for the formal decision."

Tera Pharmagenics had bet everything on Fluzenta. Frank had invested most of his personal fortune in the company. While not as wealthy as his boss, Eric had invested a sizable portion of his retirement savings. A prominent West Coast venture capital firm had invested close to a billion dollars in return for a majority stake in the company. Everyone was counting on the drug to be approved.

"You're still certain it's going to be green-lighted, right?" Frank asked.

Eric nodded, even though he was on the phone and Frank couldn't see him. "The Stage III trials looked excellent. Every indication is that it will be approved. I don't see how they could deny it."

"Call me the minute—"

"I will. Keep your phone close."

Eric hung up, turned, and looked out the window of his office. The forested mountains of Western North Carolina were just beginning to show the slightest hint of the fall color to come.

At Eric's insistence, Tera Pharmagenics had built the Panther Cove facility west of Asheville in Haywood County, near the town of Waynesville. The lab was secluded but close to Atlanta and the Research Triangle area of North Carolina. Most importantly to Eric, it was close to his eight-year-old daughter, Ali, who lived in Asheville with her mother.

He took the stairs to the second floor. Usually, companies had their executive offices on the top floor. Eric had insisted on putting the working lab and most of the scientists on the top floor. The ground floor housed his office along with the other administrative and support offices.

At the entrance to the lab, he paused a few feet in front of the black device that resembled an oversized rearview mirror attached to the wall. It was an iris scanner, the latest in biometric access technology.

Eric placed his index finger on the box mounted below and leaned his head closer to the scanner. The system quickly sampled that part of his eyes, matched his fingerprint, and confirmed his identity. Just as the green light came on and he heard the door unlock, he sensed another person behind him.

"Hey boss," said the voice. "How are you feeling?" Eric recognized it as belonging to Wally Moore, one of his two senior scientists, and turned to face him.

"Heavy-set" was being kind when describing Wally. "Obese" was more accurate. Wally had crumbs on his beard, and his shirttail was out. The pocket of the shirt, with dried remnants of a past meal on the front, was crammed with pens and pencils.

Eric's eyes traveled downward for a moment and settled on Wally's trademark lime green Crocs. He shook his head. It was the same outfit Wally wore last night. The man was unrepentant regarding his looks.

"I feel like I was overserved. What are you doing here?" Eric said.

Wally cocked his head and said, "I work here."

"I thought I told you and Nicole to take today off?"

"Yeah, so what are you doing here?"

"I had a conference call."

Wally arched his eyebrows. "No cell service up on the mountain?"

Eric grinned as he shook his head. "Guilty. But, I'm leaving soon to go to Asheville and pick up Ali. Get out of here—that's an order."

Wally saluted. "Yes, sir. As soon as I finish this regression, I'll be gone."

Inside the lab, Eric turned left to look for Nicole Peters, his other senior scientist. He figured she was at her usual spot, especially since Wally was working.

She had started with Eric eight years ago as a staff scientist and had worked her way up the ranks to the same position as Wally. Incredibly bright and ambitious, she also bordered on reckless at times.

Eric likened the two of them to the proverbial tortoise and hare, with Wally the tortoise and Nicole the hare. Wally had been with Eric from the beginning. Far from a plodder, Wally was just more deliberate and careful.

Frank had wanted to fire Wally on several occasions, but Eric refused. Despite his unkempt appearance, Wally was one of the smartest persons Eric had ever met, and he knew a lot of brilliant people. Wally had received his first degree from MIT when he was sixteen years old, and his PhD before most students start their undergrad major.

Eric turned the corner and as expected, found Nicole hunched over a lab table, her eyes glued to a microscope.

"What am I going to do with you and Wally?" Eric said as he walked up next to her.

She pulled away from the instrument and blinked several times, focusing her blue eyes on him. She was an attractive blonde, with long hair that she usually kept in a ponytail. Her features were delicate, but she was tough and unflappable. Her good looks were disarming and responsible for more than one male to underestimate her intelligence.

"Hey," she said, breaking into a smile. "What brings you up here?"

"I wanted to check before I left to make sure the both of you weren't around. I ran into Wally outside, and now here you are. Does anybody listen to me? I thought I told you both to take the day off?"

She laughed. "So, what are you doing—"

He held up his hands in surrender. "Wally's already busted my chops. I had a conference call, but I'm on my way to get Ali. Teacher's workday, so no school."

"Good for you. Tell her I said, 'Hello.'" Nicole had gone hiking with Eric and his daughter on several occasions. As a result, the two had become close friends.

"I will. Now, I want you and Wally off the premises. When I go back downstairs, I'm telling Carmen to have security escort you to your cars if you're still here in an hour."

She laughed. "Okay, okay. I'll finish up and be on my way out in thirty minutes." She returned her attention to the microscope, and he turned to go back downstairs.

Outside his office, Carmen, his assistant, handed him a stack of paperwork.

"I'm just giving it to you to put on your desk," she said. "I want you out of here in fifteen minutes, or you're going to be late."

He held up his right hand while taking the stack from her. "I promise."

She gave him another folder. "This is the itinerary for your trip. Everything's in order, and I've made a copy for you to give Kate."

In two weeks, Eric was taking Ali to London, just the two of them. With the approval of Fluzenta imminent, Eric had asked Ali where she'd like to go. Without hesitation, England had been her response.

He wasn't surprised. *The Tale of Peter Rabbit* had been her favorite book as a small child. Eric had read it to her so many times, he'd practically memorized it. Now that she was almost nine, she had discovered Harry Potter. Ali's imagination was filled with English gardens, queens, and Hogwarts, so England was a natural.

After much cajoling, he'd convinced Kate to let Ali go. Today, when he picked Ali up, he was going to surprise her with the news.

At a few minutes before the hour, he walked out of his office.

"Good thing you're leaving," Carmen said. "I was about to call security." Eric was usually one of the first people there in the morning and one of the last to go home every night.

"You just want me out of your hair so you can go shopping." Eric was aware of how hard Carmen worked, and had given her tomorrow off as a reward.

She laughed. "I do need a new pair of shoes."

He rolled his eyes and shook his head. "If—"

"I know. If the call comes in, I'll call you ASAP. If you don't have cell service, I'll leave you a message to call me." Cell phone service in the mountains was not always the most reliable.

He smiled and waved. "You're the best, Carmen. Later."

2

Kate and Bryson Edwards lived in Biltmore Forest, a ritzy, old-money enclave that was once part of the late George Vanderbilt's Biltmore Estate just south of Asheville, North Carolina. Eric took Hendersonville Road south off I-40, then turned right on Forest Road. A few minutes later, he turned again and stopped at a gated entrance, just off the street. He pressed the call button and was immediately greeted by Ali's voice.

"Who's there?" she giggled.

Eric smiled and took his cue. This was a game they'd played since she was a little girl. He lowered his voice. "I'm here for Little Red Riding Hood. Let me in."

Ali laughed and played along. "I'm not supposed to let anyone in."

"If you don't let me in, I'm going to huff and puff and—"

"Daddy," she scolded in a mature voice, "that's the wolf in *Three Little Pigs,* not the wolf in *Little Red Riding Hood.*"

Now he laughed. "Oh, that's right. I'm sorry. Let me in, and we'll get it straightened out."

He heard the intercom buzz and saw the iron gate start to swing inward. When Ali was younger, he would intentionally mix up the characters in fairy tales, much to her childish delight. Those days were long gone, but brought back fond memories.

He drove up to the house along the winding driveway, still amazed that the entrance to a personal residence could be that long. Ali was standing at the door of the house as he drove up and parked the Jeep. Kate's house reminded him of a smaller version of Vanderbilt's grand mansion only a few miles away.

As soon as he got out, she ran down the steps and threw her arms out to greet him. He picked her up and hugged her, wondering how much longer he would be greeted this way. As soon as he put her down, she grabbed his hand and led him up the steps. Kate was standing at the door.

"Hello, Eric," she said.

"Kate."

She wore dark slacks and a cream-colored blouse, which complimented her shoulder-length brown hair and matching eyes. She wore her wealth well. At times like these, he still found her attractive, and it made him wish he had worked harder at their marriage.

He'd been involved in a couple of relationships over the past three years, but neither had lasted. Recently, he'd been seeing Rae Thornton, who also was the chief financial officer at Tera Pharmagenics. She was based at the corporate office in Cupertino. That, combined with their busy schedules, left little time together. That arrangement seemed to suit them both at this point in their careers. It was too early to tell if it would last.

"Where's my iPad?" Ali said, looking up at her mom.

"Probably in your room."

"I'll be right back," Ali said before turning and running into the house.

"How are you?" Eric asked Kate.

"Fine. And you?"

He nodded. "I'm doing well, thanks. Excited about this." He pulled the copy of the England itinerary out of his pocket and handed it to Kate. "It's the details on our trip. I'm going to tell her at dinner."

Kate took it without looking at it and shook her head. "I still have misgivings. London is a long way from Asheville, and she's never been away from home this long."

"She'll be okay. It's going to be a great adventure. Beats the heck out of Disney World."

Kate smiled. "I hear you're supposed to get the Fluzenta approval any day now. I'm happy for you, Eric. I know how much it means to you, considering your aunt."

"Thanks. It's been a long time coming." He started to add that he was sorry for his obsession with work over the years but decided he didn't want to go there.

Before either of them could say anything else, Ali reappeared, clutching her iPad and a well-worn brown bear about a foot tall. Eric had given her Bear before he and Kate had divorced three years ago.

"I want to put Bear in my room at your house," Ali said. "We need to do some decorating."

"Have fun. And, be careful," Kate said. She turned her attention back to Eric. "I'll see you around eight."

Eric rolled his eyes and shook his head. The last time he'd taken Ali, they'd been two hours late getting home. Kate had been furious. She and Bryson were attending a charity event and would be late. She'd caused a scene and threatened to take him back to court once again.

He flicked Kate a wave with his free hand, then turned and walked down the steps with his daughter toward the Jeep.

They took the back roads to the Olive Garden restaurant near the Asheville Mall. It was Ali's new favorite place to eat.

As soon as the server brought the bread sticks to the table, Ali attacked them.

Eric shook his head as he picked one up and took a bite. "I've got a surprise for you," he said.

Her eyes lit up, and she glanced over at Eric's backpack, which he'd brought into the restaurant.

He laughed. "It's not in there, silly."

Puzzled, she looked at him for an explanation. "Is it in the Jeep?"

He shook his head. "No. Guess where we're going on your fall break in two weeks?"

She guessed hiking, the beach, and Disney—the usual suspects. Eric shook his head after each one.

After exhausting the possibilities, she shrugged and said, "I give."

"England."

Ali looked at him in disbelief, as if she'd not heard correctly. He repeated it, and her eyes got big. "England? Really? You're not teasing?"

He laughed. "Nope, not teasing. We're going to get on an airplane in Atlanta and fly to England. We'll see castles and gardens and—"

Ali squealed. "The Queen. Can we go to Little Whinging and see where Harry lives?"

Eric recognized the name of the fictitious town outside of London where Harry lived with his aunt and uncle. Ali had fancied herself in the role of Hermione.

"Yes, we can go to Buckingham Palace, where the Queen lives, but I wouldn't count on seeing her. I don't think Little Whinging is a real town, although I'm sure there are some small towns that look like it."

Ali accepted that and asked questions one after another during dinner. Twice, he had to interrupt to ask her to slow down. As usual, she wanted to know all the details.

After they had finished their dessert and he had answered her questions, they headed back to her house.

3

The next morning at the lab, Eric was at his desk when a grinning Carmen stuck her head inside his office door. "Dr. Zheng is on Line 2." She held up her crossed fingers and disappeared, shutting the door behind her.

Dr. Lin Zheng was with the FDA and the official Tera Pharmagenics liaison. This was the call he'd worked ten years for. It had cost him his marriage and many sleepless nights.

He took a deep breath, pasted a smile on his face, and picked up the phone. "Hello, Lin. How are you?" He tried to hide the nervousness in his voice.

"I'm all right, Eric. Thanks for asking. And you?"

For a celebratory call, her tone seemed flat and all business. Warning flags started to surface, but Eric assumed Lin was just following protocol. "Well, so far, I'm alright. I guess it depends on what you have to say."

There was an awkward pause before she continued and now the alarm bells in his head were deafening. Something was off.

"I'm sorry, Eric," she said. Her voice was soft and apologetic.

He clinched the handset of the phone, speechless for the three or four seconds that seemed like minutes.

"Sorry? For what? What are you saying, Lin?"

Zheng continued in a monotone. "The committee has denied the NDA for Fluzenta. I wanted to give you a heads-up."

"What?" He couldn't believe what she was saying. He had spent ten years, ten long years, working on Fluzenta. It had been his life. Tera Pharmagenics had proven the effectiveness of the drug in all three stages of clinical trials. The new drug application was supposed to be a formality. Without it, a company was forbidden from marketing or manufacturing the drug.

"I don't understand. How could they do that?" he asked.

"The committee felt the number of subjects in the Phase III trials was insufficient. They felt that the concept was not proven, given the adverse effects."

He shook his head and struggled to keep his emotions in check. "This is bullshit. It's a new concept, unlike previous flu vaccines. Of course there are fewer subjects. Fluzenta has the potential to save hundreds of thousands of lives. When we have another flu pandemic—when, not if—that number turns into millions overnight. We're already seeing small outbreaks. Did anyone consider that?"

"A mortality rate of 0.2 percent for the drug is publicly unacceptable, Eric."

"You've got to be kidding me? You're a scientist, Lin. The H5N1 virus has a mortality rate in humans of sixty percent. Sixty, as in six zero. So, the committee has decided a 0.2 percent mortality rate is unacceptable? Compared to what?"

"I understand your disappointment, Eric. I can't say any more. As a friend, I just wanted to let you know. You can, of course, appeal."

"When is the CR going out?" The complete response letter was the formal notification of the FDA's action and represented the official public statement.

"In the morning."

He paused, trying to collect his thoughts. The news would hit the streets first thing in the morning, and there was nothing he could do to stop it. Another idea crossed his mind.

"Somebody sabotaged us, didn't they?" he asked.

"Eric, you know better than that." Her voice took on an air of indignation. "We don't work that way. I was calling you out of respect for what you've done, and I resent your implication."

"Well, we're going to appeal. You can count on it." He slammed the receiver back in the cradle, disconnecting the call.

Now what? he thought as he massaged his stiff neck. He couldn't believe the FDA was denying Fluzenta. Ten years, down the drain. This fucking close to achieving his lifelong dream and derailed because of what he viewed as technicalities.

He stood and walked over to the window, looking out at the mountains. He'd have to call Frank with the bad news. Before he talked to Frank, he needed to find Wally and Nicole. They deserved to hear it first.

Eric stepped outside his office and over to Carmen's desk. She looked up and smiled. She started to speak, then hesitated when she appeared to recognize the devastated look on her boss's face.

He shook his head. It was a few seconds before he could get the words out. "It's going to be denied."

An incredulous look flashed across her face, soon replaced by pity. "How . . ." She shook her head. "I'm so sorry, Eric."

He shrugged, at a loss for words. At last, he found his voice and said, "Could you get Wally and Nicole here as soon as you can? Please."

He turned and walked back into his office, over to the window. Ten minutes later, he was still standing there staring at the mountains when he heard Wally walk in.

"What's up, boss? Have you heard anything from DC?"

Trying not to telegraph the news, he turned to face his lead scientist. "Let's wait on Nicole."

They didn't have to wait long. Two minutes later, with Wally pacing the floor in Eric's office, Nicole walked in, shutting the door behind her.

Eric gestured to the small conference table next to his desk, walked over, and sat in his usual seat. Following his example, Nicole and Wally sat in their seats.

"I just got off the phone with Lin Zheng," he said. They both smiled, anticipating the good news.

Eric shook his head, forcing the words out of his mouth. "The FDA is denying Fluzenta."

Incredulous, Wally glanced at Nicole, then looked back at Eric. They both realized he wasn't joking. "You've got to be fucking kidding me," Wally said, anger in his voice.

Before Eric could answer, Nicole said, "This is bullshit. There's no freaking way they can justify denying it."

Eric nodded. With words sticking in his throat like a bitter pill, he got to the point. "The committee met, and the CR is going out tomorrow. It's done."

Nicole started swearing and shaking her head. "They can't do this. Does anybody realize the consequences?"

"They can, and they did," Eric said, his voice flat.

"What are they going to do when people start dropping like flies?" Wally asked.

To everyone's knowledge, there was no alternative to Fluzenta. No other universal vaccine was in the pipeline anywhere in the world. A flu pandemic would be disastrous.

"What basis?" Nicole added.

"I don't know," Eric said, answering Wally's question first. Paraphrasing Dr. Zheng, he said, "Basically the committee decided there was inadequate evidentiary proof of achieving the primary end concept, partly because of the small number of subjects in the Stage III trials."

Nicole shook her head. "If there was a problem with the number of patients, why didn't they bring that to our attention at the time?"

"Inadequate evidentiary proof?" Wally said, his voice getting louder and his face red. "Since when does a statistically significant cure rate with acceptable side-effects not meet the standard?"

Eric held up his hand. The angry reactions of his two top scientists had a curious calming effect on him. "Trust me, I'm as upset as you about this. I'm surprised you didn't hear me screaming on the phone."

He paused for a moment to collect himself before continuing. "But . . . it is what it is. We can't change the fact that it is going to be denied. The letter is going out first thing in the morning."

"We're appealing it, right?" Nicole said, leaning forward, her intensity matching Wally's.

Eric nodded. "The minute I get the response, I'm sending a request for an end-of-review meeting. That's the first step in the appeal process and the most important. It's our best shot at getting the decision reversed."

Wally snorted and held up his index finger against his thumb. "That's the odds of a successful appeal. And you can't submit additional data, right?"

Eric tried to remain optimistic, even though he knew Wally was correct, both in his assessment of the odds and in his statement about not being able to submit additional data.

"I know of several cases where companies were successful in the review process. They have to give us an end-of-review meeting within thirty days of the denial. That will be our best opportunity, probably our only chance."

"What was Liles's response?" Nicole asked.

"He doesn't know yet. I wanted to tell you first. He's next."

After they had left his office, Eric sat there for thirty minutes, staring out the window, trying to figure out what he was going to say to Frank. At last, he picked up the phone and called Frank's cell. It went to straight to voice mail.

Goddammit, Eric thought. Frank said he'd have his phone next to him. The one time Eric needed to reach him and . . .

He shook his head and hung up. Maybe it was a good thing he didn't have to tell him yet, though it wouldn't be any easier later. This was a huge disappointment, and there was no way to put a positive spin on it.

By habit, Eric started to gather a few things from his desk to stuff in his backpack, then decided against it. *Screw it.* Everything would still be there in the morning. Checking to make sure he had his keys, he walked out of his office and stopped at Carmen's desk.

"I've got to get away," he said, his voice serious. "Hiking, fishing—something outside."

She nodded, understanding what he was saying. Carmen was Cherokee and looked it, with the straight black hair, high cheekbones, and reddish-brown complexion common to many Native Americans. To her, his comment wasn't strange. She not only believed that man could communicate with animals and nature, but she believed it to be therapeutic.

"Are you okay?" she asked.

He shrugged and then shook his head. "No, I'm in shock right now. That's why I need to leave, to clear my head. I called Frank, but it went to voice mail." He held up his cell phone. "If he calls–"

As if summoned by the gesture, the phone rang. The two of them looked at it, and then Carmen gave him a look as if to say, "I'll take a message."

He was tempted, but shook his head, and turned to go back into his office. As he shut the door, he answered.

"Eric. Where are you?" Frank said.

"In my office. I just tried to call you."

"Peggy and I are in Mendocino. We came up for a few days, and you know how spotty the cell service can be here." Frank had a house in Mendocino, on a cliff overlooking the Pacific Ocean. "Do you have news?"

Eric hesitated, not knowing how to phrase the disappointing message. There was no good way to say it. "Fluzenta is going to be denied."

There was a long pause on the line. "You can't be serious?" Frank said.

"Unfortunately, yes. Lin Zheng called me this afternoon to give me a heads-up. They're announcing the decision tomorrow morning."

There was another stretch of silence on the phone. "What the hell happened?"

Eric repeated what Lin had told him. "Bottom line from Lin is that the FDA was unwilling to buy a 0.2 percent mortality rate. That combined with a 'small number of subjects' in the Phase III trials. Soon as I get the CR, we'll request an end-of-review meeting."

"That's insane. Sixty percent versus 0.2 percent? That should be a no-brainer."

"That's exactly what I told her."

"What a cluster. I had the plane standing by to pick you up as soon as we heard. We were going to New York to meet with Chip and several other investment bankers. I was hoping it would be a chance to celebrate. Now, it's going to be a lynching."

"I'm sorry, Frank." Chip Miller was the head of the venture capital fund that had bankrolled Tera Pharmagenics.

"What do you think our chances are on appeal?" Frank asked.

Eric hesitated. He had known Frank too long and wasn't going to bullshit him. "Maybe fifty-fifty, although as you know, the track record for winning appeals is not great. We've got to sit down, take a look, and see what we can do to try and satisfy the committee."

"Fifty-fifty? Thanks for the encouragement. What a fucking disaster. Now what?" Frank asked. The anger crept through and displaced the disappointment.

"We need to tell the staff here as soon as possible."

"I need to call Liz, get her moving on damage control." Liz Manning was the vice president in charge of communications at Tera Pharmagenics. "We need to try to get out front on this. Maybe I can fly in next week—"

"It can't wait that long, Frank. We need to do it tomorrow."

"Goddammit, I can't believe this. Chip is going to freak. We have got to get this to market."

"If you can't make it, I can meet with the staff here, but we can't put it off."

"No, they need to hear it from me. Set up a video conference tomorrow, tomorrow afternoon."

"Okay, I'll set it up."

"We need to get everyone together ASAP and figure out what we're going to do. I'll talk to you later."

The line went dead as Frank disconnected.

4

Outside, Eric made his way to the old, red Jeep Wrangler parked in the fourth row of the employee parking lot. He didn't believe in reserved parking, and all employee parking at the lab was first-come, first-served. Since he'd come in late this morning, he was farther back than usual.

He opened the unlocked door and climbed in. He couldn't remember that last time he'd locked the Jeep, figuring that with an old ragtop there was no need.

When he turned the key to start the engine, he thought the starter sounded sluggish and for a moment wondered if it would crank. The engine caught, and he breathed a sigh of relief.

The Jeep had over 200,000 miles on it and needed a new battery and tires among other things. He had planned to get a new Jeep once Fluzenta was approved, but given the news he'd just received, that was probably out for now.

He pulled out of the lot and drove to I-40, heading west toward home. His house was only twelve miles away, but in the mountains, that could take twenty minutes or more. *Mountain miles,* he called it.

Eight minutes later, he exited the interstate and headed south on US 276. At Hemphill Road, he took a right. When he got to the bridge over Jonathan Creek, he thought about stopping there and fishing. He'd caught lots of trout in that stretch of water, but then he remembered his fly rod and vest were at home instead of in their usual place in the back of the Jeep.

He got to the house and quickly changed clothes, only pausing to give Felix a few treats. Putting his fishing vest on, he grabbed his fly rod and walked back outside. One of the benefits of living next door to the Park is that world-class trout fishing was only footsteps away.

Halfway to the split-rail fence marking the Park boundary, he stopped as he heard a car. A powder-blue VW convertible pulled up behind his Jeep and parked. He shook his head. He only knew of one person with a car like that. Nicole Peters.

She got out of the car, wearing shorts and what looked like a t-shirt. He watched as she slowly walked over. She stood there, hands in her pockets.

"Carmen said you went to the woods. I thought I might find you here. What did Frank have to say?"

He shrugged. "He was devastated, like the rest of us. We're scheduling a video conference for tomorrow afternoon so he can announce it to the staff. I needed to clear my head, so I decided to go fishing."

"I was worried about you."

"I'm fine. At least, I will be soon as I get over there," he said, nodding toward the fence.

"Sorry, I didn't mean to intrude."

"You already have."

A frown crossed her face, morphing into a look of hurt. The remark was cutting and ruder than he intended it to be. Silently, she turned to leave.

"Nicole, I'm sorry. I didn't mean that to be so short. Why don't you grab your gear and join me?"

She hesitated, and he added, "I could use the company if you're willing to put up with a foul-tempered old man."

"Where are you going? I don't have my stuff with me."

"My secret spot, not far. I can get another rod, or we can take turns."

She nodded toward the fence. "Let's just share. I don't have any of my gear with me, and I don't want to hold you up."

Out on the Cataloochee Divide Trail, headed toward Hemphill Bald, they paused at the edge of a steep muddy bank.

"Here's where we get off," he said. He looked down at her running shoes and frowned. "You sure? You might get those designer shoes of yours dirty."

She playfully slapped his arm. "I'm willing to risk it, Mountain Man. Come on."

With Eric leading the way, they carefully picked their way down the muddy slope to the stream. At the water's edge, they stood, admiring the pristine water gurgling next to them.

"This is awesome," she said looking from one side to another. "It's beautiful. And not a single trail leading to it. I can't believe you've never brought me here to fish."

"I've never brought anyone to this spot. I told you, it's my secret spot."

He took his rod out of its case, assembled it, and tied on an Adams Parachute, one of his most productive dry flies. Though the water was cool, the air temperature was warm and the stream shallow, so he didn't need waders.

He offered the rod to Nicole, but she shook her head. "Your spot. Show me how," she said.

He waded out into the water, stripped out some line, and made his first cast upstream. As soon as the fly landed on the water, a trout hit it, probably a rainbow. Eric was ready. He raised the rod, tightening the line and setting the hook. He could tell it wasn't a large fish, but it put up a fight, determined to spit out the fly.

As he got the fish close, Eric reached over his shoulder and grabbed the landing net. He scooped up the fish, carefully handling it to remove the barbless hook. It was a beautiful rainbow trout, around twelve inches long.

"Nice fish," Nicole said. "That didn't take long."

Kneeling, Eric gently cradled the fish in his uplifted hand, pointing its head upstream into the current. With water flowing through his gills, the fish quickly recovered. He flicked his tail and darted away.

Eric smiled and stood. He never tired of it. Fly fishing was primitive, just the angler versus the fish. No boats, no fish-finders, no fancy equipment. Although you could spend a small fortune on an outfit if so inclined, it wasn't necessary. The sport hadn't changed much over the years. To him and most fly-fishers, it was both personal and spiritual.

He handed the rod to Nicole, and they waded a few yards upstream. He stopped and pointed to a spot just above her. She nodded and stripped out some line, then cast the fly into a nice pool on the right side of the stream. "Sorry I disturbed you," she said.

Once again, as soon as the fly landed, the fish hit it. She jerked the line but was a split-second too late. "Dammit. Missed him."

Eric chuckled. "Forgot to tell you they are aggressive up here. They usually hit it when it lands." He motioned upstream. "Might as well move. You get one chance per spot."

They waded along the edge of the stream for another ten yards where he stopped again.

"You don't think the odds of winning an appeal are good, do you?" she asked.

He hesitated as he studied her face. She was hopeful and optimistic, and the naivety showed. He shook his head. "No, Wally's right. The odds aren't in our favor."

The corners of her mouth turned down. "What happens then?"

"I honestly don't know, Nicole. I'd convinced myself it would be approved. Rightly or wrongly, I refused to even think about the alternative."

"Can Tera Pharmagenics survive?" She stared at him, waiting for an answer. In the fading daylight, he was tempted to give her the corporate answer. He couldn't do it.

"Probably not."

"What will you do?"

He shrugged. "I don't know. But, I can't leave this area, job or not. Ali's here, and that takes priority."

They fished for a couple of hours, catching a half-dozen rainbows between them with little conversation. Noticing the light starting to fade, Eric said, "We should probably head back to the house. It gets dark earlier in the mountains."

They waded back downstream to where they first entered the water. Nicole took some pictures with her phone, and after a few minutes, they headed back up the muddy slope to the trail. Eric insisted that she go first so that if she slipped, he could hopefully catch her.

About halfway up, Nicole lost her footing and squealed as she started to slide down the bank. Eric reached out to grab her hand as she slid past him. Unfortunately, he had not firmly planted his feet, and he lost his balance, too.

Holding on to each other, they rolled fifteen feet or so down the bank before stopping. Both of them were covered with mud from head to toe.

"Are you okay?" Eric asked.

Nicole sat in the mud, testing her appendages. Everything appeared to be working, and she said, "Yeah, just a little—" As she looked over at him she started giggling, which soon erupted into hysterical laughter.

"What?" he said, at first wondering what was so funny, then realized that she looked like something from the *Creature from the Black Lagoon.* At that point, he started laughing.

They sat there for a few minutes in the mire, laughing so hard that they couldn't even attempt to stand.

Although he couldn't see himself, he knew he had to look as ridiculous as Nicole. Covered with layers of mud, they finally picked their way back up to the trail and headed home.

When they got close to the house, Nicole turned and gave him a questioning look.

"Oh, no," he said, pointing to the stairs on the left of the front door that led directly to the deck. "Straight to the shower."

When they got to the other side of the house, he pointed to the outdoor shower at the far end, by the bedroom. "You first," he said as he stooped down to remove his dirt-encrusted hiking boots.

She shrugged, marched down to the shower, and turned it on to get the hot water going. She sat on the small bench and took off muddy shoes and socks. Then, without hesitation, she stood and slipped off her muddy clothes, leaving them in a puddle next to the shower as she stepped underneath the showerhead, completely naked.

Eric couldn't help but watch as she calmly turned around underneath the stream of water, rinsing off every speck of mud. Casually, she shampooed her hair and bathed every inch of her body with the bath soap before rinsing off.

She shut the shower off and turned to face him, making a feeble but unsuccessful attempt to cover herself. "Any towels?" she asked.

He hesitated for a moment as he tried to process her question, still admiring the sight before him.

"Hello?" she asked.

"Uh, yes, just inside the sliding door behind you."

"Thanks. You're up," she said as she turned to open the door to the master bath and step inside.

He froze, waiting for her to emerge. A few minutes later, she came out wearing his bathrobe and a towel wrapped around her head. She shook her head. "Are you going to wash that off, mud man, or is that your new look?"

He chuckled and walked over to the shower. Nicole passed him, going over to the table, where she sat.

He turned the shower on and kept his back to her while he peeled off his muddy clothes. Dropping them on top of hers, he stepped under the shower and rinsed the mud off, determined to be just as cavalier about it as she had been. As he turned, he was conscious of her watching him just like he had watched her.

After he had finished, he went inside and toweled dry. He put on a pair of shorts and a t-shirt, then returned to the deck. Nicole sat at the table, drinking a glass of water.

He gathered the dirty clothes and took them inside, dumped them in the washing machine and started it.

"I put the clothes in to wash," he said when he returned to the deck and sat across the table from her. "You can dry your hair now and . . ."

She shook her head, still laughing. "Mind if I borrow some clothes?"

He hadn't thought about that. "Uh, I'm not sure mine will fit."

She laughed again, tugging at the lapels of the bathrobe she was wearing, exposing a brief glimpse of cleavage. "Well, I suppose I could wear this until my clothes are done. But, I'd rather put something else on."

"I've got some shorts and a shirt you can borrow. Probably be quite loose on you, but you're welcome to them."

"Thanks," she said, getting up and exposing a fair amount of leg in the process. She stood, waiting for him. When he didn't move, she continued. "Do you want me to just rummage through your closet or is there something in particular you had in mind?"

He bolted out of the chair. "Sorry, just not thinking." He walked with her into his bathroom, acutely conscious of her pleasant scent. She stopped at the sink, unwrapping the towel from around her head as he continued to his closet.

In the closet, he reached for a white dress shirt, then realized the only bra Nicole had was currently in the washing machine with the rest of her clothes. *Not good,* he thought as he replaced the white shirt with a dark t-shirt that he hoped wouldn't accent her chest. He held it up and shook his head. *Too clingy.* Returning it to the closet, he grabbed a blue dress shirt with a checked pattern. It was thicker and would fit looser.

He grabbed a pair of hiking shorts and returned to the bathroom, where Nicole was drying her hair. Her robe had loosened at the top, exposing a patch of bare skin below her neck.

Trying to avert his eyes, he lay the shorts on the counter and then hung the shirt on the doorknob. As he turned to walk out, he hesitated as it dawned on him that she didn't have any underwear. *Nothing he could do about that,* he thought.

Returning to the deck via the kitchen, he decided he needed a drink. He opened the door to his wine refrigerator and quickly removed the first bottle of red he found. He opened it, poured himself a healthy portion, and then took a big swallow. Hoping the alcohol would settle his nerves, he brought the bottle and two glasses with him to the table on the deck.

After sitting, he took another large swallow, almost emptying the glass. He wondered why he was so nervous.

Duh, he thought, answering his question. Nicole was a beautiful, young woman who had just paraded naked for him moments ago on this very deck. The problem, he reminded himself, was that she worked in his division and reported directly to him. In his head, he heard the voice of his first boss and mentor saying, "Don't fish off the company dock."

He wondered if Nicole's actions were deliberate. It seemed so innocent. Yes, he had spent a lot of time with her and no doubt they had become close friends. He had never entertained any such thoughts about her and couldn't believe that she would think that about him. After all, there was a good fifteen years difference in their ages, enough that Nicole could theoretically be his daughter.

When she appeared, he was relieved to see that the shorts were baggy and that his shirt, with only the top two buttons undone, was mercifully chaste. He figuratively patted himself on the back for reining in his runaway imagination.

"You started without me," she said as she sat. He poured her a glass of wine and toasted their muddy adventure.

Since she couldn't very well go out in public dressed in his clothes (and wearing no underwear, he reminded himself), he proposed that they have a simple salad and pasta for dinner. As they sat and relaxed, he heard the roar of an engine coming up his drive.

It took him a moment to realize it was Harlan, his Aunt Gertrude's husband and next-door neighbor.

5

The four-wheeler shut down and Eric waited for Harlan to make his way around the corner and up the steps to where they waited.

"Hey, Eric–" The elderly man froze when he saw Nicole, his left foot midway between the top step and the deck. "Oh, I'm sorry, didn't mean to interrupt. I was wondering whose car that was."

A little too loudly, Eric said, "Oh no, you didn't interrupt. Come on up and have a seat."

Harlan hesitated as if mulling over the idea before he limped over to the table. Eric and Nicole stood as Eric introduced them.

"Harlan, this is Nicole Peters. She, uh, works at the lab. Nicole, this is Harlan Burgess, my Aunt Gertrude's husband. They live next door."

Harlan looked Nicole up and down, no doubt wondering why she wore what were obviously Eric's clothes. He looked over at Eric and gave him a thin smile. Eric swore the man winked.

Eric insisted that Harlan join them, and quickly went inside the house to fetch him a glass of water. When he came back out, the two were sitting at the table laughing.

"I was just telling him what happened on our hike," Nicole said.

God, I hope she left out the part about the shower, Eric thought as he laughed nervously.

"I was just coming over to see if Ali was here and invite y'all to supper," Harlan said.

Eric shook his head. "No, I was just showing Nicole one of my fishing spots over in the Park when we fell and got all muddy and then had to clean up."

Harlan nodded, that same knowing grin crossing his face.

Eric felt his face flush. He looked over at Nicole, sitting there all too comfortably, barefooted, wearing Eric's shirt and what was obviously a pair of his shorts. He could imagine what Harlan was thinking.

"Well, now, Gertrude's got plenty cooked. Y'all are welcome to come over and eat with us. That is if y'all don't already have plans," Harlan said as he glanced at Eric and smiled.

"We'd love to," Nicole answered.

* * *

After the meal, on the way back to the house in Eric's Jeep, Nicole reached over and patted Eric's hand. "No offense, but that was way better than a salad and pasta."

He had to agree. As usual, Gertrude had put out a spread. Cornbread, fried chicken, mashed potatoes, and fresh vegetables. She and Nicole had hit it off. After dinner, Nicole had insisted on helping Gertrude do the dishes, which won her major points with the elderly woman.

Then, Gertrude had insisted on coffee and dessert and visiting afterward. Eric was helpless as he watched his entire day continue to spin out of control. His only regret was that since Gertrude didn't drink alcohol, there was no wine with dinner. Harlan, however, had taken Eric out to the barn for a little nip of moonshine, which Eric greatly appreciated, and Gertrude pretended to ignore.

Eric pulled his Jeep under the carport and switched it off. There were no lights on in the house, and as always, he was amazed at how dark it was in the mountains of Western North Carolina, far away from any metropolitan area.

They got out of the Jeep and leaned up against it, looking up at the stars, waiting for their eyes to adjust. It was a new moon, and there was very little ambient light.

"This is so amazing," Nicole said, as she sidled up next to him. Instinctively, he put his arm around her, not thinking.

"Are you cold?" he asked.

"I'm fine now, just a little chill is all."

They stood that way, watching as more and more stars became visible, neither of them saying anything for the longest time.

"Oh my God," she said, pointing up above. "That's the Milky Way, isn't it?"

"Yes, it is. Beautiful, huh? Hard to see that in southern California."

She elbowed him in the ribs.

"Let's go sit out on the deck. You better lead the way," she said, taking his hand.

As they sat out on the deck, he asked if she wanted anything to drink.

"A glass of wine would be nice. And, a blanket," she replied.

As he stood up to go into the house, she grabbed his arm. "Don't turn on any lights. I want to keep looking up at the sky."

As he slid open the door and walked into the kitchen, he knew Felix was close by and stopped.

"Okay, Felix. You can see better than me, so stay out of my way. I don't want to trip over you, you big oaf." He stood still for a few seconds, then felt the big cat rub up against his leg, even though he couldn't see him in the dark. Now that he knew where Felix was, he made his way toward the kitchen.

In the dim glow of the nightlight over the kitchen counter, he could make out the opened bottle of wine and the two wine glasses they had used earlier. Glasses in one hand and wine in the other, he gingerly made his way back to the sofa, careful not to trip over Felix, who he knew was somewhere close. He stopped to pick up a blanket, put it under his arm, and went outside.

Back on the deck, he was puzzled to see no one at the table. He looked around, wondering where Nicole was, and then heard her say, "Over here." He turned and could barely make her out, sitting on the bench up against the wall of the house.

He poured them each a glass of wine and then sat next to her, pulling the blanket over them. She cuddled up next to him, and he could feel her warmth.

"To a good day fishing, in spite of falling in the mud," she said, raising her glass.

He laughed and raised his glass. "A good day fishing."

Eric remembered that he had not put their clothes in the dryer. It was late, and she was still wearing only his shirt and shorts. Preparing to get up and do so, he said, "I need to go put your clothes in the dryer."

"In a minute," she said.

He was suddenly aware that only a very thin layer of cloth separated them. He tensed when he felt her hand on his bare leg underneath the blanket. She let it rest there for a few minutes until he relaxed. Then, she lightly moved it up his leg. His breathing quickened, and he felt aroused, unable to fight it. All he could think about was her showering and the water glistening off her incredible body.

Sensing his reluctance, she took his hand and put it inside of his shirt, the shirt she was wearing. He vaguely knew that more than a couple of buttons were unfastened, but he didn't remember how that happened. All he knew now was that he could feel her nipple stiffen as his fingers touched her breast, and he heard a faint moan escape her throat.

Eric closed his eyes and surrendered, knowing he was helpless to resist.

* * *

The next morning, Eric awoke, trying to clear the cobwebs from his half-asleep brain. Even though he was in his bed, he was disoriented. Nicole was lying next to him, her head on his shoulder. As his body awakened, he realized they were naked underneath the covers.

She stirred and blinked her eyes open. “Good morning,” she said as she snuggled closer.

He couldn’t help but grin. “Good morning.”

Her smile reassured him there were no regrets, at least now, at least for her. He wasn’t so sure.

They lay there for another fifteen minutes, neither of them saying anything. Eric was feeling awkward, unsure of what to say or do. Nicole seemed content in his arms, but at some point, one of them was going to have to get up out of bed.

Deciding to be chivalrous, he declared, “I’m going to go make us some coffee.”

He pulled his arm free and sat on the edge of the bed. His clothes from last night were nowhere in sight. *Oh well,* he thought. He stood and walked out of the bedroom, not looking back. In the bathroom, he stopped to pee, then went to the closet and found some sweats to slip on before making his way to the kitchen.

Felix was waiting for him. He gave the cat a small handful of treats, then made coffee. He heard Nicole in the bedroom and was wondering what to say to her when she appeared. He started the coffee, then took two mugs out of the cabinet.

"Are you okay?" she said as she walked into the kitchen.

He turned to look at her. She'd found another of his shirts, thankfully a loose-fitting flannel one, and was wearing a pair of his sweatpants. "I—we shouldn't have done that," he blurted.

She looked at him with a hint of sadness and pity. She walked over and put her arms around his waist. Reflexively, he started to put his arms around her, but then took her shoulders and gently pushed her away. He stared into her blue eyes, trying to remain detached. "Nicole, we can't—"

She raised up and kissed him, then pulled back, a look of satisfaction on her face. Before he could speak, she placed her finger against his lips and smiled.

"I know. I understand, believe me, I do. But I'm not going to say that I didn't enjoy it and that I didn't want you because that would be a lie. And don't tell me you didn't enjoy it, either."

He tried to speak, and she pressed her finger harder.

"Let me finish." She lowered her finger and took his hand. "I don't have any regrets, and I don't want you to, either. It happened, and we can't undo it. Let's agree to accept it for what it was and move on. We've got to focus on how to get Fluzenta to market, right?"

He nodded, relieved to hear her say that. It was a mistake, and they both agreed. Now, the challenge was to move past it.

6

The next day at work was chaos. The disappointing news had spread throughout the lab like a virus. As soon as Eric got to his office, he shut the door and called Lin Zheng.

"Dr. Zheng's office. May I help you?" Eric assumed the pleasant voice belonged to Lin's secretary.

"Hi. This is Dr. Carter, with Tera Pharmagenics. Is Lin available? I just need a minute, please." He didn't like to use his title but hoped that it and the reference to Zheng by her first name might facilitate his route past the gauntlet of a protective assistant.

"I'm sorry, she's in a meeting right now. May I take a message?"

He wasn't sure whether Lin was in a meeting, or she had given orders not to put calls from Eric Carter through. He couldn't blame her if it were the latter.

"Yes. Would you please tell her that I called to apologize for my rude behavior yesterday? I was caught off-guard and acted like an ass—you can quote me on that. If you could put me through to her voice mail, I would appreciate it."

There was a snicker, and he heard the clicking of keys on the other end. Hopefully, the woman was entering the message verbatim. "Just a minute, and I'll put you through to her voice mail."

Eric thanked her and left a short, but apologetic message for Lin and asked her to call him at her convenience, leaving his cell number. He didn't expect her to call back, but he was hoping the gesture would impress her with his remorse.

Meetings and phone calls filled the rest of the morning. Frank called to say that he scheduled an emergency management meeting the next day in Cupertino. Since he didn't offer the company plane, Eric had Carmen book him a direct flight out of Atlanta.

It was a morose group of Tera Pharmagenics employees gathered together in the Panther Cove cafeteria at one o'clock for the video conference. The room was abuzz with whispered conversation when on the wall-sized screen, Frank Liles strode across the small stage to the podium. The room quietened as the camera zoomed in on the face of their leader as he adjusted the microphone, preparing to speak.

"Good afternoon," he said, flashing his trademark smile. The last vestiges of conversation in the cafeteria died down, overpowered by the amplified voice of their CEO.

He gripped the edges of the lectern and gazed out over his virtual audience, seeming to let his eyes pause for a few seconds several times as if recognizing a familiar face.

"I apologize for not being able to speak to you in person, but it was important that we get together as quickly as possible."

Eric had to admit, the man was charismatic. He knew Frank was looking at a monitor, but the feeling in North Carolina was that Frank was in their midst, talking to each of them individually.

"I'm sure most of you have heard the news by now. The only thing faster than the Internet is the Tera Pharmagenics grapevine." A few chuckles rose from the live audience. "For those of you who haven't heard, the NDA for Fluzenta has been denied." Frank paused to let the news sink in.

Standing near the entrance, Eric looked around the cafeteria. There were nods, and everyone was waiting for the other shoe to fall. He felt a twinge of guilt when he saw Nicole and Wally standing near the door. He regretted last night, but as she said, they couldn't undo it. He was determined to put it aside.

Frank continued, not bothering to look at his notes. "Everyone is abuzz about what this means to Tera Pharmagenics and each of us as stakeholders. That's why I wanted to meet with you, so you hear it straight from the top."

He paused for effect. "Fluzenta has undergone rigorous testing over the past six years. It has proven to be a safe and effective drug to treat multiple strains of avian flu, the first such drug to do so. Since this is a unique drug involving a new concept for flu vaccines, we underestimated how to effectively convey that message in our application. We have requested a review meeting, and are confident that in the appeals process, we will prevail."

Eric shook his head and allowed a thin smile. He could see Liz's hand in this. It was smart to publicly admit it was the company's fault and not bash the FDA. Tera Pharmagenics didn't need any enemies on the committee.

"Let me assure you, while this is undoubtedly a setback, this is *not* the end of Tera Pharmagenics. We are firmly convinced that the world needs Fluzenta and we intend to vigorously pursue our appeal. It is too important, and we can't afford to waste time. We need to be stockpiling the vaccine now, so we're all ready for the next outbreak."

Frank let the applause fade away before continuing to speak. "At the same time, we also have other drugs in various stages of development. Those efforts are still on track, and we remain optimistic about the future of Tera Pharmagenics."

Once again, employees applauded, both in the cafeteria and on screen. Eric maintained a neutral expression. He knew that Tera Pharmagenics had cannibalized the other projects to get Fluzenta to the finish line, counting on this drug to finance the others. He guessed that most of the employees in this room knew that as well. Without Fluzenta generating much-needed cash, there was no way to ramp back up on the other ventures in time to save the company. Frank was putting a smiley-face on the disaster.

"We will continue to keep you posted. As always, we appreciate your hard work and your support. Thank you."

The image on the screen faded and was replaced by the Tera Pharmagenics logo.

It was short and to the point. Eric watched the crowd as they filed out. He knew most of them by name, acknowledging everyone as they passed. They were his family, and he felt like he was letting them down. They had depended on him, and he had failed to deliver.

He walked out the door to where Nicole and Wally stood.

"Liles did a good job," Nicole said.

Eric was relieved to see no trace of the previous evening in her demeanor. Same old Nicole, for which he was thankful. It made it easier for him to reciprocate.

He nodded. "He's got a good stage presence, always had. I've got to go to Cupertino first thing in the morning for a management meeting. Let's go down to Frog Level and figure out what I'm going to say," Eric said. "I've got to run back to my office for a few minutes, and I'll meet you there."

When Eric got to back to his office, he stopped at Carmen's desk.

"I thought that went well," she said.

"Considering . . ."

He raised his eyebrows. "Not the announcement I had hoped we'd be making. I'm meeting Wally and Nicole at Frog Level. Why don't you take the rest of the day off?" Carmen didn't drink, and Eric had long since stopped inviting her to their informal get-togethers there.

"Thanks. I think I'll take you up on it. You need anything before I leave?"

He shook his head. "No, I'm set. Have a good evening. I'll call you in the morning on the way to the airport."

He went to his office and locked several files in his desk, security conscious as always. Looking at the stack in his inbox, he decided it could wait until he returned.

On the corner of his desk, he had a separate pile of folders relating to the FDA application. He needed those for the meeting tomorrow, so he stuffed them into his backpack before making his way down to the parking lot.

Not surprisingly, the lot had already cleared by the time Eric got in his Jeep. Apparently, no one was working after the video conference. He couldn't blame them since there was little to be done this afternoon.

He drove to Waynesville, still in shock. Frog Level Brewing was the oldest brewery in Waynesville, named after the low-lying section of town down by the railroad tracks and alongside Richland Creek. When it had first opened eight years ago, it became the de facto hangout for Eric and his team.

As he parked on the street in front of the brewery, he saw Wally's old green AMC Gremlin and shook his head.

It was a 1978 model, the last year they were made. Eric was amazed the thing still ran. The odometer quit working years ago, along with most everything else in the vehicle. Nobody, including Wally, knew how many miles it had on it.

Not bothering to lock his door after he got out of the Jeep, he saw Nicole's VW convertible parked in the small parking lot and smiled. They had both got there ahead of him, which was typical.

He walked through the front door and spotted his two scientists sitting at a table with Clark Williams, the proprietor. Clark, a local and a retired Marine Corp First Sergeant, still came in almost every day. The discipline instilled in him by the Corps was hard to shed, even though he'd turned over most of the day-to-day operations to others.

"The big dog still working?" Eric asked as he walked over to the threesome and put his hand on the Marine's shoulder.

"Got to, Captain," he replied, referring to Eric's former Army rank. "Don't make enough to pay somebody else. How are things out at the Cove?"

Eric exhaled and eyed his two scientists. "You haven't heard?"

Clark cocked his head. "Apparently not. But I was wondering why these two were so quiet and in here so early in the afternoon."

Eric looked around, then remembered the news was now public information. "The drug we've been working on the last ten years? The FDA denied it."

"Damn," Clark said. "Sorry to hear that."

"So are we," Wally said.

A perky blonde walked up, bringing another glass of beer over to the table for Eric.

"Thanks, Maryann," Eric said as he pulled out a chair and sat.

As she walked off, Clark finished his beer. Using his kebbie for support, he stood, wincing. "Enjoy. I'll let you guys talk shop. I'll be back later."

Eric watched as his friend limped toward the bar. Eric never heard him complain, even though he knew he was in pain more often than not. The degenerative spinal disease was taking its toll.

Nicole took a sip of her beer and then looked directly at Eric. "What are we going to do?"

"That's what I wanted to discuss."

Over several beers, the three of them talked about any options they might have. They focused on what were essentially two issues: Evidence of achieving primary end concept and the number of study subjects.

Fluzenta was the first universal flu virus, designed to combat multiple strains. Up to this point, flu vaccines were developed specifically for individual strains when they appeared, a costly and time-consuming process.

There were four types of flu viruses. Type A viruses were called avian flu because birds served as natural hosts for that form. Type A viruses were categorized into subtypes, based on two surface proteins: HA, commonly abbreviated as H, and NA, abbreviated as N. They had developed Fluzenta based on earlier work with the H4N4 virus, an avian flu virus that had not yet appeared in humans.

Tera Pharmagenics had proven the effectiveness of Fluzenta against several other viruses that had surfaced in humans, to demonstrate its universal capabilities. But, since this was a new approach, they were getting penalized for what would be considered a small number of subjects in a traditional flu vaccine trial. They had to sell the approach first before convincing the committee they had achieved the primary end concept.

There was nothing they could do about the number of study subjects. There were four study groups for the Phase III clinical trials, but the NDA only required two. Like everyone else, Tera Pharmagenics submitted only the two with the most favorable outcomes. In their case, that was Group One and Group Four. According to the rules, this application could reference nothing from the other two study groups.

"I've been thinking," Nicole said. "Maybe we could 'adjust' the data that we've already submitted."

Wally gave her a skeptical look. Eric remained neutral, curious as to what she had in mind. "How exactly would we do that?" Eric asked.

Nicole looked around, then leaned forward and continued in a low voice. "First, we make the argument that we can legitimately exclude data from certain patients in the two cohort groups we submitted."

"You know we can't do that," Wally replied. "The study parameters have been fixed for a while. We can't go back and change the considerations now."

Eric started to comment, but Nicole held up her hand. "Just hear me out first." She waited to make sure Wally wasn't going to interrupt again before she continued.

"While an applicant can't submit additional data, the FDA does allow you to 'correct' data, right? I'm simply maintaining that we can incorporate those exclusions in the dosing instructions."

Wally snorted beer out his nose. "You are so full of it. You're backing into the outcome. You. Can. Not. Do.

That." He slammed his fist on the table to emphasize his point.

Eric stared at her. "Doesn't that make the problem of too few study subjects even worse?"

"Let me finish," Nicole said. "We have data with different administration frequencies. We could shave a day off the dosage frequency and eliminate certain patients."

Wally shook his head, disgusted. He took a long drink from his beer and then wiped his mouth on the back of his hand as he set the glass down. "That's going to be a huge red flag for the committee."

"They usually give some latitude on frequency," Nicole said. "After all, it's a double-blind study, so . . ."

Wally shook his head. "It won't make any difference. I reran the data on Group Four, shifting the administration interval both ways. There's no statistical difference in outcomes. That's the problem and reducing the time between doses by a day won't change things."

"It worked in Group Two," Nicole responded. "I checked. And, there are more patients in Group Two, especially if we revise the restrictions and change the dosing."

"Doesn't matter, Blondie," Wally said. "We didn't submit data from Group Two, remember? We can't provide *any* additional data. Period."

Nicole looked at Eric. "We can say we meant to submit Group Two instead of Group Four. It was a mistake in the original application, and we're *correcting* it." Her words hung over the table like a dark cloud, the silence deafening.

Eric considered the implications of her suggestion. What Nicole was suggesting was outright perjury.

"We—we being Frank and I as officers of Tera Pharmagenics—certified that the application was accurate and truthful. You're suggesting that we admit otherwise?"

"It was a mistake. Companies make mistakes all the time," Nicole said. She looked at Wally. "Blame it on me. I'm okay with that if it gets Fluzenta approved."

"Still doesn't make it right," Wally said, crossing his arms.

Eric held his hands out, palms down, and lowered them to the table. "We're brainstorming, and that's healthy. But let's get back on track." He looked first at Nicole, then Wally. "There are things we can do for the appeal. I don't mind being aggressive in interpreting the rules. But we have to be careful that we don't cross a line here."

"What if I told you that I know for a fact Bearant Pharmaceutical did it for their blockbuster cholesterol drug?" Nicole said.

Eric sat back in his chair. He wasn't naïve enough to believe that some companies wouldn't resort to that and he'd heard the rumor about Bearant. Everybody in the industry suspected as much.

"How would you know that?" he asked.

Nicole lowered her voice, looked at Wally and then back at Eric. "One of my classmates works for them. They did it and were successful. Why can't we?"

Eric pushed his chair back from the table and rose. "Let's take a five-minute 'comfort' break. When we come back to the table, let's refocus our efforts on what we *can* do."

Walking to the bathroom, Eric felt like they needed to take a timeout. He didn't question Nicole's information but was troubled by the fact that she suggested doing something that he considered unethical. He wanted to chalk it up to panic and shock from the news they'd received yesterday. Maybe he was foolish and naïve.

As he left the men's restroom, he passed Wally coming in. Eric got back to the table where Nicole still sat. He didn't relish being alone with her, even for a few minutes in a public place. He braced himself for what she was going to say, afraid she was going to bring up last night.

"I'm sorry if I crossed a boundary a few minutes ago. I was just trying to think outside the box," she said. "And if they can do it . . ."

Eric nodded, relieved she said nothing about yesterday evening and pleased to hear her admission. "I know. This has been very stressful for all of us. And, I've always encouraged you to be creative. We just have to be cautious and not do anything we might regret." *Anything else,* he thought.

When Wally returned to the table, Nicole said, "I have another idea, since that one went over so well."

Eric chuckled, and even Wally had to smile. Nicole had broken the ice. She explained that when you drilled down to the individuals, there were a few who deviated enough from the rest to potentially skew the data for the entire group. The guidelines allowed the applicant to exclude singular data if there was sufficient evidence to justify the exclusion. Why not at least do that much?

"Maybe you should recheck your math, Wonder Boy?" she said to Wally, unable to resist the jab.

Eric smiled. The good thing about Wally's lack of filters was that it usually worked both ways. Wally ignored her shot at him, probably thinking it didn't merit a response.

"Wally?" Eric asked.

He shrugged. "I'll take another look at it. But that could backfire. If we are successful in reducing the number of subjects, doesn't that play into their hands on that issue?"

Eric looked at Nicole, awaiting her reply.

"What I'm suggesting is to prove our end concept. I think that will overshadow the argument about the insufficient number of subjects. I also suspect it will reduce our percentage of side effects."

Eric nodded. One of the troublesome issues with the two trials submitted was the severity and number of side effects. That was problematic and what was probably behind the committee's comment about not enough subjects in the Phase III trials.

Over the next hour, they suggested several hypotheses that could give them a slight edge, including strengthening the dosage restrictions and indications.

Around 9:45, Eric adjourned the meeting. He was pleased that they had identified several areas that had the potential to help their appeal. Wally and Nicole excused themselves, and after they had left, Eric moved over to the bar where Clark was sitting on his stool on the other side.

"Another?" he asked as Eric sat and placed his empty glass on the bar.

Eric shook his head. "Thanks, but I'm done for the evening. I'm still recovering from the other night. From hero to zero. Let me settle up."

Clark slid the tab across the bar. He took the towel off his shoulder and started wiping the bar down. "Looked like a serious meeting."

Eric pulled out his credit card and laid it on top of the check. "It was. Trying to figure out next steps for the drug that was shot down."

Clark continued wiping the bar down, studying him. "What's bothering you? Something's on your mind, I can tell."

Eric cocked his head and looked at his friend. "When you were in, what'd you do when you had to 'bend' the rules to get something done?"

Clark slowed, then stopped, waiting for Eric to continue.

Eric shook his head and sighed. "I've got two choices—neither of them good." He paused before continuing. "It's not right. It's a good drug. It has the potential to save lots of people. I'd bet my own life on it."

Clark threw the towel back over his shoulder. "What about selling it to another company? Get them to bring it to market?"

"I wish it were that simple. We checked around. They're a bunch of fucking hyenas. They know we're badly wounded. Why pay retail when you can pick it up for ten cents on the dollar at the bankruptcy hearing?"

Clark let out a low whistle. "That bad, huh?"

Eric nodded. "As they say, 'We're all in.' If we don't bring Fluzenta to market, we're screwed. We're tapped out, my friend. It's game over."

"Don't you have other drugs in the pipeline?"

Eric shook his head. "We've cannibalized everything for this one. *Everything.*"

"Maybe you could find another investor? Keep things afloat until you can get it approved?"

"We've looked. With the denial, no one's willing to take a flyer. Everyone's spooked. They're just settling in to watch the train wreck."

"I take it Panther Cove would be shuttered."

Eric laughed, and it was hollow. "The entire company would be shut down, including Panther Cove."

There was a long pause before Clark finally spoke. "You said you had two options. I'm guessing the first option is to appeal with what you've submitted. I take it you don't think that option has much chance of success. What's the other choice?"

Eric looked around, confirming nobody was within earshot. The place was empty, except for Maryann, seated at the far end of the bar. He watched as she flipped pages of a magazine she was engrossed in, oblivious to the two of them.

"We have the possibility of refiling another study."

Clark wrinkled his brow. "Go on."

"We would need to 'tweak' it a bit. That part doesn't bother me. We do have the latitude to change the administration frequency and dosage warnings. But, we'd have to say that we filed the wrong study in error."

"So, you'd have to lie?"

Eric winced, then nodded. As usual, his friend didn't mince words, and the starkness of it was like a splash of cold water. The first sergeant was simply calling a spade a spade.

Eric looked at him and in a quiet voice asked, "What would you do? What did you do?"

Clark folded his arms across his chest and leaned back on his stool. "You're convinced the drug will save more people than it'll hurt?"

"Absolutely. Exponentially more."

Clark leaned forward and looked him directly in the eye. "I'd tell you to lie your ass off."

7

Early Friday afternoon, as soon he got off the plane at San Francisco International Airport, Eric found a nearly empty gate and stopped to call Wally and Nicole.

When he left Atlanta, he believed that Nicole's strategy was the wrong thing to do. He worked the entire flight, scratching out notes on half of a yellow pad, what he normally did when wrestling with a difficult decision. By the time they landed, he'd changed his mind. If he was going to save Fluzenta, changing the data was their only chance.

With the two of them on the phone, he consulted his notes and ran the approach by them. Last night at Frog Level, Eric had dismissed Nicole's suggestion to "amend" their application. He had agreed with Wally, who was vehemently opposed. It was wrong, and it was unethical. If called out, it would reflect on all their reputations. "Sleazy" was the word Wally used.

But his conversation with Clark had made him rethink the issue. He reluctantly agreed that this was their best shot at getting it approved. If he truly believed that Fluzenta would benefit the greater good, then he had to do whatever he needed to get this drug to market.

He could tell that Wally still wasn't convinced, but by the end of the call, they were all on the same page.

He stuck his phone into his pocket and made his way to the escalator leading down to the baggage claim area. At the bottom of the escalator, an indolent young man with a ponytail held a sign with Eric's name on it. Eric introduced himself and held up his overnight bag as proof of his only luggage. The driver, who introduced himself as Mark, took Eric's bag and said that his car was just across the street.

Since it was the middle of the day in California, Eric told the driver to take the 101 instead of the 280 down to Cupertino. Although it was a shorter distance, it usually took longer due to the congestion and ever-present construction on the old freeway. It was only 1:35, and since the meeting didn't start until 3:00, they had plenty of time.

A few minutes later, Eric told the driver to take the next exit. The driver, apparently accustomed to taking orders from his passengers, nodded, not questioning where they were going.

As they exited the freeway, Eric told him to take a right and go down two blocks to the In-N-Out Burger. The driver smiled and nodded, not surprised at the request.

Eric was hungry and made his pilgrimage to the legendary California-based chain whenever he came out west. While he usually tried to eat healthily, he figured an occasional In-N-Out burger wasn't going to kill him. Given the events of the last week, he didn't care if it did.

Thank goodness, the chain hadn't made it east of the Mississippi. Yet.

As they pulled into the parking lot, Eric leaned forward in the Town Car and handed his credit card to Mark. "Would you please get me a cheeseburger—Animal Style, fries, and a chocolate shake. And get you something, too. My treat."

The driver parked the Town Car and left it running while he went inside to pick up the food. A few minutes later, he came out with a tray containing two drinks and a bag full of food.

It turned out, Mark was an In-N-Out fan too. Eric told him that they had plenty of time to eat before getting back on the road.

Fifty minutes later, the driver stopped in front of the main entrance to the Tera Pharmagenics office complex.

"Thanks for lunch, boss," Mark said as Eric exited the car.

"My pleasure," Eric said. "Thanks for the ride."

Inside, Eric stopped at the security desk, where he showed his driver's license and signed in.

The guard, a new person Eric didn't recognize, checked Eric's identification against the log. Satisfied that Eric was who he said he was, he then handed the license and an access badge to him.

"They're expecting you in the sixth-floor conference room, Dr. Carter. You know the way, I assume?"

"Yes, thank you."

Eric picked up his bag and Friends of the Smokies backpack, then went through the turnstile to the elevator bank. It was 2:47 p.m., Pacific Time, so he was on schedule for the three o'clock meeting.

Before going into the conference room, he stopped in the restroom next to the elevators. The meal was satisfying but messy, and he wanted to check and make sure he wasn't wearing any of it. Satisfied, he relieved himself, washed his hands, and then headed toward the executive conference room.

Opening the door, he was surprised to see only four people in the spacious room. Most meetings at corporate were attended by the major players and their key subordinates, resulting in a crowd. Not this time.

Chip Miller, the chairman of Tera and CEO of West Coast Capital, was seated at the head of the table. West Coast Capital was the biggest investor in Tera. The fact that Miller was there was a surprise and underscored the gravity of the meeting.

Eric had expected Frank, who sat on Chip's right, and Aiko Tanaka, the vice president of operations. She sat across from Frank on Miller's left.

Rae Thornton, the CFO, was seated next to Frank. Eric had assumed she would be there, but she'd made no mention of it when he had talked with her last week.

After greetings, Eric took a seat next to Aiko, across the table from Frank and Rae. Rae gave him an almost imperceptible shake of her head, with her look conveying that this was new to her as well.

Frank nodded toward the food on the table along the wall. "We've got food if you're hungry."

Eric nodded and smiled. "Thanks. I had my In-N-Out fix on the way in from SFO."

"Since the four of us were already here," Frank said, staring at Eric. "I decided it would be better to have you join us in person. Liz is busy trying to manage the fallout from the FDA's announcement, so she'll join us later."

Eric tried to keep his face neutral. He knew Miller lived in southern California, so his presence was indicative of a hidden agenda. Frank's comment about the four of them being there was a cautionary warning. Eric was determined to tread lightly in the beginning and see how this meeting was going to unfold before he said too much.

Frank nodded to Eric. "Would you update everyone on exactly where we stand on the appeal?"

Eric didn't have to even look at his notes that he'd studied on the flight out to the West Coast. Just to be certain he had the latest information, he'd called Carmen on the way from the airport to make sure he wasn't going to be blindsided by anything new.

"We've requested an end-of-review meeting, which is the first and most important step. The FDA encourages settling disputes at the division level. End-of-review meetings have the greatest probability of success, with almost half of them getting a favorable dispensation."

He noticed Aiko nodding in agreement. A good sign.

"What if that isn't successful?" Chip asked.

"If that isn't successful, then we can file a FDRR, or formal dispute resolution request." Not waiting for the obvious question, he took a deep breath and continued. "Once you're past the divisional level, the odds are much less promising. The last few years it's been less than ten percent."

There was a collective sigh around the table.

Chip was shaking his head. "What I'm hearing is that our best, and apparently only shot, has a fifty-fifty chance of succeeding. How long before we know the outcome of this review meeting?"

Eric shrugged. "The majority of divisional meeting requests are granted within thirty days with the decisions communicated within thirty days after that. Since we filed last week, I'd guess that we should expect a meeting by the end of the month with a decision the following month."

He nodded to Aiko, wanting to draw her into the discussion. "But, as Aiko knows, the FDA is not always reliably predictable." He waited for her to contribute.

She agreed with Eric's assessment and concurred that Tera Pharmagenics's case was as solid as she'd seen. "I'm slightly more pessimistic on his notification time frame, but as he pointed out, that is hard to predict."

Eric continued. "Let's make it the end of next month. I'm comfortable that we should have a decision no later than then."

Frank cleared his throat before speaking. "What is our strategy for the appeal?"

"I met with my two senior scientists to discuss our approach," Eric said. "Without boring you with a lot of arcane detail, I'll summarize."

He explained that the rules allowed minor modifications to data already submitted, or corrections, but with no new data. At first, they were going to tweak the data from the two cohorts in the application, which would result in slightly better outcomes. However, upon further review, they realized that with the changes, Group

Two showed better results than Group Four. Tera Pharmagenics would have to be willing to admit they made a mistake and wanted to replace Group Four data with Group Two.

Aiko appeared suspicious. "Is the committee willing to make an exception? This appears to go against the rules." She was questioning the approach without directly confronting Eric.

Eric nodded. "We think so, although we have no way of knowing until we submit the revision before the review meeting. We do know that other companies have done this, so there's a precedent."

"Who?" Frank asked.

"Bearant, for one. They did it on their cholesterol drug."

"Really?" Frank's eyebrows shot up at the mention of their competitor.

The group spent the next two hours debating Eric's strategy.

"This meeting is off the record, correct?" Aiko said.

"Absolutely," Frank replied. "There are no minutes and no official record."

She looked at Eric and then Frank. "You two are on record as certifying the New Drug Application." She let the words hang, without taking the logical next step.

Frank looked at Eric, then back at Aiko, choosing his words carefully. "Mistakes are made. NDAs, like many government forms, are extremely complicated. Ours wouldn't be the first, and I doubt it will be the last." He shifted his look to Eric. "Sounds like we made a mistake."

Eric wanted to ask if the mistake he was referring to was considering perjury.

"We've got close to a billion dollars invested in this drug," Chip said. "I'd suggest that we take our absolute best shot at getting it approved. Now is not the time to get conservative, especially if our competitors have done the same thing before."

Chip was making it very clear what he thought, Eric mused.

Frank pushed forward. "If we weren't convinced of the effectiveness of Fluzenta, we wouldn't be having this discussion. In my opinion, we're just giving them more accurate information. It sounds like we're all in agreement, then, on how we'll proceed?"

Eric was quiet for the ride up to Bella Vista, a quaint, roadside inn up in the hills overlooking Silicon Valley. Before leaving the office, he'd called Nicole and Wally to tell them about the decision. Wally was disappointed, as expected, but they would start working immediately on the appeal. By the time they reached the fog-shrouded restaurant on Skyline Boulevard, Eric had mentally sketched out the details.

Bella Vista was one of his favorite restaurants, one of those places that never changed and never disappointed. He looked forward to pan-fried abalone along with a good California wine. Eating at Bella Vista was one of the highlights of coming to the area.

Eric found himself seated next to Chip Miller. After everyone had ordered cocktails, the investment banker turned to Eric and said, "I sense that you're not very confident about the appeal, even with changing the data."

Eric was surprised at Chip's perception. He wasn't confident but felt like he'd put on his game face during the meeting. He was unsure about how to respond and answered cautiously.

"I probably am a little spooked. I believed they were going to approve the original application, so my read is admittedly suspect."

Chip nodded, seeming to appreciate Eric's candidness. "What's our fallback if they deny the appeal?"

Eric didn't rush to answer, although he'd given that considerable thought on the flight out. Further appeals were futile, even he admitted that. Unless West Coast Capital was willing to invest significant additional dollars, the only option left was to sell Fluzenta. Selling Fluzenta meant the end of Tera Pharmagenics.

The server appeared with their drinks and then took dinner orders, which bought Eric time to formulate his response. After Frank had toasted their anticipated successful appeal, Chip turned to Eric, waiting for an answer.

Eric chose his words carefully. "There are only two options. One, we find additional capital and restart the application process." He paused, wanting to gauge Chip's response.

"And the second?" Chip said, his face remaining neutral.

"We have to sell. Rights to Fluzenta, assets, maybe the entire company."

"What about selling off Panther Cover?" Chip asked.

The question caught Eric off guard. He studied Chip's face and got the impression that Chip was already considering such a move.

"Panther Cove is the heart and soul of the company," Eric said. "If you sell that, you might as well close shop."

Chip held up his hand. "I agree. We're just talking hypothetically. Although Frank did mention to me before the meeting that someone had expressed an interest in the North Carolina property."

Eric shrugged. "News to me."

"Don't worry," Chip said. "That would be a last resort."

Over dessert, Eric thought about Chip's remark. He wondered why Rae hadn't mentioned it.

After dinner, the limo returned to Cupertino, stopping first at the hotel where Eric and Rae were staying. Rae offered to buy nightcaps for all, but Aiko and Frank were anxious to get home. Chip had an early morning flight, so he passed as well.

Eric stood motionless next to Rae as the limo pulled away. He was tired, mentally and physically.

"How about that nightcap?" Rae asked as they walked into the lobby.

* * *

Minutes later, they were in Eric's suite. They had both traded their street clothes for robes and were seated next to each other on the small sofa, each of them holding a glass of port.

Rae snuggled up next to him and put her free hand on his leg beneath the folds of his robe. "It seems like you've had a change of heart on how to handle the appeal."

He shrugged and took a sip of his wine. "Not really."

"I didn't want to get into it in the meeting, but I didn't think we could file new data."

"We're not," he snapped. "We should've submitted Group Two to begin with."

Rae held up her hand. "I'm not challenging you. I'm just asking for my edification."

"It is all in how you interpret the rules. We're just applying the same interpretation that others have used."

"Okay, you know more about that than I do. I'm sorry."

"Are you?" He looked at her, wondering how sorry she was. He was frustrated and angry, spoiling for a fight.

Rae removed her hand and stared back. "What is that supposed to mean?"

Eric shook his head. "What do you know about selling Panther Cover?"

He could tell that he had surprised Rae with the question and she was weighing her response.

"What have you heard?"

"Answering a question with a question is supposed to be a sign of deception." He paused. "Chip told me that someone had expressed an interest in buying it."

Rae exhaled. "I think that's an exaggeration, based on what I know. The CEO of Bearant is looking to build a facility in the southeast. He apparently told Frank on the golf course that if we ever wanted to sell, they would be interested. That's it. Frank told me that this morning."

He nodded. "I told you. I'm not leaving Western North Carolina, with or without Tera Pharmagenics. Not as long as my daughter is there."

He tried to take consolation in the fact that Frank and Chip were reaching out to some prominent politicians to salvage Fluzenta, but he couldn't hide his disappointment that Frank may be looking to sell the lab. Tera Pharmagenics would have no presence in North Carolina. And Eric would be out of a job.

"Speaking of Ali, when do I get to meet her?" she asked.

"You've already met her."

"You know what I mean."

Eric had introduced her to Ali at a company picnic two months ago as a work associate. Other than the fact they both worked for the same company, there was no reason to hide their relationship. He just wasn't ready to introduce her as anything more, especially now.

"It's not that simple, and you know it. I want Ali to know first, and then we'll break the news to everyone else."

Rae snorted, which infuriated him further. "Have you told Kate we're seeing each other?"

"No, I haven't told anyone. Have you?"

"I told you I wouldn't say anything without your permission and I haven't," she said.

Rae was intelligent and attractive, with short brown hair and dark brown eyes to match. But it was her sense of humor that first attracted Eric. She had a sharp tongue and a dry wit to match.

They had first met at a company meeting, and her sidebar comments during a boring presentation by the treasurer kept him laughing. At the reception later that evening, Eric rescued her from an inebriated co-worker who was trying to convince her that she was his soulmate. They sat together at dinner and the relationship quickly blossomed. Rae was the first person he had cared about since Kate.

Even though they didn't work in the same area, seeing her was somewhat problematic since they were both senior officers in the company. Frank wouldn't have a problem, but Eric wasn't sure how others would react to the news.

Rae took a deep breath, apparently deciding to defuse things. "Let's change subjects, why don't we? I know you're upset about what Chip said. I *am* sorry, and I didn't give Frank's comment a second thought. Chip's right, it is in everyone's best interest to get Fluzenta approved. That's our first priority. I think everyone's just thinking out loud, trying to come up with options."

Eric's anger had subsided a bit, and he nodded. "Sorry. I don't mean to take out my frustration on you. It caught me by surprise."

She smiled and moved closer, putting her hand back on his leg. "When are you going to take me hiking?"

He looked at her, wondering if she was serious. "Anytime. You know how much I love hiking in the park. When are you coming to North Carolina?"

She shrugged and took a sip of wine. "I'm not sure. Hopefully soon. You already have a hiking buddy, anyway."

Eric studied her face and tensed. For a fleeting moment, he thought that Rae knew about that regretful night he spent with Nicole. Although he and Rae had said from the beginning of their relationship that there was no commitment, he felt guilty just the same. Sleeping with Nicole was wrong, and he had vowed never to repeat it. He hated keeping secrets from Rae, but he wasn't about to confess.

"I assume you're referring to Nicole," he said.

Rae arched her eyebrows and stared at him, encouraging him to continue.

"Yes, she goes hiking with us, and yes, she goes fly fishing with me as well. *But,* she works for me, and that's all there is to it." He meant what he said, and hoped that would be the end of the discussion.

Rae pulled away and turned to face him. A combination of anger and hurt flashed across her face. "*Us?* You're telling me that Ali has met Nicole? And goes hiking with you and your daughter?" The temperature in the room seemed to drop ten degrees.

Eric gritted his teeth, realizing that his guilty conscience had pushed him deeper into a hole. While he'd previously told Rae that he and Nicole occasionally went hiking and fishing, he'd obviously neglected to mention that she'd gone with him and Ali. That was what Rae was upset about.

He was now on the defensive. In a nonchalant tone, he tried to recover. "It's no big deal. Ali has met Wally, too. They both work for me, and naturally, we all spend a lot of time together."

"So, does he go hiking with the two of you? And fishing with you, too?"

He spent the next thirty minutes trying to convince her that Nicole was a coworker, not a threat. His highly anticipated reunion with Rae was a disaster.

Acknowledging that they were both tired and stressed, they agreed to a reluctant truce and went to bed. Each of them took full advantage of the space afforded by the king-size sleeping accommodations. Eric tossed and turned. He could tell that Rae was doing the same, yet neither of them spoke. Exhausted, Eric finally drifted off to sleep.

Early the next morning, he awoke and was surprised to find Rae in his arms. Sometime during the night, they had moved closer.

Despite the previous night's disagreements, the proximity of their thinly-clad bodies overrode any differences of opinion and nature took over. With little foreplay or emotional involvement, they satisfied their physical needs and not much else.

Afterward, Eric hoped that ruffled feelings had been smoothed. Slightly, he sensed, but not completely. The conversation was stilted. At breakfast, he felt compelled to offer an olive branch before they parted.

"When are you coming back east?" he asked.

She shrugged, and between mouthfuls of yogurt, said, "I'm not sure. Is that an invitation?"

He reached out and put his hand over hers. "Look, I'm sorry about last night. I apologize for not telling you about Nicole hiking with Ali and me." He felt her hand stiffen. "It wasn't intentional. I do want you to come to

North Carolina and stay at the house. When you come, I'll try to arrange for you to meet Ali, okay?"

She eyed him suspiciously. Seeming to sense he was apologizing, she smiled. "I would like that."

"Good. Me, too. Just try to give me as much notice as possible. Kate can be difficult at times."

8

Eric worked the entire time on the flight back to Atlanta. By the time they landed, he'd realized how much work was going to be involved in preparing for the Fluzenta appeal.

On the northeast side of Atlanta, darkness had fallen, and traffic started to thin out as he drove toward Waynesville. As he approached the end of I-985, which simply transformed into a four-lane divided highway with intersections, traffic lights, and a lower speed limit, he began to relax, glad to be escaping the tentacles of Atlanta.

He thought about his upcoming trip to London with Ali, trying to convince himself that he could make it work. There was only a five-hour time difference, just an hour more than Cupertino. With the Internet and cell phones, he'd be in constant contact with his team. He shook his head as he realized that was the problem—he'd be unable to give his full attention to Ali. It wouldn't be fair. There was no way he was going to be able to take a week and go to London before the review meeting. The trip would have to wait.

Ali would be disappointed, but he'd make it up to her. Kate, however, would be furious. He could hear her now, reminding him that once again, work takes precedence over everything else.

It was dark as he drove up the winding gravel driveway to his house. The usual lights operated by his timers were on. As he opened the front door, Felix sat there waiting on him, as if to say, *about time you got home to feed me.*

He fed the Maine Coon, put his bag down in the bedroom, and replaced his travel outfit with sweatpants and a sweatshirt. His body wasn't sure what time it was or what time zone he was in, but his stomach insisted that he was hungry. He realized he hadn't eaten since breakfast that morning with Rae.

Exhausted, he prepared a cup of hot tea and a ham sandwich on a baguette he retrieved from the freezer and toasted. After he'd assembled the sandwich and found a half-full bag of chips, he went out on the deck and sat with his meal. Whatever the label, it was delicious, further proof that if someone was hungry enough, anything tasted good.

The night air was crisp and clear and markedly cooler. As he ate, he marveled at the number of stars visible. Brighter than everything else, Venus was noticeable in the western sky.

Subconsciously, he'd been mulling over the best approach to take on the Fluzenta appeal. The restrictions were hard and fast: they couldn't introduce any new data. He had to remind himself that now they were going to submit Group Two. Since they hadn't previously submitted that data, they had a limited opportunity to "clean" it.

The challenge, then, was to figure out how to massage the Group Two data to result in something as favorable as possible or present a new way of looking at it. Both of those were tricky, which was why the success rate for appeals was so low.

The other option was to find a mistake in the committee's reasoning, but that was even more difficult. The members were knowledgeable. After having been embarrassed a few times over the years, they were much more meticulous in their review. As a result, loopholes were hard to find.

The more he'd studied it, the more unsure he was about the appeal.

He finished his sandwich and tea, then decided to turn in. Maybe his subconscious would come up with some brilliant solution while he slept.

* * *

The next morning, he awoke refreshed, but with no profound insights and more pessimistic than ever. Everything rested on the review meeting.

On his way to the lab, he called Carmen and asked her to round up Wally and Nicole for a meeting in his office as soon as he arrived.

Twenty minutes later, as he walked by Carmen's desk, she said, "They're waiting inside. How was your trip?"

He shrugged, not wanting to go into details yet. "Okay. My internal clock is still kind of screwed up, so check on me during the day and make sure I don't fall asleep at my desk."

In a hushed voice, he told Carmen that he needed to reschedule his trip to London with Ali.

Carmen raised her eyebrows and asked, "Are you sure?"

Reluctantly, he nodded. "I know. I hate to do that, but . . ." He nodded toward his office. "After I finish with them, I'm driving over to Asheville to deliver the news in person. Cancel my appointments for this afternoon."

"How was your trip?" Nicole asked when he walked in.

"Too far for such a short meeting. The only salvation was In-N-Out." He paused and then continued. "I've decided that we're going to submit Group Two to replace Group Four."

Wally's jaw dropped, and Nicole smiled.

"Wally, I realize you're not in favor," Eric said. "To tell the truth, I have a lot of misgivings about doing this."

"Why are you doing it, then?" Wally asked.

Eric had been expecting this. "We have to get FDA approval. We've come too far." He paused. "Sometimes, you have to make hard decisions for the greater good."

"So, you've rationalized it?" Wally said.

The words stung because they were true, and Eric hated to admit it. He nodded. "That's one way of looking at it. I think we're all convinced of Fluzenta's benefits. I think we'd regret it if we didn't do everything in our power to get it to market. It's that simple.

"I want you both to understand that this is my decision and mine alone."

Nicole shook her head. "I said that I—"

Eric held up his hand to silence her. "It is *my* decision, not anyone else's." He fixed her with a stern look until she nodded in agreement.

"Now, we need to polish Group Two until it shines. Agreed?" This time he looked at Wally first, then Nicole, getting their commitment.

The three of them worked the entire morning, repeatedly writing and erasing on the whiteboard in his office. The best they could come up with was using cohort group two and also excluding certain subjects. While none of them were certain it would be enough, there was a palpable air of optimism by the time they finished.

The biggest obstacle he saw was defending to the committee why they had not classified it that way originally. An objective observer might say that they had backed into the result they wanted, which is exactly what they would be doing.

As Clark had said, Eric was going to lie and lie big time. Eric was betting his reputation on this. He hoped it was worth it.

He crammed a stack of papers in his backpack and walked out. Too bad the drive over to Asheville was only thirty minutes.

* * *

Frank Liles looked at the numbers again, hoping to spot something positive or a crack somewhere. Nothing. He knew the answer but didn't want to believe it. Without

Fluzenta, Tera Pharmagenics was bankrupt, figuratively and literally.

Chip Miller, representing West Coast Capital, the largest investor in Tera Pharmagenics, would personally close the doors and turn out the lights. If he did, the millions Frank had invested would evaporate.

He set the file down, took off his glasses and rubbed his face with his other hand. He was too old to start over. Unbeknownst to Susan, his wife, he had mortgaged every piece of property they owned, planning on getting it back when they struck gold with Fluzenta.

The pilot's voice crackled over the speaker. "We're starting our descent into Asheville. Fifteen minutes before touchdown."

Frank looked out the oval window and saw the mountains below. After the meeting in Cupertino Monday, yesterday, he'd flown to New York to meet with bankers. On the way back to the west coast this morning, he'd decided to make an unannounced visit to Panther Cove. He wasn't sure what he expected to gain, other than reassurance that the appeal was going well.

So close, he thought, turning his attention back to the file. He wondered if there was any way they could present the data in a more positive light. Packaging, he called it. He liked Eric and respected his work, but Eric could be so matter-of-fact sometimes. On more than one occasion, he'd told Eric that you had to properly package the message.

Frank wasn't suggesting falsifying the raw data. He just wanted to make sure they were presenting it a positive light, highlighting the good things and minimizing the not-so-good. That was just smart business, he rationalized.

He believed the drug was beneficial and would be proven over the long-term to be dramatically effective. It would be a shame to block it from coming to market when it would help so many people around the world.

He picked up the aircraft phone and called Eric's cell. It went straight to voice mail. He disconnected and pressed the button that connected him directly to Gwen, Frank's assistant.

"Yes?" she answered, even though it was only seven o'clock in California.

"See if you can find Eric for me." He started to disconnect and added, "Please."

"Certainly," she replied.

A few minutes later, the phone buzzed, Gwen calling. "Eric took the rest of the day off to spend with his daughter."

Frank frowned. Not that he begrudged Eric taking time off to spend with his daughter. In fact, it was Frank that had encouraged him to take time off when he and Kate were having problems. But he hated it when Eric wouldn't answer his cell phone.

"What about—"

"Wally?" Gwen had worked as Frank's assistant for ten years and was adept at completing his sentences.

"No, not him. The other one." He couldn't stand dealing with the slob. It was too distracting.

"Nicole?"

"Yes. See if you can find her. When I get there, I'd like to have a little chat with her about the project." He had quit referring to it as anything more than the "Project." Since that was the only thing the Panther Cove facility was working on, it was sufficient.

Two hours later, Frank was working in the first-floor conference room door at the Panther Cove lab when there was a knock at the door.

"Yes?" he said.

He looked up to see Nicole Peters standing in the doorway. The petite blonde was more attractive than he remembered. Her hair looked shorter since he'd last seen her and she had lost some weight. He motioned her in.

"Come on in, Nicole. Have a seat," he said, as he cleared the papers in front of him on the small conference table.

"Carmen said you wanted to talk to me about the Fluzenta project?"

"Yes, yes. I understand Eric is spending the afternoon with his daughter, which is a good thing." He picked up the papers he'd shoved to one side and put them back in the folder. "I had a few questions and didn't want to bother him."

Nicole nodded. "I'll try to answer if I can."

"Good. I'm frustrated, as I know you are, that Fluzenta was denied. That was a bad decision, but we've got a chance to redeem ourselves, and I want to make sure we do. We have got to find some way to convince the FDA of the value of this drug. It would be socially irresponsible to deny it."

"Believe me, Mr. Liles, I agree. I've spent the last eight years working on this project, and I know how much good it will do."

He nodded. "Good, glad to hear you say that. What, then, can we do to convince the FDA?"

She squirmed in her chair. "We—Eric, Wally, and I just met this morning to discuss that." She hesitated, and her eyes wouldn't meet his. "I'm not sure . . . I don't want to say anything . . . anything out of school."

Frank nodded, certain she had something more to say, and he wanted to hear it. He flashed her his best made-for-television smile and shrugged.

"I would never ask you to say anything out of turn, Nicole. This is just a casual conversation between us. I have the utmost respect for Eric and . . . Wally, but sometimes I like to speak directly with the troops on the ground, individually. I just want your ideas, fresh and unfiltered. Rest assured, this is in the strictest confidence."

She considered his request and then nodded enthusiastically. "Okay, sure." She seemed eager to accept the challenge and relieved he'd given her permission to speak freely.

"Apparently, Eric has agreed to submit a different study group, Group Two," she said.

He nodded. "He mentioned that in Cupertino, although he didn't seem very convincing."

"I think he's . . . he's a little uncomfortable with it, but according to what he told us this morning, that's what we're doing."

"What is your feeling?"

She smiled. "I agree that Group Two has a better chance of succeeding if we 'admit' that we made a mistake in initially categorizing the data. That gives them a plausible out. Our position is that this is the way we should have correctly presented the data in the initial application. This gives them a story to support changing their decision without conceding any error on their part—the perfect solution for bureaucrats."

Frank cocked his head. "Your choice of adjectives concerns me. What do you mean by 'better'? We need assurances that whatever strategy we pursue will result in approval."

Nicole shrugged. "I'm not convinced that even with this approach, it's a done deal. It's up to the committee, and that's out of our control."

Frank nodded. "In my younger days, I used to be a pretty decent pool player, 'hustling' is what we called it back then. I was putting myself through school, and the extra money came in handy. One Saturday night, I drove to a little town a couple of hours from where I lived and dropped in for some local action where no one knew me."

He watched her closely for a reaction, then continued. "It was getting late, and I had upped the ante by that point, going for the big win. We were playing for a hundred dollars, which was a lot of money to a poor college student."

"That sounds like a lot of pressure."

He smiled. "That leads me to my point. I was in a new town with a pool hall full of strangers, playing a game of eight-ball for a hundred dollars."

She nodded, wearing a puzzled look as if he were stating the obvious. He waited for another beat and then delivered the punch line.

"But I only had fifty dollars in my pocket."

He watched her face as she grasped what he was saying. Real pressure was when one could not afford to lose. At any price. And that was precisely where they were.

"We've got to find a way," he said. "I'm not willing to leave our future up to a bunch of bureaucrats in Washington. Not when lives are at stake."

Nicole nodded. "I think I understand." She shifted in her chair. "There may be another option . . . one that might be considered more unconventional."

Frank studied her face, sensing that she was hesitant to continue. He leaned forward, meeting her eyes. "This is between us, Nicole. If you've got an idea, I want to hear it, regardless of how 'unconventional' it may be. Now is not the time to be shy."

She returned his stare and then grinned. "What if I could show you a way to control the pool table in your favor?"

"I'm all ears."

She shifted again in her seat and leaned across the desk. "We have the cure. All we need is a disease, right?"

Frank shook his head. "I'm not sure I understand what you're saying."

"What if I told you we could reverse engineer a virus, a virus for which the only known cure was Fluzenta?"

He sat back in his chair, trying to digest what she was saying. From an engineering perspective, her proposal was logical, but the obstacles had to be enormous.

Nicole continued. "Creating a vaccine is tough. First, you have to figure out how the virus works, then design a safe and effective way to thwart the virus. That takes a lot of time and false starts.

"It's a lot easier to start with the solution and work backward. We know how Fluzenta works and we know it is safe, so we're ahead of the game. We take a known virus and modify it so that Fluzenta 'fits.' Think about it like this: Is it easier to design a key to fit an unknown lock or design a lock to fit a specific key?"

"Theoretically, what you say makes sense, but I see two major problems. First, the time and effort required. We don't have that luxury. Second, and more importantly—so what? Assuming you could do as you say, then where do you go from there?"

Nicole nodded. "What if I told you that I've already been working on a virus to 'fit' Fluzenta? And I'm closer than anyone knows."

Now his curiosity was piqued. "Okay, for the sake of argument, let's assume such a virus exists. What about the second problem?"

Looking him in the eye, she said, "You release the engineered virus."

Frank swallowed hard and stared at the blonde scientist in front of him, wondering if he'd heard her correctly.

"Let me get this straight. Are you talking about releasing an engineered virus? So, people have to buy our vaccine? That's insane."

"It's not as horrible as it sounds. Hear me out. We pick a virus that has low lethality, not Ebola or something like that. A virus that hasn't made the jump to humans. Yet. All we're doing is jumpstarting Darwinism. Every avian strain of flu out there that affects humans has made that transition.

"And remember, we have a known cure. We know it works and exactly how because we've already tested it. If they don't allow Fluzenta to go into production, a lot of people will die from avian flu. If we do this, there may be some collateral loss, but it will be far less than the number that would die anyway. You have to consider the greater good."

Frank shook his head. "You're playing God."

She sat back in her chair. "You wanted a sure thing. This is it."

9

Kate had suggested Nine Mile on Montford Avenue. It was an “in” spot, which didn’t surprise Eric, but the food was excellent. He parked and saw Kate sitting at a table outside, wearing sunglasses and as elegant as always. She was sipping on a glass of white wine.

“Hello,” he said. He leaned over and gave her an air-kiss, figuring that was appropriate for the setting.

Bestowing a cheek and a half-hearted pucker his direction, she replied, “Hello to you, too.”

Before he got comfortable in his seat, a server swooped in to take his drink order. As he walked away, Kate pulled her sunglasses down and stared at Eric. “It must be important for you to ask me to lunch in the middle of the week and drive over.”

He shook his head and forced a smile. She exuded an “air of superiority” that never failed to irritate him. He could ask her the time of day, and her haughty reply would piss him off.

Determined to keep the conversation civil, he took a deep breath and replied, “It is. And thank you for meeting me on such short notice.”

He started by telling her the news about Fluzenta, figuring she already knew.

"Bottom line, this appeal is our last chance, and it is fifty-fifty, maybe sixty-forty. I worked on it all the way back from Cupertino yesterday, and I'm sorry, but there is no way I can take a week off. I'm going to have to postpone our trip to London."

She shook her head slowly, her eyes pitying him over the top of her sunglasses. "She's going to be heartbroken, you know?"

Eric snorted. Typical Kate, she didn't stop at sticking the knife in. She had to twist it a bit. He bit his tongue.

"I realize that. That's why I wanted to tell you first. I'd like to pick her up from school so I can tell her myself."

With her index finger, she pushed the sunglasses up on her nose, tilted her head back, and sneered slightly behind her disguise. The entire motion was as if she found him repulsive. "I thought you had changed, at least I was hoping. Hoping that you had finally realized your family was more important than your precious career." She let the words dangle, snaking their way through his gut.

She picked up her keys and stood. "I've lost my appetite. You're on the list to pick her up. Just have her back home no later than five o'clock. It's a school night." She turned and walked away.

The server came over, looking at Kate's back and then at Eric.

"Was there a problem, sir?"

Eric shook his head. "No, not with you."

With a heavy heart, he picked at his lunch, managing to get half of it down. While he waited for the server to bring his credit card back, he checked his watch. He still had a couple of hours before Ali got out of school.

He drove to Malaprop's Bookstore on Haywood Street, one of his favorite independent bookstores. Between the cappuccino and browsing, the time passed quickly. He had to hurry to get to Ali's school on time. Familiar with the drill, he took his place in the conga line of soccer moms waiting to pick up their charges.

As he got close to the canopy, he could see Ali looking for her mom. His faded red Jeep stuck out in the sea of Lexus and Mercedes sedans, and when she finally noticed it, she strained to see. When he was three cars behind, he stuck his hand out and waved. Her grin broke his heart. She was so glad to see him. He dreaded telling her that he was postponing their trip to London.

As his turn was up, the chaperone walked out to the Jeep with Ali. Recognizing him, the teacher smiled and waved. Ali threw open the door, grinning from ear to ear.

"Daddy," she exclaimed. "What are you doing here?" She settled in the seat, fastening her safety belt and throwing her backpack in the rear seat.

"I wanted to surprise you. Thought we could make up for our ice cream date we had to miss the other week."

They went to Cold Stone Creamery since it was near Ali's school. As usual, Ali had her vanilla ice cream with sprinkles. She talked incessantly about her day at school, relaying every detail to him.

It made him realize how much he missed her and the day-to-day happenings in her life. Maybe Kate was right, he thought.

"Did you see Mom?" she asked.

He girded himself as he prepared to broach the real reason for his visit. "Yes, I did. I met her for lunch."

Ali eyed him curiously, now suspecting something after that revelation.

"I needed to talk to her and with you."

Her eyes narrowed, confirming her suspicions. He could think of no other way to break the news. He took in a deep breath then exhaled.

"We're going to have to postpone our trip to London, Sweetie."

Her expression sank as she absorbed what he'd said. She didn't say a word.

"Something very important has come up at Daddy's work," he said, using the phrase he'd rehearsed on the way over to Asheville.

"What, Daddy?" Her tone was like a dagger between his ribs. It expressed genuine concern, not for delaying the trip, but for him. His heart was breaking, and he was tempted to chuck it all.

"You know that I've been working on a special medicine, right? One to keep people from getting sick?"

She nodded.

"Well, I have to go to Washington to answer some questions about it. Then, the people who need the medicine can get it."

She looked at him, her brown eyes reflecting her processing the simplistic explanation he'd given her. After a few seconds, she said, "That's okay, Daddy. I understand."

He told her maybe they could go to London around Christmas, even though he had not cleared it with her mom. That was one of the things he wanted to discuss with Kate at lunch but never got to it before her abrupt departure.

"London would be fun at Christmas," she said, a trace of her smile returning.

"It would be. We'll have to make sure it's okay with your Mom, though. I didn't get a chance to ask her at lunch."

When they finished eating their ice creams, Ali asked if they could go to the Nature Center. She loved to see the animals, especially the black bear and the playful river otters.

Eric looked at his watch. "Sure, but we have to have you home by five. It's a school night." He wasn't about to risk further alienating Kate.

Once inside the Nature Center, Ali headed straight to Otter Falls, the first exhibit on the grounds. Today, two of the otters were playing chase, scampering across the rocks and sliding down into the water, over and over. Ali laughed as she watched.

Then, she tugged on Eric's hand. He knew she was going over to see the bear. The solitary black bear was sleeping when they got to his enclosure.

"He's lonely," Ali said. "He doesn't have anyone with him like the otters."

Eric shook his head. *Out of the mouths of babes,* he thought.

"He would be happier in the Park, wouldn't he, Daddy?" She was referring to the Great Smoky Mountains National Park.

He didn't know the story behind this particular bear, but he couldn't help but agree with his daughter. Even she knew something didn't seem right about imprisoning a wild animal in a cage.

Trying to put a positive spin on it, he said, "Maybe, but there are some advantages to living here. He gets plenty to eat, and he doesn't have to worry about another animal bothering him."

She wrinkled her brow as if weighing the advantages and disadvantages. "I think he would rather be in the Park. He would probably have friends there."

He nodded, proud of his daughter. He had to agree with her logic.

They walked around, pausing for a brief time in front of the other exhibits. Eric looked at his watch and shook his head. Time to go. He was determined not to be late.

When they got to Kate's house five minutes early, Kate was late getting to the door. Not waiting, Ali opened it, and dragged Eric inside. Kate was coming down the hall as he closed the door behind him.

Ali announced, "We had ice cream and then went to the Nature Center. The otters were funny, but the bear was sad." She mentioned nothing about the canceled trip.

Kate looked at Eric, her eyes asking if he'd told Ali.

Eric nodded. "I told Ali that I couldn't take her to London next week."

"Yeah, he has to work on his medicine for people. But he said we might go for Christmas, right Daddy?"

Kate's neutral face turned sour. Before she could say anything, Eric held up his hand. "I told Ali 'maybe,' and we'd have to check with you first. It's too early to tell." He held his breath, hoping Kate would calm down and not make a scene.

She relaxed a tiny bit and looked down at Ali. "We'll see, honey. I'll talk to your Dad about it later."

Mollified, Ali turned and stuck her hands up toward Eric. "Thank you for the ice cream. And taking me to see the animals."

He reached down and picked her up, hugging her tightly as she planted a wet kiss on his cheek. "You're most welcome. I love you, Ali."

"Love you, too, Daddy."

10

Eric drove back to Waynesville with a heavy heart. Although he was glad that Ali seemed to understand why they were delaying the London trip, he hated to leave her after delivering the bad news. Sometimes the simplest things were the hardest, like today. It was only a few hours, and all they did was eat ice cream and see the animals, but it was a priceless afternoon to him. There was no way he was moving to California.

His phone buzzed, and he picked it up out of the console. Frank Liles. He debated on whether to answer, then pressed the Talk button.

"Hello, Frank."

"Hey, Eric. Where are you? Still in Asheville?"

"No, about halfway home. Why?"

"I wanted to see if you had time for dinner."

Eric was confused. "Dinner? Are you in Asheville?"

"No, at the lab. At the last minute, I decided to stop by on my way back to Cupertino. I'm going back in the morning."

Eric scowled, wondering what this was about.

"Let's have dinner at that restaurant downtown," Frank said. "The place with the trout. What's the name?"

"The Sweet Onion?"

"Yeah, that's it. How far out are you?"

Eric looked out the car window to get his bearings. He'd just passed the Canton exit. "I'm probably fifteen minutes away."

"Good. I'll meet you there." The call disconnected.

Sweet Onion, just off Main Street, was one of Eric's favorites in Waynesville, only a few blocks up the hill from Frog Level. He found a parking place in front of the restaurant, got out and walked inside. Before the hostess could assist him, he saw Frank sitting to his right, in the far corner.

"How is Alison?" Frank asked as Eric slid in opposite him.

"She's doing well, considering. I delivered the news about skipping our London trip next week."

Frank nodded. "That wasn't good news for any of us. You'll be able to make it up to her. We just have to get this denial reversed as soon as possible."

After they had ordered, Frank told him about talking with Nicole.

"She said you'd decided to go along with resubmitting Group Two. I think it's a splendid idea, don't you?"

Eric had given it a lot of thought on the way over to Asheville. It was tempting, he had to admit, but somehow it seemed disingenuous.

"It's backing into the answer, Frank."

Frank sat back and held out his hands. "So? You don't think every other pharmaceutical firm doesn't do this? They all do."

"I'm sure they probably do, but—"

"But?" Frank leaned across the table and lowered his voice. "We've invested almost a billion dollars in Fluzenta, Eric. Billion with a capital *B*. I've got probably fifty, sixty million in it, and you've got, what, a couple of mil?"

Eric shrugged, then nodded.

Frank continued. "Fluzenta goes to market, we make ten times that. Your couple of million turns into twenty million, Eric. That's twenty million for you and Ali." He leaned back to let that sink in.

"Fluzenta doesn't get off the ground, you know what we've got?" He paused for a few seconds, then held up his thumb and forefinger touching. "Zero. Nothing. Not even what we've put up. We don't even have enough in the bank to pay what we owe, let alone pay the investors."

"I understand what's at stake, Frank, believe me, I do."

Frank took a sip of his wine and continued. "How much do you know about West Coast Capital? Chip Miller?"

Eric shrugged. "Not much. What you've told me. It's a West Coast-based venture capital fund headed by a very rich Chip Miller. I know they've invested a lot in Tera. Why?"

Frank's eyes darted nervously about the restaurant. Eric looked around, thinking for a moment that Frank saw someone. The place was almost empty. The next closest person was several tables away.

Before he could say anything, Frank lowered his voice another notch to little more than a whisper. Eric had to strain to hear him.

"West Coast Capital has $850 *million* invested in Tera Pharmagenics." Frank paused for a moment. "Do you have any idea where Chip got his fortune?"

Eric shook his head. "Investments? Inheritance? I don't know. I haven't thought about it. Why should I care?"

"Wrong answer. You do care, trust me." Frank stared at him for an uncomfortable length of time. "Chip's money is 'family' money."

Eric threw up his hands. "So? He comes from a rich fam—"

"Listen to what I'm saying. Chip is from New Jersey. Fifteen years ago, his uncle was shot and killed while having dinner at a restaurant on Mulberry Street in the city. Little Italy." He sat back in his chair. "Capiche?"

Eric shook his head. As he was about to say something, he realized what Frank was saying. *Chip's money came from the mob.* He cocked his head and said, "You're saying *the* family? As in—"

Frank held up his finger to his lips, silencing Eric, and nodding.

Now Eric was whispering. "You're telling me that our biggest investor is the mob?"

"They are involved in a lot more legitimate businesses than many people realize," Frank said. "You heard the discussion in Cupertino. They want their money back, preferably with appreciation. Losses are unacceptable to these people."

Eric shook his head. "But that's crazy. Investing in new drug development is a gamble at best. We don't control—"

"I understand that. And I've tried to make sure they did, too. But we've led them to believe it was going to be approved. Everyone thought that. We have to find a way to get this on the market, Eric. We have no other option, understand?"

Eric studied his boss. "We're doing everything we can. If they deny us in the review meeting, we can appeal it further."

Frank pushed his plate away, finishing the last bite of his trout, thinking as he chewed. "We both know this review meeting is our only chance. How do you see our odds if we can convince the committee to accept Group Two?"

Eric had spent a lot of time thinking about this since his trip to San Francisco. Even with tweaking the data and resubmitting, the odds weren't as good as he would've liked. He gave Frank his best guess.

"Sixty-forty. Sixty percent chance we'll be successful."

Frank eyed him incredulously, his mouth open. "Sixty-forty? Are you serious? That's not much better than what you said in California. We might as well go to Las Vegas. And that's with tweaking the data from Group Two?"

"That's my best guess." He'd been in this business long enough to know that the FDA was not as predictable as people thought. Witness the denial of Fluzenta. "I want this as much as everyone, Frank. But I can't control the FDA."

Frank looked off into the distance, focusing on nothing.

"We cannot afford to strike out, Eric. We can't."

11

Thanks to a last-minute opening, the date for the review meeting arrived sooner than Eric had expected. Working round the clock, Eric and his team had reworked the Group Two data and submitted it as a "correction" to the original NDA.

"Almost show time," Eric said, trying to diffuse the tension. He, Nicole, and Wally were in a limo, going to their supervisory review meeting with the committee that had denied the NDA for Fluzenta.

They were in Silver Spring, Maryland, just outside the Beltway. They had flown into Washington Dulles International Airport on one of the Tera Pharmagenics jets. Reagan National was closer, but the hassles of flying private aircraft into that airport were considerable, so Eric had opted for Dulles.

He recognized the low brick sign ahead on New Hampshire Avenue as the limo driver slowed and turned into the entrance to the Federal Research Center at White Oak, home to the Food and Drug Administration. A block away stood a sprawling four-story brick building, which was Building 1 and their destination.

Earlier in the week, he and Frank had a heated argument about whether Frank would attend. Frank had insisted on coming, but Eric felt that his presence would be interpreted as a strong-arm tactic and possibly backfire. This meeting was about the details and Eric convinced Frank that he was more effective working behind the scenes.

They entered the lobby, signed in, and received their Visitor badges. The receptionist instructed them to have a seat in the vestibule, and someone would be down shortly to escort them to the meeting room. After only ten minutes, a smartly dressed young man walked up to the group.

"Dr. Carter?" he said, looking first at Wally, then to Eric. Despite the fact that Eric had insisted Wally clean up and at least wear slacks and a shirt with a collar, he still didn't look the part of the sponsor.

Eric stood and took the proffered hand. "I'm Eric Carter." He introduced Wally and Nicole as his senior scientists.

"I'm Quentin Farmer. If you'll follow me, please."

They followed Farmer past a security guard to the bank of elevators and walked into a waiting car. The young man pressed four, the doors closed, and they were on their way.

On the fourth floor, they exited and walked down a long hallway to a door on the right. Farmer ushered them in.

Five people sat at a large, oval-shaped conference table, with Lin Zheng in the power position. She stood, greeting Eric with a warm "Hello" and handshake, clasping his wrist with her free hand. Eric was relieved to see that her eyes were warm and forgiving. She appeared to harbor no ill feelings over their last phone conversation where he hung up on her.

Lin introduced the committee as Eric and his team took their seats. She opened the meeting with a brief summarization of the application and the response letter. It was concise and unemotional. She concluded by yielding the floor to Eric.

Although he had his notes in front of him, he didn't need to reference them. He'd rehearsed his opening remarks many times. He was more interested in trying to read their faces when he proposed that they had submitted the wrong cohort group.

He kept his remarks short and to the point, merely establishing the opening. He was ready to engage with this group and see where they stood.

In addition to excluding certain patients as Nicole had suggested, Tera Pharmagenics had also added more label warnings and additional restrictions on who should not be taking the drug. They had reduced the potential mortality rate by a third of what it was before.

Finally, Eric got to the elephant in the room.

"As you can see, we have submitted data from another cohort group." He took a breath, glanced at Nicole, and then continued.

"I realize this is highly unusual." He deliberately chose "unusual," wanting to convey that there was a precedent without saying so directly. "This is the direct result of a clerical mistake on the original application, for which I take full responsibility. I am embarrassed to say that in our haste to get the NDA to you on a timely basis, I inadvertently approved the incorrect trial. You should consider this as an amendment, which is allowed under the rules, and not as additional data, which is precludable."

Dr. Zheng paused to look at the folder in front of her, pulled out a sheaf of paper, and held it up.

"So you are saying Group Two should have been submitted instead of Group Four?"

He nodded. "Again, Dr. Zheng, I apologize. In preparing for this meeting, we—I—noticed that somehow Group Four had been submitted instead of Group Two. This was completely my mistake, and I take full responsibility. As you can see, we have been completely transparent about this error. We conducted the Group Two trial according to the same rigorous criteria as all of the studies. With the additional warnings and restrictions, we feel that we have resolved the committee's issues on the original application. "

Four of the committee members nodded, but their faces remained neutral. The fifth person at the table, a PhD introduced as Orson Mitchell II, scowled. Eric sensed trouble.

Mitchell, a preppy-looking WASP wearing a bowtie, cleared his throat. Assuming an air of importance, he held up his copy of the documents as he spoke.

"Even though you and your CEO, Mr. Liles, certified on the NDA that it was complete and correct, we are to believe that submitting Group Four was a mistake?"

Eric gritted his teeth and nodded. The FDA was going on record and covering their ass. If this blew up later, Eric Carter and Frank Liles would be the scapegoats, not the committee. They wanted him to restate the obvious in his own words.

"Yes. It was a simple clerical error, and for that, I humbly apologize." He wanted to add that other companies had done the same thing, but he didn't want to appear confrontational. That would ensure certain denial of the Tera Pharmagenics appeal.

Mitchell dropped his documents on the table and snorted. "This is highly irregular. I find it hard to believe that you and your team could make such an elementary mistake. Is this your first application?"

Eric looked at the other members of the committee. This was a rhetorical question, intended to embarrass him. He was tempted to ignore it, but shook his head.

"No, this is not my first time, which makes it all the more embarrassing. Again, I apologize."

He got the distinct impression that the committee was bored with the proceedings at this point and disinterested in what Mitchell was saying. Orson Mitchell II was the designated bad guy. His assignment was to deliver the official scolding, as well as the unrefutable assignment of guilt.

Mea culpa, mea culpa, Eric thought. He understood that no further explanation was required or expected regarding the substitution. This was for show.

Two hours later, Eric and his team concluded their remarks. Since the committee had asked their questions during the presentation, the conclusion was brief with only a couple of additional questions for clarification.

As everyone said their goodbyes, Eric was feeling encouraged. The questions had been positive, and the group indicated a general acceptance of the answers.

"That ended a lot better than it started," Wally said as soon as they got in the limo for the trip to the airport.

Nicole looked at Eric. "I thought it went well after they made it clear you were going to be the sacrificial lamb."

Eric shrugged. "All of that was for the record. If it blows up, Frank and I are going to be hung out to dry. But I don't care as long as they give us the approval for Fluzenta."

It was almost an hour later when the limo dropped them off at Signature Flight Support at Dulles airport. The Tera Pharmagenics jet was on the apron, refueled and ready to leave. As soon as they were onboard, the co-pilot closed the door and went to the cockpit where the pilot started the engines.

In the main cabin, Eric, Nicole, and Wally sat in the middle seats. Eric and Nicole sat next to each other, facing Wally.

Soon after they were airborne, Eric unbuckled his seat belt and rose. "Excuse me, but I'm going to move up front and call Frank."

He moved forward to another seat next to the cockpit. He picked up the satellite phone and called Frank's cell phone.

"I was beginning to wonder," Frank answered. "I thought maybe they'd kidnapped you."

"I wanted to wait until I was on the plane to call. You never know who's listening."

"Well?"

He relayed the highlights of the meeting, including Mitchell's tongue lashing.

When he'd finished, Frank said, "What a prick. Sounds like it ended well. Maybe, I should've—"

"It wouldn't have made any difference, Frank. In fact, it was probably better that you weren't there. They would have delighted in raking the CEO over the coals in person. I took the lashes for both of us. We had a good story, and I think they bought it. Did you have any luck with the senator from North Carolina?"

"I finally had a chance to speak with him, briefly. He was receptive and promised he'd have one of his staffers look into it. Of course, he's a politician, and we know how reliable that is. But, I believe it's on his radar, and we do contribute to his war chest. How soon will we get an answer?"

"They normally have thirty days, but we waived that as a measure of good faith. According to Zheng, it will probably be sooner."

"Okay. I need to call Chip. Later," Frank said and ended the call.

Eric replaced the handset in its cradle and stared out the window. It was only an hour and fifteen minutes to Asheville. He walked back into the middle cabin and collapsed into his former seat.

"How did that go?" Nicole asked.

Eric nodded. "Good. He had spoken to the senator from North Carolina, so that's encouraging, too."

"Where does that leave us?" Nicole asked.

"I feel good about it. We've got a great drug, and we gave it a good shot. Let's hope the FDA agrees."

"Just wait till we have an avian flu outbreak. Then they'll be breaking our door down," Wally said.

Nicole nodded. "If by chance they do deny it, we can continue the appeals process, right? That was just the first step."

Wally snorted. "Keep dreaming, Blondie. Each step in the appeals process has lower odds of succeeding. That was our best chance."

Eric held up a hand. "C'mon guys. Let's don't get ahead of ourselves just yet. You did good in there. Think positive."

Eric didn't want to say out loud that Wally was right. If the supervisory review they just finished confirmed the initial denial, it was over. Fluzenta was dead, and so was Tera Pharmagenics.

12

Eric drummed a pencil on the conference table in his office. Underneath was the certified letter from the FDA he'd just received an hour ago, announcing that the committee had reaffirmed their denial. They refused to accept the substitution of Group Two.

The only good news was that they hadn't waited the entire thirty days. It had only been two weeks since he had been in Washington, pleading their case.

The committee's position was that if Group Two should have been filed, then Tera's application was careless, and a careless process was no excuse. That comment was a slap in the face to a seasoned professional like Eric. The unspoken message was that they thought his argument was crap.

He picked up the phone and called Dr. Lin Zheng's office. He wasn't angry this time, just confused and needing clarification.

Her assistant answered and put him on hold. Eric was already composing his message, figuring Lin wouldn't talk to him.

"Hello, Eric," Lin said, answering the phone. Eric was surprised and had to regroup.

"Hi, Lin. Thanks for taking my call. I promise not to be a rude ass this time."

She chuckled. "I was expecting your call. I've only got a few minutes before I have to go into a meeting." She didn't ask what he wanted.

"What did I miss, Lin? Help me out. When we left, I had the distinct feeling that the committee was leaning our way." He picked up the FDA letter. "Then, I received this."

There was a hesitation on the line before Lin spoke. "You read it correctly. The committee was poised to approve your refiling and accept your explanation."

"Really. What happened?"

"All I can tell you is that one of the committee members got a call. Someone challenged giving Tera an exception and hinted that if we did, it was going to be all over the news."

"Who would do that?" Eric asked. It was a rhetorical question, and he didn't expect an answer.

"I can't say any more. I've probably said too much as it is, but you and I go way back. I just didn't want you blaming yourself. I'm sorry, Eric, but there's nothing I can do. It's above my pay grade. On that note, I have to run. Call me sometime when you're in DC and let's get together."

He thanked her and hung up the phone. Time had run out. There were no rabbits in the hat and no options left that he could think of. Nobody would be riding in on a white horse to rescue Fluzenta.

He stared out his office window. The leaves were changing color. Fall was in the air, and it was getting dark earlier. If it weren't so late in the day, he'd go to the woods under the pretense of trout fishing.

Before long, the dead of winter would be upon them. And Eric would be without a job. The Panther Cove lab would either be closed or the newest location for another company.

Out of respect, he'd told Nicole and Wally a few minutes ago, pledging them to secrecy. He hadn't called Frank yet, dreading the conversation.

He stood and walked out, telling Carmen he would be unreachable and would be in tomorrow morning. Thirty minutes later, he walked into Frog Level Brewing. An older guy, a regular Eric recognized, was seated at the far end of the bar, nursing a beer. A couple was just settling their bill and preparing to leave. Tuesdays were always slow.

Clark was sitting behind the bar in his usual spot, closest to the street. He looked up, saw Eric, and nodded.

Eric walked up and put his keys on the bar. He pulled out a stool and sat as Clark placed a caramel-colored beer on the counter in front of Eric.

"Where's your fan club?" Clark said, smiling.

Eric belted down a large swallow from the glass. "Just me. Where is everybody?"

Clark pulled his stool over and sat, taking a sip of the half-full glass of beer he'd just drawn from the tap. "Just Clarence," he said, nodding toward the man at the other end of the bar. "It's Tuesday. Slowest day of the week."

Eric downed the rest of his beer, sliding the empty glass toward Clark.

"Thirsty today?" Clark asked.

"Celebrating."

"What's the occasion?" Clark asked with a puzzled expression.

"My unemployment."

Eric told his friend what had happened.

Clark poured him another beer. "Maybe you could commute to California for a while. Buy yourself some time."

Eric shook his head. "You don't understand, that's not going to be an option. I told you before, the whole company will be down the tubes. Everything, and I mean everything, was based on this drug."

The two friends talked for hours, Eric drinking two full beers for every half that Clark drank. Around nine, Eric got up to go to the bathroom and almost fell. Weaving his way across the room, he realized he'd probably drunk too much, especially without eating.

When he staggered out of the bathroom and made his way back over to the bar, he saw Clark on his phone, nodding, and then hanging up.

"One more," Eric said, as he sat and almost missed the stool. Clark didn't say a word, just took a fresh glass out of the cooler and drew yet another beer.

Eric was having a hard time trying to get the words out coherently. Squinting with one eye, he looked at his glass. It was still half full. "I think we need to . . . to settle after dis one. I gotta go to bed."

"Sure thing, brother. Just relax, no rush."

After what seemed like an eternity, Eric finally downed the rest of his beer and slammed the glass down on the bar. "Did I pay you yet?" he asked Clark, slurring his words.

"We'll settle up later. Just sit tight."

Eric stuck his hand in his pocket, looking for his keys. They weren't there. With much effort, he tried the other pocket. Same result. He looked up at Clark. "Have you seen my keys?"

"You don't need—"

Eric slapped the bar. "They were here. I put them right here, I 'member. Somebody stole my keys."

He felt a hand on his shoulder, and he clenched his fist. He snapped around, ready for a fight. It was Nicole.

"Heya. What you're doing here?" he said, reaching out to hug her and almost falling off his stool.

"I'm going to take you home. You ready?"

He looked at Clark, confused, then back at Nicole. "But I don't have my keys."

He heard a jingle and saw Clark handing a set of keys to Nicole. "The Jeep will be okay down here. We'll sort it out in the morning. Thanks, Nicole."

Eric wasn't much help to Nicole as she somehow managed to get him into her car. He remembered attempting to tell her something, then next he knew, she was shaking his shoulder, trying to get him out of the car.

"Where . . ." He recognized they were at his house. Struggling to help him walk, she got him up the steps and inside. He wanted to fall on the couch, but she kept pushing him forward.

"No, no. Keep going. You stop now, and I'll never get you to bed."

Laughing, he squeezed her shoulder. "You're taking me to bed. That's good."

She laughed. "No, not like that. Not tonight, cowboy. I'm trying to get you to bed before you pass out."

The last thing he remembered was lying on his back in bed, grinning. Nicole was taking his pants off.

* * *

The smell of bacon frying woke him up. The simple task of opening his eyes hurt. His head was throbbing, and with the amount of sunlight in the room, he knew it had to be late. He forced himself to shift his head so he could see the bedside clock. 8:37. With a groan, he closed his eyes, wishing the pain in his head to go away.

He tried to recall last night, remembering Nicole taking his jeans off. Reaching down underneath the sheet, he felt his boxers. He wondered where she was.

"You ready for coffee, yet?" Nicole asked, walking into the bedroom.

With one eye partially open, he turned toward the sound of her voice. Nicole was dressed and wore slacks and a blouse. *Business casual* was the term that popped into his befuddled brain.

"If you've got some aspirin to go with it," he mumbled.

Her laugh made him smile, which also hurt. "I'll be right back."

He attempted to sit on the edge of the bed, careful to keep the sheet over his shorts. The jackhammers inside his head were pounding away wide open now.

Nicole returned with a mug half full of coffee and two aspirin in her hand. He wondered why she gave him only half a cup, but when he took it and saw how much his hand was shaking, he understood. He downed the aspirin with a slug of coffee, almost burning his tongue. "Thank you."

"Think you can make it to the kitchen?"

He nodded. Although that hurt, it didn't seem to hurt as much as talking. He wanted to put on some more clothes but realized that was impossible at the moment. He stood, letting the sheet fall away. Not seeming to notice or care, she put her arm around his waist and helped him to the kitchen.

Grateful for the stool and the counter to lean on, he closed his eyes. The noise of kitchen utensils clanging and scraping sounded like a commercial construction site. At last, it stopped, and he heard a plate on the counter in front of him. He peeped and saw a plate of eggs, toast, and bacon.

"Eat what you can. I'm hungry," she said.

He slowly swiveled over to see her sitting next to him, a full plate in front of her.

There wasn't a lot of conversation as they ate. Eric didn't quite know what to say, and besides, it hurt too much to talk. Nicole was busy eating and seemed content to do so in silence.

After he had got a little food down, along with more coffee, he started to feel better. "Thanks for coming to get me last night. I was obviously over-served."

She smiled at his feeble attempt at humor.

"You're welcome. Clark would've brought you home, but he didn't think you could make it until closing time."

"Good call. I owe him. And you."

She laughed, but it was gentle. "You would've done the same for me." She reached over and patted his hand, not leaving it there. "You okay?"

It was his turn to laugh, or at least attempt to. Laughing still hurt.

"I've got a hell of a hangover, but I don't think that's what you're asking. No, I'm not." He glanced outside, the morning light hurting his eyes. "I spent ten years of my life on that drug, Nicole. Ten fucking years. And, a considerable amount of money, at least for me. But you know the worst thing?"

She narrowed her eyebrows and shook her head.

"I think about all the lives it could save. And now, it won't."

She put her hand over his and this time let it stay. "We're not through, Eric. We can appeal. Maybe we can sell it to another company. We can't give up."

He looked at her in disbelief, slowly shaking her head. "All of that takes money and time. We're out of both."

"Yes, but—"

"I probably shouldn't tell you this, but do you know how much of his money Frank Liles has invested in this company?" He didn't wait for her to answer. "Probably close to a hundred million dollars."

Her eyes got wide, and he continued. "He's mortgaged everything he owns."

He let that sink in and pressed on. "Hell, I've got probably two million of my own money invested. And all of it is gone."

An awkward silence grew between them.

Eric said, "I guess the silver lining is that most of the money belonged to the venture capital firm—Chip Miller's company."

"Maybe you could talk him into waiting until the end of the year?"

Eric shook his head and snorted. "Miller's not willing to wait. He'll be ready to pull the trigger as soon as he hears the news. West Coast Capital wants their money back, and if they have to sell off pieces to get it, they will."

Nicole stood behind him and put her arms around his neck. She hugged him, then stepped back and put her hands on her hips. "This is such bullshit. There's got to be something we can do to get Fluzenta out there. Too many people need it."

13

On her way to the lab, Nicole dropped Eric off at Frog Level to pick up his Jeep. He saw Clark's truck parked out front and decided to go in and say "hello."

He walked into the empty bar and to the open doorway of Clark's office, just inside. Clark was sitting in front of his computer screen and looked up when he heard Eric tapping on the wall.

"Hey, brother," Clark said. "You look better than I thought you would've at this time of the morning."

Eric nodded. "Thanks. And thanks for looking out for me last night. I appreciate it."

"Hey, what are friends for. You feel any better?"

"No. My gambit to substitute data didn't work. The company's down the toilet, and I'll soon be out of a job. Other than that, everything's fine."

"Yeah, you told me all that last night. I didn't want to say anything to add to your misery, but I heard something yesterday that you might want to know."

"Pile it on, brother. Why not?"

"I heard that your company is shopping the lab property."

"Panther Cove? Really?" Eric was surprised. He thought about his conversations with Rae and Chip, but he'd not heard anything lately about selling the Panther Cove facility. Frank had not said a word about it.

Clark nodded. "From what I hear, it's officially for sale, and priced to sell, too."

"Who's shopping it? Someone local?"

Clark hesitated as if debating on whether to say anything more. "You didn't hear this from me."

Eric nodded.

"Bryson Edwards."

* * *

Eric left Frog Level and headed to work. He felt betrayed. Betrayed by Frank, betrayed by Kate, betrayed by everyone.

Panther Cove was his baby and they were going to sell it out from under him. His fingers tightened on the steering wheel of his Jeep.

The bluegrass ringtone chimed. He wasn't in the mood to talk with anyone, but picked up the phone and glanced at the screen.

Rae. How convenient. He clicked Answer, waiting for her voice on the hands-free speaker.

"Hey. How are you?" she said.

"I've been better. Of course, I'm sure you know that."

There was a pause on the line. "I'm not sure I know what you're talking about. What's wrong?"

He was in no mood to play games. "Is Tera Pharmagenics selling off Panther Cove?"

"What? Where did you hear that?"

He noticed that she didn't answer his question. He asked her again.

"Are you selling Panther Cove?"

"No, I'm not aware that we're selling it. Why?"

"Because I heard from a reliable source that the company is shopping it."

"Well, if we are, that's news to me. No one has mentioned that subject since we were in Cupertino, at least in my presence."

Her tone turned indignant as she realized he was accusing her of withholding information from him. "Look," she said. "I'm in Atlanta. I called because I wanted to come up and spend the weekend with you. Maybe that wasn't such a good idea."

He started to come back with a smart-ass reply, then held his tongue.

"Sure. Come on up."

He heard Rae take a deep breath over the phone. "I tell you what. Forget it. Maybe some other time." There was an audible click as she hung up.

He shook his head. Maybe she didn't know, maybe she did. He'd taken his anger out on her, but now he felt bad. He wanted to see her.

When he got to the lab and parked, he called her back.

His call went straight to voice mail. He left her a message saying he was sorry and would she please call him back and that he would love for her to come to North Carolina for the weekend.

An hour later, his cell phone rang.

"I was tied up on a conference call," Rae said when he answered. "Besides, we both probably needed to cool off. I can understand why you're upset and I get that you're taking it out on me." Her voice was calm and measured. "But I promise you I knew nothing about any attempt to sell Panther Cove."

"I'm sorry," he said. He had been an ass, and he knew it. "I had just found out before you called, and jumped to the conclusion that you knew about it. To top it off, I also heard that Kate's husband has the listing."

"Kate's husband? Where did you hear this?"

"Clark told me, but you can't repeat that."

"Well, I intend to get to the bottom of this first thing in the morning."

"No, Rae, please don't. He told me this in confidence, and I don't want to betray that. It doesn't matter."

"I *am* going to find out, but don't worry, I won't disclose that you told me anything. I'm the fucking CFO, Eric, and I sure as hell should know if we're trying to sell off a multi-million-dollar asset."

Eric had to smile at Rae's use of the f-word. She didn't normally use that one and to him confirmed that she didn't know about selling the lab.

"I apologize for taking it out on you," he said. "I'd like to see you this weekend if you're willing to put up with a grouchy old man."

"Maybe I could exorcise the grouch," she said.

He could hear the smile in her voice and he in turn smiled. "Well, you've been forewarned. What time will you be here?"

* * *

When he got to the house the next afternoon, he fed Felix and tried to straighten up a bit before Rae got there. He had suggested going out to dinner, but she countered with wine and nibbles at the house.

On the way home, he'd stopped and got several different kinds of cheeses, olives, crackers, and fresh North Carolina apples. He took a quick shower and put on some clean clothes, finding himself excited about her visit. He glanced at the clock. Rae would be here in fifteen minutes.

He splurged and opened a bottle of Caymus, one of his favorite Cabernet Sauvignons, to let it breathe. He unwrapped the cheeses, slicing them and arranging everything on a tray with the fruit, olives, and crackers. Determined to make up for his grumpy demeanor over the phone last night, he set two places at the table on the deck, along with two wine glasses.

He stepped back and nodded, satisfied with the arrangement. It was going to be a beautiful fall evening. A little on the cool side, but not so much as to be uncomfortable with a light wrap. He started to go inside to get a light blanket for Rae when he heard a car pulling up out front. He smiled and walked down the deck stairs instead to greet her.

The ubiquitous silver rental car, Rae at the wheel, parked behind his Jeep. She shut off the car and stepped out.

Eric's eyes widened. All he saw was legs. Rae stood next to the car, one arm draped over the door. She was wearing the shortest skirt he'd ever seen her in. She removed her sweater, revealing a slinky, gold top that went well with the black mini-skirt.

She held her hands down on her hips, palms facing him, and smiled. "Do I get a hug and kiss or are you going to just stand there and gawk?"

"Wow," he answered. "Right now, I'm enjoying ogling this gorgeous brunette that just drove up in my yard."

She laughed and smiled as he walked slowly toward her. "So, you like my new outfit?" she asked.

He answered by taking her in his arms and kissing her passionately, letting his hands roam over her body.

When they finally separated, she caught her breath and said, "I take that as a 'yes.'"

Eric grinned, holding her at arm's length. "You just made me forget all of my problems."

"That was the idea," she said, still smiling, obviously pleased with her entrance.

He reached into the car, grabbed her bag and sweater, and shut the door. Holding up the sweater, he said, "I think you are going to need a few more clothes to sit out on the deck. It's going to be a little cool once the sun goes down."

He took her hand and led her to the house. "Or, we could just stay inside?" he said at the front door.

She laughed again. "After the way you acted on the phone, you're going to have to beg forgiveness first, big boy."

"I can do that—no problem."

Inside, he took her bag back to the bedroom. When he came out, she was kneeling, petting Felix. Once again, he was struck by her long legs, almost completely exposed.

"I hope you weren't wearing that outfit at your meeting."

She stood, tugging on her skirt. "Why? Are you jealous?"

He laughed. "Yes, and if there were any men in the meeting, I know what they were looking at. And they probably think you're the mild-mannered accountant."

She came over and kissed him again. "I bought this in Atlanta, especially for you. Once I crossed the line into North Carolina, I stopped in Franklin and changed. You should've seen the looks I got when I came out of the restroom at the convenience store."

He nodded, grinning. "I can imagine. They'll be talking about that in Franklin for a while."

Stopping to get the hors-d'oeuvres and bottle of wine, they went out to the deck and sat, Eric unable to take his eyes off her.

"Eat fast," he said.

Munching on the appetizers and enjoying the wine, they watched as dusk crept into the mountains. When it got cooler, Eric covered her shoulders with a blanket.

"I hate covering up my view, but I know you're getting chilled."

She smiled and nodded. "Thank you. You'll get the completely unobstructed view later."

They talked about everything but work, laughing and relaxing. He was glad Rae was there. She had lifted him out of his funk.

After darkness had settled and most of the wine was gone, Rae stood and held out her hand. She led him back into the bedroom, where the only light spilled over from the kitchen. He tried to kiss her, but she pushed him back on the bed. She stood facing him, just out of reach, and dropped the blanket from her shoulders.

Deliberately, she raised the top she was wearing over her head and slipped it off, tossing it over in the corner. She lowered her hands down to her side, letting him savor the view. She wore a sheer black bra, thin enough that he could see her erect nipples.

Without rushing, she put her thumbs underneath the top of her skirt and wriggled out of it, exposing a black thong that barely covered anything. Wearing only the bra and panties, she turned a complete revolution, letting him fill his eyes from every angle.

When she faced him again, he reached his hands out to her. Smiling, she shook her head. She was in no hurry and enjoying teasing him. Carefully, she reached up and unhooked her bra, managing to keep her hands in front of her breasts. Then, she let the bra fall to the floor.

As he stared at her bare breasts, she lowered her hands, and hooked her thumbs under the thong, sliding it down over her hips.

He extended his hands once again and said, "Come over here so I can kiss you."

That night, the sex was incredible. As promised, she had done things to him that made him feel better, much better.

After the second time, he shook his head, lying on his back with Rae's face on his shoulder. "I won't be able to do it again for a week," he said, laughing. "You've worn me out."

She reached down and squeezed him. "We'll see about that."

They cuddled up, satiated, and soon drifted off to sleep.

The next morning, after making love once again, Rae asked, "Are you going to take me hiking today?"

Shaking his head and laughing, he said, "I'm not sure I can get up out of bed. What are you trying to do, kill me?"

She grinned. "Just trying to take your mind off things."

"You've succeeded. I'll do anything you want."

She snuggled up next to him. "Then fix me breakfast and take me to the woods."

They had never gone hiking together. Of course, they hadn't spent any time together here in the mountains. Usually, it was in a hotel room on the road or in Rae's condo in California.

Rae had mentioned going hiking before, but Eric didn't think she was serious. He never thought of her as the outdoors type. Then again, thinking back to last night, he'd never thought of her as the sultry seductress, either.

After a big breakfast, they sat out on the deck and enjoyed another cup of coffee, letting their meal settle.

"Where would you like to hike today?" he asked.

"Anywhere. Take me to one of your favorite spots."

He looked at her, sizing up her physical ability. Rae was in good shape, and he knew she worked out regularly. He didn't think she'd have any difficulty hiking up to Hemphill Bald and then maybe over to the Purchase.

She held his stare. "What? You don't think I can keep up?"

He smiled, amazed that she knew his thoughts. Before he could answer, his phone buzzed. He picked it up, thinking it might be Ali. Sometimes, during the weekends she wasn't with him, she'd text. He read the screen.

Up for trout?

The message was from Nicole. He started not to answer but knew she'd persist if he didn't. He texted back that he was sorry but busy this weekend.

Her reply was terse.

K. Ltr

He set the phone down and saw Rae looking inquisitively. He felt guilty and was unsure of what to do. Convincing himself that transparency was the best course in this case, he said as casually as he could manage, "It was Nicole, asking if I wanted to go fly fishing. I told her I was busy this weekend."

Rae considered the news, then shrugged. "If you want to go fishing . . ."

"No, I want to spend time with you."

She searched his eyes as if looking for any unspoken conditions attached to his comment. Her face relaxed, and she said, "I still want you to teach me how to do that. Sometime. It doesn't have to be this trip."

"I will. I promise."

They packed a lunch and hiked over to Hemphill Bald. As he predicted, Rae had no trouble keeping up and seemed to enjoy it.

On top of Hemphill, sitting at the picnic table, Rae looked around, enjoying the view. "Is that the ski resort over there?" she said, pointing at the mountain just southeast of them.

"Yes, that's Cataloochee. A small resort, nothing like you see out west, but it certainly is convenient."

"You'll have to take me skiing there."

Eric raised his eyebrows. He didn't know Rae skied.

Seeing his surprised look, she laughed. "You didn't think I could hike, either, did you?"

Busted, he shook his head. "Guilty, as charged. Of course, I've never seen you dressed like you were last night. You're just full of surprises this weekend."

Rae broke out into a big grin. "You liked that, huh?"

"Oh yeah, couldn't you tell?"

She reached over and put her hand on his. "I enjoyed that a lot. I like doing things with you. Everything."

"Me too." He studied her face and grinned. He did enjoy her company, and she had delivered him from his foul mood. The cause of that dejection crept back into his mind like a thief in the night. His smile faded.

Rae squeezed his hand, sensing his sudden change of attitude. "Don't worry. Everything will work out."

"I can't leave this area, not with Ali here."

She nodded. "I understand. I'm here for you, don't forget that. Regardless of what happens, I'm not going anywhere."

He turned his hand over and laced his fingers between hers. "Sorry." She shook her head, and he continued. "Thanks for coming. I'm glad to see you."

She drew him closer and then kissed him. She pulled away and said, "Thanks for bringing me hiking. I love this place. It's beautiful. I can understand why it's one of your favorite spots."

That brought a thin smile to his face, and he squeezed her hand. "I'm glad you like it. The Park is huge, and I've got lots of places to show you. And next trip, I want you to meet Ali."

She nodded. "I'd like that."

He kissed her hand and said, "Are you up to a hike over to another of my other favorite spots?"

Rae grinned, accepting the challenge. "The question is whether or not you're up to it." She raised her eyebrows, driving home the innuendo.

He laughed. "Me and my big mouth. I may need a nap to recover. Come on, let's pack up and hit the trail."

They hiked over to Purchase Knob, and as they walked out next to the Science Center with the 270-degree view unfolding, Rae gasped. On the way over, he'd told her the story about Purchase Knob and the McNeil-Gilmore family donating the 535-acre tract and buildings to the Great Smoky Mountains National Park.

"Oh my God, what an incredible view," she said, taking it in.

Eric nodded. "I never get tired of it." It reminded him of his aunt's cabin in north Georgia, where he grew up. Not as high, since there are no 5,000-foot elevations in Georgia, but just as beautiful. There was something peaceful and relaxing about the mountains, which is what attracted him back to this part of the country.

"Tell me about your Aunt Ida," she asked.

He smiled as he thought about his Aunt Ida, Gertrude's sister. He knew Rae was trying to cheer him up, and it worked.

"She was a simple woman, but strong. She took me in when my parents died." He told her about growing up on a farm. "It was hard work, and being a kid didn't exempt you from chores. But it taught me a lot. She's probably the reason for me being where I am today."

He told her about raising chickens and his suspicion that she died from avian flu. "That was before there were flu vaccines. Aunt Ida's chickens were free-range before that was cool. They never got anything, no hormones, no antibiotics—none of that stuff. Nowadays, eighty percent of all antibiotics in this country are given to farm animals. It's big business."

Eric smacked himself in the forehead. "Wait a minute," he said. "It *is* big business. It's huge. We could sell Fluzenta in the veterinary market."

Rae looked at him and shook her head. "What do you know about the veterinary market?"

"Nothing. But I know someone who does."

He explained that a classmate of his ended up going to work with LeConte Pet Products, the largest veterinary products company in the U.S. "K.T., short for Kathy

Towson. I ran into her a few years ago at a conference on viruses."

"Maybe you could sell the veterinary rights and retain the rights to the human market."

Eric was nodding. "Exactly what I was thinking. And raise enough cash to keep us afloat until we could refile the application properly and get it approved for people."

"Sounds like a plan to me."

"I need to call Frank. We have to delay selling Panther Cove."

He was excited. This may be a way out of their dilemma.

14

After texting Eric, Nicole went back to the lab to work. She knew he didn't have Ali this weekend and wondered what he was doing. She desperately needed the time to finish her work on the engineered virus, but she was disappointed that she wouldn't see Eric.

As soon as they had received the denial from the FDA, Frank Liles had sent her a text, giving her the go-ahead for the plan she had outlined to him in North Carolina. He wanted to implement it within thirty days. The schedule was doable but tight, and there was no time to spare.

Unknown to everyone, she had been working on her own "Skunk Works" project as a fallback position. The term, coined by the legendary Kelly Johnson at Lockheed, referred to small teams, thinking outside the box and working below the radar to develop revolutionary new aircraft. It had become synonymous with top-secret teams physically removed from the regular corporate workplace, working with almost total freedom and few restraints.

For Nicole, the team consisted of one member. Her. Something Eric had said about having a key, but no lock, had triggered the idea months ago.

On paper, reverse engineering a virus to fit a cure they already possessed seemed much easier than creating a new medicine for a virus. If you have the cure, all you need is a disease.

Fluzenta was the cure, so she had set out to research the possibility of modifying a virus to fit Fluzenta.

The H4N4 virus was a logical candidate for several reasons. First, Tera Pharmagenics had a wealth of information on it. Their early research and trials were based on that strain and proved that Fluzenta was very effective against H4N4. Based on Tera Pharmagenics's experience, Fluzenta was ninety-five percent successful with H4N4 in the avian population.

Second, H4N4 was still avian, and no confirmed cases had been documented in humans. Since that strain hadn't made the jump to humans, Tera Pharmagenics had shifted their focus to H5N1, which had. All the effort since the early years had been with the H5 virus. The H4 trials had been forgotten.

Another good thing about H4N4 was that the mortality rate was not nearly as bad as some of the other viruses, like H5N1 for example. H5N1 had already made the jump to humans, and the mortality rate was sixty percent. H4N4 was half that, at least in birds, and there was no reason to think it would be anywhere near that of H5 in humans.

Last, since Tera Pharmagenics had done extensive research with H4N4, the virus was readily accessible to her in the lab. Monitoring was less stringent on viruses that had not spread to humans. This meant that Tera could work with the virus in their Biosafety level 3 labs with few questions.

However, the fact that H4N4 was avian was also a negative. It would have to be modified to make it viable in humans and at the same time retain the characteristics that made it succumb to Fluzenta. This was turning out to be more complicated than she'd realized.

Zoonoses were diseases that jumped from animals to humans. Microorganisms, such as bacteria and especially viruses, were incredibly adaptive and were capable of evolving quickly to survive. Zika, Swine flu, and Ebola were well-known examples.

Eventually, everyone knew H4N4 would make the jump. It was a matter of time. Nicole rationalized that all she was doing was accelerating the process, speeding up the clock if you will. Giving Darwin a little boost.

Nicole carefully handled the dropper containing the modified H4N4. In her notes, she named it H4h for short. H4h had been modified to work in humans, at least in theory. The next step was to test that hypothesis.

With no infected humans, there was no way to determine if Fluzenta would be effective with the humanoid version. She needed a volunteer.

Carefully, she deposited a tiny quantity of the H4h in a small vial and sealed it. Removing it from under the BL3 hood, she gingerly set it upright in a tray with several other similar vials that contained benign samples.

"What are you working on?"

"Fuck," she said out loud, not hearing Wally walk up behind her. It was a good thing she didn't have the tray in her hands or she would've dropped it. "Why don't you wear a bell or something? Ever heard of announcing your presence?"

"Whoa, aren't we jumpy. What are you doing?"

She took a quick breath and tried to hastily compose herself before turning to face him.

"I was working on some animal samples, asshole. I'm trying to update our data for a potential veterinary proposal. Like we discussed on the call, remember?"

"Aren't you jumping the gun? You heard what Eric said. He hasn't even talked to his contact at LeConte yet. Do you think anyone's going to buy Fluzenta for veterinary use?"

"I don't know, but if anybody can sell it, Eric can."

"Whatever."

"Speaking of Eric, what's he up to this weekend? I texted him about going fishing, and he replied that he was busy this weekend. I know he doesn't have Ali."

Wally shrugged. "I don't know. Maybe Rae's in town."

"Rae?"

Wally nodded matter-of-factly. "Rae what's-her-name. The CFO. From Cupertino."

Nicole raised her eyebrows. "Tera's CFO? Really? I didn't know—"

Wally held up his hands. "A friend of mine saw them out at dinner a few months ago in Asheville. They looked pretty cozy from what he said."

Nicole quickly tried to wipe the surprised look off her face. She did her best to portray a nonchalant attitude and shrugged. "Good for him. Did you need something, or may I get back to work?"

"I was going down to the cafeteria to grab a snack. Want anything?"

Momentarily taken aback by his rare show of courtesy, she rallied to answer. "Thanks, I would like a latte, double-shot with one raw sugar, please."

"Sure." He spun and walked away.

She held out her hand. It was still shaking slightly. She'd have to be more careful. She couldn't afford a mishap at this stage.

And what the hell was this with Eric and Rae? She hadn't known they were seeing each other and wondered how long this had been going on. He hadn't mentioned anything to her about it, and neither had Ali.

She shook her head and refocused on the tasks at hand for now. She'd have to come back to that later. Right now, she had work to do.

There were two questions about the H4h virus to be answered: First, would it infect humans?

She had compared the avian version of H5 to the human one, looking for the subtle differences. Again, there was a wealth of research on how it had transmutated and what the dissimilarities were at a molecular level.

The easy part was genetically modifying the H4N4 flu and endowing it with the same characteristics that the human H5 strain had acquired. This should ensure that the new H4h virus would infect humans.

The second question related to the first: would Fluzenta work in humans against H4h? If Fluzenta had the same success rate in H4h as it had in avian H4, it would be a colossal achievement.

Nicole believed she now had the answers to both questions. She had endowed H4h with the mutations that allowed H5 to infect humans. And, she was supremely confident in the efficacy of Fluzenta.

She was almost ready to proceed with her abbreviated clinical trial.

15

Monday morning, sitting at his desk, Eric heard a tap at his office door. He looked up to see Nicole standing there.

"Got a minute?" she asked.

He motioned her in. Out of habit, he got up from behind his desk and went over to the small conference table. He usually didn't like having informal meetings across his desk, feeling like it impeded the conversation. This time, he hesitated when he got to the table, wishing he'd stayed behind the safety of his desk.

Nicole closed the door behind her. "How was your weekend?" she asked as she came over to the table and sat opposite him.

"Good," he said, without divulging any more details. "Yours?"

"Busy. I worked most of the weekend. I got your email. As you asked, I did a little research on veterinary products," she said.

He cocked his head. "I'm listening," he said. "What did you find out? What are the FDA requirements for veterinary drugs?"

"It doesn't matter. The FDA doesn't regulate veterinary biologics."

He wrinkled his brow. "I thought drugs for animals were the responsibility of the FDA?"

She smiled and shook her head.

"Drugs are, *but*—this is the key—veterinary *biologics* are specifically *not* regulated by the FDA but by the Department of Agriculture."

She opened the slim manila folder she had brought with her and pulled out a sheaf of papers. She slid the top page in front of him, pointing to the first line.

"See. Biologics are under the purview of the CVB. Center for Veterinary Biologics, part of APHIS."

"APHIS?"

She pulled out the second page and slid it across the table. "Animal and Plant Health Inspection Service, an agency of the Department of Agriculture."

He picked up the sheet, skimmed it, and then sat it down on the table. "That's interesting. I never knew that."

"But we're not set up to manufacture veterinary products. We don't have the proper licenses, and we don't have the animal studies—"

"I'm not thinking about us doing it. Instead of closing Tera Pharmagenics or selling out to another biopharmaceutical firm, we could partner with a company already in the veterinary space. They have all the licenses, contacts, distribution, etc. We would license Fluzenta to them."

Nicole had a puzzled look. "But I don't see what that buys us, other than maybe a little cash. We don't have anything else in the pipeline."

Grinning, he said, "Think about it. Here's the key—we only give them a license for the veterinary market. The money from veterinary sales could fund the necessary new studies for a human vaccine so we could resubmit our application to the FDA."

He snatched up a sheet of paper off his desk and tapped his fingers on the row of numbers.

"Look. This is safe enough to be given to animals. As part of our trials, we did do a lot of work with birds, work that could probably be massaged to comply with the Department of Agriculture requirements."

"How do you know that?"

"Goddammit, Nicole, I don't." He dropped the paper on the desktop. "But I have a contact at LeConte Pet Products in Vermont and she would. Why are you so negative? I'm trying to find a way to keep Fluzenta alive."

"I'm not. This is just so . . . so out of the blue. I'm just surprised, is all."

He got up and walked over to his desk, signifying the meeting was over. "Get with Wally and pull up all of the data we have on our animal trials. I'm going to call my contact at LeConte and then call Frank."

As Nicole walked out, he called the number he had for LeConte.

"Huber Animal Health, may I assist you?" said a cheerful female voice.

Eric was confused. "Huber? I'm sorry, I was trying to call LeConte Pet Products," he said. He was preparing to hang up, but the person on the other end said, "LeConte was acquired by Huber earlier this year. How may I direct your call?"

"Oh, I didn't realize that. Yes, I'm trying to get in touch with Kathy Towson, Doctor Kathy Towson."

He heard a clicking of keys and the person said, "I'm sorry, we don't have anyone here by that name. Is there someone else who could assist you?"

Eric shook his head. Although he hadn't talked to K.T. in probably a year, he hadn't heard anything about her leaving LeConte. Of course, he didn't realize that Huber had acquired LeConte.

He recognized Huber, of course. A German company, they were one of the largest pharmaceutical firms in the world. He wondered if the acquisition had displaced K.T.

"Are you sure?" he asked. "Dr. Kathy Towson, she was in the animal medicine department at LeConte when I last spoke with her, probably a year or so ago."

"I'm sorry, but our directory doesn't show anyone with that name."

Eric hung up the phone, perplexed. Now, he was at zero with the veterinary option. He typed in "Huber Animal Health" on his computer as he called Frank.

"I've got a way to save Fluzenta," Eric said as soon as Frank answered. "How much do you know about veterinary products?"

He told Frank about the veterinary idea. Frank's reaction had been the same as Eric's, thinking that they would still have to deal with the FDA. When Eric explained that there was a completely different route for veterinary *biologics,* Frank seemed more receptive.

"I'm betting that some of our earlier trials would suffice for the animal market. I have a contact in the veterinary market, and I want to explore it with her. But first, you need to slow down on selling Panther Cove."

"What . . . what are you talking about?"

"Don't bullshit me, Frank. I know you're shopping it."

"Who told you that?"

"Doesn't matter. We both know you are. But if we have a chance to salvage Fluzenta, it would buy us some time to refile and get Chip off our back."

"We're just testing the waters, is all."

"Fine, just don't do anything until we've fully explored this. That's all I'm asking."

"Who's your contact with?"

"She was with LeConte Pet, but Huber has acquired them. Now it's Huber Animal Health." Eric was scrolling through the Huber Animal Health website as they talked, trying to find K.T. "Bearant also has a veterinary division and you know the CEO there."

Frank was silent. Eric could hear the wheels turning in Frank's head. He continued.

"It would provide some cash coming in for Chip. And, it would give us some breathing room to resubmit our application to the FDA. We could keep Fluzenta alive, Frank."

"I'll see what I can do."

Eric was still skimming the Huber website as he hung up, trying to find a list of key personnel. Like most high-tech firms, they only listed people at the very top, trying to make it more difficult for other companies to poach personnel.

There was no mention of Dr. Kathy Towson.

* * *

Frank hung up the phone. He had to admit that Eric's veterinary proposal was creative. If things didn't work out with Nicole's engineered virus, the vet option might be a fallback. He couldn't see any harm in exploring it.

He pulled out his cell phone and texted Nicole.

Call me when you can

He wanted to find out what she knew about Eric's plan and also get an update on the virus. Chip had called and wanted to know where they stood.

16

Thursday afternoon, Eric left work at five, early for him. He drove into town and parked in front of Frog Level.

There weren't many people there, yet, which was fine with him. He'd deliberately not invited Nicole or Wally, wanting some alone time.

He walked inside and found no one sitting at the bar. He stopped at the open door of Clark's "office," a narrow makeshift structure with plywood walls that ran parallel to the entrance, and stuck his head inside.

Clark was seated at the far end working at the computer.

"Anyone working here?" Eric asked.

"Nope," his friend answered, not taking his eyes off the computer screen. He finished what he was doing and then looked at Eric. "You solo today?"

Eric nodded.

"Give me a few minutes, and I'll join you," Clark said.

"I'll be outside." Eric walked over to the bar as Maryann greeted him.

"The usual?"

"Yes, please."

She opened the tap for Nutty Brunette, one of Clark's regular amber ales, and mostly foam emerged. "Damn. Sorry, I need to change kegs. It'll take me a few minutes."

"No problem. I'm going out back to the creek. To meditate a bit."

She laughed. "Okay, I'll bring it to you."

"Thanks."

He walked on through the place, past the big, shiny brewhouse tanks on his left behind Plexiglas walls above the old bar, which at the time was the only bar. He thought back to when he'd first met Clark five years ago. He chuckled when he recalled the single, small brew house on wheels that was housed there against the outside wall.

Eric had stumbled into Frog Level at a spring festival, curious. He'd struck up a conversation with the goateed man sitting behind the bar and soon found out he was the proprietor. Thus, began a friendship that had endured to the present day.

Maryann appeared, bearing a fresh beer, and set it on the table in front of Eric. She also set a small porter down opposite him for Clark. "Sorry for the delay. He's on his way."

"No problem," Eric said. "I don't think I would've thirsted to death."

She laughed. "I know, but we have to take care of our regulars. Enjoy."

A few minutes later, Clark made his way down the steps and sat across from Eric. He picked up his cup, and said, "Cheers," then took a swallow. "What's on your mind today?"

Eric smiled. "What makes you think something's on my mind?"

Clark shook his head. "I know you too well, my friend. It's written all over your face."

Eric took a drink before answering. "That obvious, huh?"

"Work? Or women? Or both?"

Eric laughed. "You should be a psychologist."

"I was close—a drill instructor."

They both chuckled, and drank in silence for a few minutes. Clark didn't press, seeming to recognize that Eric was trying to sort out his mood.

"Work is still the shits," Eric finally said. "We're making one last stand. We may have a chance to sell the drug to the veterinary market. If this play doesn't pan out, I think it's game over."

"Knowing you, you're doing everything you can. That's all you can do."

"I had to cancel mine and Ali's trip to London. That's bumming me out. And Kate is clubbing me like a baby seal with it."

"Ah, the women part."

"If that were all, it'd be enough."

Clark gave him a quizzical look but didn't comment.

Eric debated on how much to tell his friend. "Let's just say I did something really stupid. I should know better. Now, I've got to extricate myself."

A few minutes passed, then Clark said, "Suck it up. If it's any consolation, it probably wasn't the first time for you or any of us. And, it won't be the last."

Eric had to chuckle. On more than one occasion, he'd heard Clark mutter those three words *suck it up,* a motto of Marines. "Next you're going to tell me to improvise, adapt, and overcome." That was also one of Clark's favorites, another slogan of Marines.

Laughing, Clark said, "I have to admit, that did cross my mind. I heard that every day when I was in."

Three beers later, Jenny, Clark's wife, showed up to take Clark to dinner.

"Why don't you come with us, Eric?" she asked.

He shook his head. "Thanks, but I've got to head home. Felix will destroy the place if he doesn't get his treats. You guys enjoy."

After they had walked away, Eric finished his beer and stepped inside to settle with Maryann. He handed her a twenty, told her to keep the change, and headed for his Jeep.

* * *

Friday, Eric went to Asheville to pick Ali up for the weekend. Kate made a brief appearance to remind him to have Ali back promptly Sunday evening. Not wanting a confrontation in front of their daughter, he simply agreed.

On the way to his house, Ali proceeded to give him the schedule for the weekend. Tomorrow, they were spending the afternoon at Cataloochee. She wanted to see the elk.

"Can Nicole come with us?" she asked. He could feel her eyes on him, watching for a reaction.

He had expected this. He knew he couldn't completely avoid Nicole, but he didn't want to send the wrong message to his scientist. When it came up, he'd decided to take the coward's way out and let Ali call Nicole herself and ask.

"Fine with me. Why don't you call her when we get to the house?"

Ali smiled, pleased that her dad had so quickly agreed.

After they got home, and Ali had given Felix his treats, she asked Eric for his phone. The day that Eric had to dial the number for his daughter was long gone.

Like an expert, she pulled up Nicole's number and made the call, putting the phone up to her ear like a grown-up.

"Hey, Nicole, it's me—Ali."

Eric had to laugh, sure that Nicole was grinning as well. He was proud that Ali had used good etiquette, but doubted that she needed to identify herself to Nicole. He heard Ali ask about tomorrow, then saw Ali's look of disappointment. Apparently, Nicole had turned her down.

"Okay," Ali said, still wearing her frown. "Maybe you can come Sunday before I go home." A smile creased her cheeks. "Okay. Bye."

Ali put the phone down on the island bar and announced to Eric that Nicole had to work tomorrow, but maybe she'd see them Sunday.

Eric was relieved and curious. He wondered if Nicole had just used work as an excuse since he couldn't imagine what she'd be working on that would require going in on Saturday.

"Can I ask Uncle Wally to go with us?"

"Sure." Since they would only be exploring the buildings over at Cataloochee and waiting on the elk to make an appearance, Wally might accept. No real hiking would be involved.

She grabbed the phone and called.

"Uncle Wally. It's me, Ali." She recited her pitch again to Wally and squealed with delight when he apparently accepted.

"Okay, let me ask Dad." She turned to Eric and asked, "What time does Uncle Wally need to be here?"

"Around two."

"Around two," Ali repeated into the phone. "Okay, see you then. Bye."

She set the phone down and announced the results, pleased with her success. "Uncle Wally is coming with us."

"Good." He supposed that since there were no children Ali's age nearby, she considered Nicole and Wally her playmates.

Not surprisingly, Wally was better with kids than adults. In many ways, he was childlike, and that seemed to resonate with the younger set. Ali had always been fond of him, and he appeared to enjoy being around her.

Wally showed up a little after two the next day. Ali heard him drive up and ran out on the deck to greet him. He was holding a grungy, well-worn backpack, which he set down so he could pick Ali up.

"Hey, Princess. How's my favorite little girl?" He had always called Ali 'Princess,' and she loved it.

"Uncle Wally," she said as she wrapped her arms around his neck. "I'm so glad you're coming with us."

He hugged her and then held her up at eye level. "You're getting too big for me to do this much longer."

She giggled and wriggled her way down to the deck, eyeing the backpack. "What's in there?" she asked.

"I don't remember," he said, grinning. He always brought her a surprise, and she had come to expect it. Eric was amazed at the things he came up with, wondering where he came up with the ideas.

She bounced from one foot to the other, looking first at her dad and then at Wally. All Eric could do was laugh.

"Can I open it?" she asked.

"Ali . . ." Eric said, a mild rebuke in his voice.

"I asked."

Wally knelt. "Yes, you did. And yes, you can." He glanced up at Eric and nodded.

Ali reached for the zipper and quickly opened it, pulling apart the two sides of the pack. She looked in and then looked back up at Wally.

"Go ahead," he said. "It's for you."

Ali reached in and pulled out a small, stuffed bunny. "Peter Rabbit," she said, holding it up for her dad to see. "Thank you, Uncle Wally."

"That's not all," Wally said, reaching back into the pack. He pulled out a Harry Potter PlayStation game.

Now, Ali was excited and threw her arms around Wally's neck. "Thank you." This time, the words carried more conviction.

Beaming, he hugged her tight.

Eric shook his head. More points for Uncle Wally.

They packed up a lunch and drove over to Cataloochee. Once there, they toured the old buildings for the hundredth time with Ali acting as the tour guide.

Wally was the perfect tourist, asking her questions and listening patiently to her explanations. *If only he were that polite to adults,* Eric found himself thinking.

They stopped at the restrooms, and while Ali was inside, Eric asked Wally, "So, what is Nicole working on today?"

Wally shrugged. "I don't know. I told you, she's awful secretive these days. I asked her yesterday what she was doing this weekend, and all she said was 'working.' No further details."

Ali emerged from the restroom, cutting their conversation short. She grabbed both their hands and pulled them toward the Jeep. "Time to go see the elk," she said.

They weren't disappointed. At the end of the road by the meadow, they set up their camp chairs. As if on cue, near dark, Ali spotted the first one emerging from the woods.

"There," she said, pointing directly across the field. "See him?"

Sure enough, a large bull had materialized at the edge of the trees, making his way across the meadow toward them as he grazed. By the time the first one had stopped no more than thirty yards away from them, there were another dozen or so spread out across the field.

They went back to the house and grilled hamburgers. Sitting out on the deck after dinner, Ali yawned. Eric knew she was fading, though she'd never agree. Ali was one of those children who had only two settings: wide open and out. He'd already got her to brush her teeth and change into her pajamas.

She crawled up in Eric's lap and nestled up against him. It was only a matter of minutes before she was sound asleep.

"I'll be back in a few minutes," he told Wally as he rose to put Ali to bed.

"The Harry Potter game was a hit," Eric said when he returned. "Thank you."

Wally smiled. "Yeah, I figured she was getting a little too old for stuffed animals, so I picked up the game on my way over. Hey, it was a nice day. Thanks for inviting me." He rubbed his ample belly. "The burgers were delicious."

Wally had a fresh beer, and Eric poured himself another glass of wine.

"What do you think about the veterinary option?" Eric asked.

Wally shrugged. "Worth a shot. What have we got to lose?"

"Not much at this point. It would give us a little breathing room, though."

"I suppose. What we need is a good flu outbreak."

Eric shook his head. "No, don't say that. I'd rather prevent one happening with a vaccine. Flu causes too much human suffering, more than most people realize. Prevention is always preferable to reaction."

"I hear you, but that's not the way things work, and you know it. Unfortunately, it usually takes a disaster to wake people up. The next pandemic is out there. It's not a matter of if, but a matter of when."

Changing the subject, Eric asked, "What do you think Nicole is working on?"

Wally shook his head. "Don't really know, boss. Whatever it is, she's keeping it close."

Eric had thought it odd that Nicole told Ali she had to work today. He'd originally chalked it up to other reasons, but now he wondered. He made a mental note to ask her about it next time he saw her.

* * *

Sunday morning after breakfast, Ali asked Eric if she could call Nicole. Anticipating his response, she was already reaching for his phone.

"Sure." They were sitting out on the deck. Eric was enjoying the last cup of coffee before the day started in full.

"Hey, Nicole. It's me, Alison." Her face lit up as she talked. "Are you going to come hiking with us?" Ali nodded, then looked at Eric. "She said 'yes.' What time?"

"Tell her we'll pack a lunch and go up to the Purchase. Noon."

"Noon," Ali repeated into the phone. "Will you bring pimento cheese?"

Eric shook his head. Ali was determined if nothing else. She hung up the phone and announced to her dad that Nicole was bringing pimento cheese for sandwiches.

He started to say something to Ali about asking Nicole to make pimento cheese, but decided to let it slide. After all, Nicole was like family.

Shortly before noon, Nicole arrived, ready to go hiking and bearing her trademark pimento cheese. She set the container on the island.

"Sorry, I didn't have any bread, so I couldn't make the sandwiches at home."

"That's okay," Ali said. "We have bread, don't we, Daddy?"

"Yes, we do. You girls can make the sandwiches while I fill up the water bottles."

"We went over to Catloochee yesterday with Uncle Wally," Ali said as they pulled out bread and opened the pimento cheese. "We saw a lot of elk."

"Cool. Wish I could've seen them."

"So, what were you busy working on?" Eric asked.

Nicole shrugged. "Just trying to wrap up some loose ends for the veterinary proposal. Organizing the files and trying to anticipate what data we might need to update. Did you get in touch with your contact at LeConte?"

He shook his head. "Apparently, she doesn't work there anymore. I haven't been able to track her down, yet. I did find out that Huber has acquired LeConte."

"Huber as in Huber Pharmaceuticals?"

Eric nodded. "LeConte is now known as Huber Animal Health."

"Interesting," she said.

17

Monday morning, Eric called his counterpart at Huber, Dr. Franz Weber. Franz wasn't familiar with the animal products side of the house but offered to check and see if he could find out what happened to Kathy Towson.

Later, Frank called. "Bearant's not interested," he said.

"What do you mean, 'not interested?'"

"I talked with Lewis Griffin, the CEO, and mentioned the veterinary idea. It's a non-starter. No interest in a license restricted to veterinary-only use. They want the whole enchilada or nothing. He did hint that they were interested in the Panther Cove facility, however."

Eric exhaled. They're like fucking vultures, circling the dying animal. What Bearant wanted was Fluzenta, but they would be soon able to buy the entire company. In the meantime, they wanted to cherry-pick pieces, sensing they could get them at bargain-basement prices, further reducing what they'd be willing to pay for everything else later.

"What did you tell him?"

"I hedged. I told him that we had considered selling it and might be interested in entertaining any offers."

"Good. Don't do anything rash. I'm waiting to hear back from Huber."

"Speaking of them, I did find out something interesting about LeConte. Guess who was one of their investors?"

"Not a clue. Who?"

"West Coast Capital."

"Really? That's a good thing, right?"

"Not anymore." Frank went on to explain that he'd called Chip. West Coast Capital had cashed out of LeConte Pet Products. They had provided the startup capital and sold out their position to Huber.

Eric slammed his hand on the desk. "Shit," he said out loud. "Did you tell him about the veterinary idea?"

"Briefly. He was less than enthusiastic, but wanted more details."

Eric was surprised. He figured Chip would be anxious to get any money he could out of Tera at this point.

"Call me as soon as you hear from Huber," Frank said.

An hour later, Franz Weber called.

"I found your friend," he said. "She's still with the company. She got married and is now goes by K.T. Marshall. I've got a number for you."

Eric thanked Franz and as soon as he hung up, called the number Franz gave him.

"K.T. Marshall," she said when she answered.

Eric recognized the voice belonging to the tall woman with shoulder-length blonde hair and bubbly personality he met at the conference. "K.T. Hi, this is Eric Carter, in North Carolina. We met at the CDC conference on viruses last year."

"Oh, yes, I remember. You're with Tera Pharmagenics outside of Asheville."

They chatted and briefly updated one another on their respective lives. When Eric told her that he had difficulty finding her when he called for Kathy Towson, she laughed and told him about getting married to a pediatrician in Vermont.

"Congratulations," he said, knowing you weren't supposed to congratulate the bride. He thought that was an archaic rule of etiquette and found that most women these days didn't care about that. While they could have chatted longer, he soon got to the point of his call.

"I was calling to ask about the veterinary marketplace." He went on to explain about Fluzenta and their denial by the FDA. "We're exploring the possibility of licensing the drug to a veterinary products company, and I wanted to know what advice you might have."

Kathy seemed very interested, and they spent another forty-five minutes discussing it. They agreed to touch base by the end of the week and discuss next steps.

Eric hung up the phone, elated. He looked up to see Wally standing in his doorway.

"Come on in," Eric said, moving over to the conference table for their usual Monday meeting.

"Who was that?" Wally said as he sat.

Eric shook his head but didn't say anything. As usual, Wally had no qualms about asking questions about things that were none of his business.

A few minutes later, Nicole strode in. He motioned for her to close his office door before she joined them.

"Good news. I just got off the phone with K.T. Marshall," he said, "my contact at LeConte Pet Products, now Huber Animal Health."

Both of his scientists looked at him expectantly.

"The veterinary option looks good." He went on to explain that he'd met K.T. at a conference in Atlanta. She was now in charge of biologic product development at Huber. "She seemed very interested in the potential."

"That's awesome, boss," Wally said. "What's next?"

Nicole was quiet.

Eric said, "She's going to float the idea around Huber to gauge the level of interest, and we're going to talk again at the end of the week."

"Have you discussed it with Frank?" Nicole asked, breaking her silence.

"Briefly, before I spoke with K.T. He'd contacted Bearant, but they weren't interested."

"If we license it to Huber, where does that leave us?" Nicole asked.

"I don't want to get our hopes up this early, but as we discussed, we would sell them a veterinary license while we resubmit our application to the FDA for the human version."

"Do you want me to finish updating the files?" Nicole asked. "I'm almost done."

Eric looked at her and nodded. "Yes, of course." He started to question why she would ask but chalked it up to her being in a pissy mood.

He rose, indicating the short meeting was over. "That's all I have for today. I'll keep you posted."

Wally looked at his watch. "I think we should celebrate. Let's just go to Frog Level. I'm buying."

Nicole folded her arms across her chest and slid back in her seat. "I've got work to do."

"Whatever," Wally said.

"Hold on, guys," Eric said. Enough was enough. Something was eating at Nicole, and he wanted to get it out. Wally froze mid-step.

Eric fixed her with a stare. "Nicole, what's the matter. You're acting like someone stole your candy."

She shrugged. "As I said, I've got work to do."

"Nothing that can't wait until tomorrow. You seem out of sorts lately. What's going on?"

She looked down at the table and then back up at Eric. "I just feel like everyone's bailing on Fluzenta. We seem to be more interested in selling it instead of focusing on getting it approved."

"That's not the case." Eric softened his voice, realizing he was reacting too aggressively. "This is an interim step, a survival tactic, nothing more. I think it's the only way to save Fluzenta, which is what we all want."

He looked at each of them in turn. "I've devoted ten years of my life to Fluzenta. It's cost me a marriage and my daughter living under my roof. Don't think for a minute that I'm 'bailing' on Fluzenta. Quite the contrary. I'm doing everything possible to keep it alive."

He waited for a reaction. Wally nodded, then Nicole unfolded her arms and also nodded. Eric said, "Let's go down to Frog Level, get a few beers, and relax. I think it would do us all good. We're all getting a little stressed out."

When Eric arrived at the brewery, there was a good crowd for a Monday. Clark was sitting behind the bar, engaged in a conversation with someone Eric didn't recognize. He acknowledged Eric with a slight nod and Eric flipped him a salute.

Not seeing Wally or Nicole anywhere inside, Eric walked through the bar and out on the deck, overlooking Richland Creek. His two cohorts were seated at a table down next to the water, a beer in front of each of them.

As he started down the steps, Maryann passed him on her way inside.

"Your buddies beat you here. Your usual, I presume?" she asked, stopping for a minute on the steps.

He nodded. "Thanks, Maryann. You're the best."

He sat on a stool between Wally and Nicole, facing the water. "Thanks for waiting," he said as he eyed their half-empty glasses.

They both rolled their eyes in reply. They chatted about the weather for a few minutes, then Maryann showed up with Eric's beer.

"Here's to Fluzenta," Eric said, raising his glass. They nodded, and after touching glasses, everyone took a healthy drink.

"How long before you think we have an answer on Huber?" Wally asked.

Eric shrugged. "Hard to tell. I think we'll have a good indication by the end of the week. Hammering out the details will probably take a month or two, maybe."

"You think we can hold out for that long?" Nicole said.

"If we have good faith intentions, yes."

"What if Huber's out? We already know that Bearant is a no-go." Wally said.

Eric shook his head. "Try to find another buyer. Maybe sell off Panther Cove. Rob a bank."

Wally and Nicole laughed. Eric was glad to see them start to ease up. Over several beers, they brainstormed. The suggestions got more outlandish with every additional round. When Wally suggested that they get Clark to buy the lab and convert it into a branch location of Frog Level called "Beer and Bugs," they decided they'd had enough. Nicole asked Maryann for the check and excused herself to go to the restroom.

"If you go to work somewhere else, I want to know," Wally said, getting serious.

Eric smiled and nodded. "I will, but you and Nicole need to look out for yourselves. You're both young and can easily get on with another company. Plus, unlike me, you're not restricted to this geographic area." He started to add that he'd probably destroyed his credibility with the appeal, but thought better of it.

"I'm not sure I could work for someone else," Wally said.

Nicole's phone, setting on the table, dinged, indicating a text message. Reflexively, Eric glanced over at the screen. It was a text from Frank Liles, the sender's name in larger letters than the text.

He tried not to stare but was puzzled. *Why would Frank be texting Nicole?*

"Well?" Wally asked.

Eric turned to look at Wally. "I'm sorry, what did you say?"

"I asked what you thought of Bearant?"

As Eric tried to focus on answering Wally's question, Nicole came back and sat, looking down at her phone. She picked it up and typed in a short response, then set it down again closer to her, out of Eric's view.

"Sorry," she said, not offering any further explanation. She didn't bother to mention that the text was from Frank.

Everyone finished their beers, and Nicole stood. "I've had enough if I'm going to drive home."

Wally chimed in and also stood. "I'm going to catch up on Warcraft. I haven't played in three days."

Eric and Nicole laughed at his obsession with the popular online game.

"See you guys tomorrow. Drive safe," Eric said.

* * *

As soon as Nicole got in her car, she called Frank Liles.

"I was with Eric and Wally. What's up?" she asked when he answered.

"How are things going with our 'project?'"

"I'm concerned," she said. Nicole told him about Eric speaking to the head of biologic product development at Huber Animal Products. "According to him, they're very interested in licensing Fluzenta."

"I think we can stall that. How long before the virus is ready?"

"Three, maybe four weeks. But you know how Eric is. He's zeroed in on this veterinary track. He's not going to give up on it that easy."

"Then you've got to move faster."

"Faster?" Nicole was as impatient as Frank, but she was already fast-tracking it as much as she dared. "We need to do some controlled tests on it, Frank."

"Look, Nicole, you said yourself that we have the cure, so what's the holdup? We're running out of time."

She ended the call. She knew Eric had Ali this weekend, so maybe she could move things up a week.

18

Tuesday morning, Eric woke up thinking about Nicole getting a text from Frank Liles.

Nicole hadn't mentioned it, and neither did Frank when Eric talked to him yesterday evening. He was beginning to think he may have misread the name on her phone. After all, it was a quick glance, and the screen was at a ninety-degree angle. He wanted to ask, but it was obviously none of his business and would let them know he'd been eavesdropping.

He had called Rae last night when he got home from Frog Level, but it had gone to her voice mail. As usual, he didn't bother to leave a message. She would know that he called and return it when she could.

He looked at the clock. 7:18. It was only four a.m. in California. Taking his phone with him, he went into the kitchen, gave Felix his morning bribe, and prepared coffee. Once the machine had produced enough to fill his mug, he poached a cup and went outside on the deck.

He turned his thoughts back to Tera Pharmagenics and Panther Cove. They were going to sell the lab, and he couldn't see any way of avoiding that. Based on Clark's insight, it was probably going to happen soon. He could think of nothing to derail the sale.

He wasn't ready to give up on Fluzenta. The drug was too important. As he sipped his coffee, he asked himself if he was objective. It was his baby after all.

After the first pot of coffee, along with some eggs and country ham, he had yet to come up with any brilliant solutions. Maybe it was time to throw in the towel.

His phone rang, and he picked it up to see who was calling this early. Rae. It was almost nine o'clock, which meant six a.m. if she was on the West Coast.

"Good morning," he said when she answered. "You're up early."

She laughed, and it made him smile. "It's not quite that bad. I'm in Denver, so it's only seven a.m. here."

She explained she'd flown in last night for a meeting with several of the investors in Chip Miller's venture capital firm.

"We had a late dinner, then drinks after. You know the drill."

"I hope it's not the same drill as ours," he said, laughing.

"You know you don't have anything to worry about. How are you?"

He sighed. "Depressed. Everything's spinning out of control, and I feel helpless."

"I'm sorry, Eric. Everyone has tried their best. Not looking very good at this point."

"So I've been told." The conversation was dragging him down. "Have you found a buyer yet for Panther Cove?"

There was silence on the line. To him, it confirmed she knew. He was anxious to see if she admitted it.

"I think so, as of last night," she finally said. "Frank specifically instructed me not to say anything about it to you."

He wanted to lash out, but he knew she was conflicted and just doing her job. That was the problem with seeing someone that worked at the same company, especially when it was as small as Tera Pharmagenics.

"You didn't. I heard it from someone here in Waynesville. Small town, you know."

"I didn't—"

"It's okay. I understand you were doing your job. Not your fault, but I feel like it's piling on."

This time *he* hesitated, not wanting to put her in an awkward position, but needing to get it out. "While I'm on a roll, I'd like to ask you something. You don't have to answer if you don't feel comfortable."

Her voice was hesitant as she answered, "Yes?"

"Why would Frank be texting Nicole?" He wished he could see her face, but knew he'd have to rely solely on audible cues.

"What do you mean?" she asked. The quickness of the response and the tone indicated she was surprised by the question. He told her about seeing Nicole's phone when they were at Frog Level yesterday afternoon.

"Neither one of them has said a word to me about it, which seems a little strange."

"Are you sure it was Frank Liles?"

"Positive. Well, at least that's what it said on her phone."

There was a brief pause, then she said, "I don't know. I have no idea, Eric, and that's the truth. What do you think?"

"I wish I knew."

"Why don't you ask her?"

"Maybe I'm just paranoid. On a different subject, I had a good conversation yesterday with the head of bioscience development at Huber Animal Products. I think they may be our answer."

He told Rae about the conversation and felt that it went well. "Very interested. She said she'd get back to me by the end of the week."

"That's great. See, I told you things would work out."

"Not done yet, but I am optimistic. I think it would be a win-win."

After he had hung up with Rae, he wasn't sure if he felt better or worse. Neither of them could come up with any good reason for Nicole and Frank to be texting. Rae suggested maybe something was going on between them, but he privately wondered if that was perhaps wishful thinking on Rae's part.

That afternoon, K.T. Marshall called.

After exchanging pleasantries, she said, "I met with the head of our division yesterday after we talked." She paused. "He seemed to be very receptive. He wanted to talk to his boss and said he'd get back to me ASAP."

When she didn't continue, Eric said, "And?"

"I'm sorry, I'm still trying to sort it out. It was odd. Yesterday, he was all over it. In fact, I almost called you back last night. This morning, we had a meeting, and he wouldn't even discuss it. All he would say is that there was a lack of interest at the corporate level. When I asked about the change, he just said the company was not going to pursue it."

Eric sat back in his chair. He knew K.T. was being honest with him. She was just as surprised as he was. Somebody up the ladder had killed it. The question was "why?"

"I'm sorry, Eric. I thought it was a great idea. But without my boss's support, my hands are tied."

He thanked her for sharing and hung up. He was puzzled. He called Frank.

"Do you know anyone at Huber?" Eric asked when his boss answered.

"Not well, but yes, I know the CEO. Why?"

Eric explained what had happened. "Yesterday, when I talked to K.T. Marshall, she was very interested. She just confirmed that. But when she kicked it upstairs, she got stonewalled. Somebody killed it."

"You know how big companies are, Eric. It's just going to take time to get to the right people in Huber." Frank sounded disinterested and unconcerned.

"We don't have the time. If you know the CEO, then why don't you call him?"

"I don't know him well enough to call and question his handling of internal management issues."

"Well, I'll call him, then."

"Goddammit, Eric, don't go stirring up trouble."

Eric was frustrated. He felt as if he was the only one with a sense of urgency. He couldn't understand why Frank wasn't more aggressive. "I'm trying to find a solution, Frank, and I've got one. We just need to pursue it—aggressively."

Frank exhaled loud enough for Eric to hear him. "Let me talk to Chip, first, before you go making any calls. I'll get back to you as soon as I talk to him, okay?"

Eric hung up the phone, hoping that maybe Chip would get fired up.

* * *

Wednesday morning, before Eric left the house, Frank called.

"I spoke with Chip," he said when Eric answered the phone. "He doesn't want any conversations with Huber. Period."

"What? That makes no sense. First, you tell me that Chip's going bananas, wanting to get his money back. Now, that we've got somebody interested, somebody with money, he wants us to stand down? What the fuck is going on, Frank?"

"I'm not sure, Eric. Chip is keeping his cards close to his vest."

Eric exploded. "Keeping his cards close? What about us? What about Tera Pharmagenics? What about getting Fluzenta to the market? What happened to all of that?"

Frank sighed. "Look, Eric. I'm just the messenger here. You and I both know we made a pact with the devil. These venture capital people are a different breed. The only thing they care about is the money. I suspect that he's pursuing selling the company and he doesn't want us mucking it up."

"That's unacceptable. I'm going to call K.T. and see if we can—"

"Eric." Frank interrupted. "Listen to me. Chip doesn't want us pursuing this. Remember our conversation at dinner that night? About the source of Chip's wealth? Trust me, you do not want to get on his bad side."

"I don't care. What have I got to lose? If he's going to sell the company anyway, I don't care."

"Don't be foolish, Eric. If he sells it, we get our money back."

"Thanks for the advice."

Eric hung up the phone, then called K.T. He wasn't going down without a fight. If there was a chance to save Fluzenta, he was going down swinging.

19

Friday after lunch, Eric left work to pick up Ali for the weekend. He'd had a couple of terse conversations with Kate during the week, and he had wondered if she was going to let Ali come even though it was his weekend. She was still pissed about him canceling the London trip with Ali.

As usual, Ali was waiting for him at the front door, along with her mother. Before Eric got to the top step, Ali was running out to greet him, arms outstretched. He grabbed her and easily swung her up into his arms, holding her tight.

"You're getting so big, I can hardly pick you up anymore," he said, looking at his daughter's smiling face.

"You'll always pick me up, won't you, Daddy?"

He smiled back. "As long as I can."

Satisfied with his answer and naïve to the realities of human mortality, she wriggled down and ran over to get her suitcase next to Kate.

"Hello, Eric," Kate said.

"Kate."

Ali looked at her mom, swiveled her head toward her dad and back again. "We're having supper with Gramma and Harlan," she announced.

"Dinner," Kate corrected.

"They call it supper, don't they," Ali said, looking at Eric for confirmation, a defiant look on her face.

"Yes, they do, and growing up, that's what I called it," he said, daring Kate to pursue it. He knew for a fact that Kate had grown up referring to the evening meal as supper and he was primed for an argument.

Sensing his mood, Kate wisely changed direction. Bending down and holding out her arms, she said, "Give me a hug, Pumpkin."

Ali obliged, then dragged her suitcase over to her dad. "I didn't pack too much, did I?"

Eric smiled and shook his head. "You never pack too much for me."

"How are things at the lab?" Kate asked.

"You should know," Eric snapped.

"What's that supposed to mean? I was just trying to make conversation." She seemed genuinely surprised at Eric's reaction.

He searched her face and saw nothing but hurt. *Maybe she didn't know,* he thought. Softening his voice a notch, he forced a smile and said, "Lots of changes in the wind. I'll explain later."

She gave him a puzzled look, but he grabbed Ali's hand and turned to leave. "We'll be back Sunday evening at eight," he said over his shoulder.

He threw her suitcase in the back of the Jeep and strapped Ali in the passenger seat.

"Hungry?" he asked as he climbed into the driver's seat.

She nodded enthusiastically. "What's Gramma cooking?"

He shrugged. "Don't know, but I bet it'll be good."

Traffic was thick on I-40, and it took them close to forty-five minutes to get to their exit. They made their way up the mountain, and as they pulled up to the house, Gertrude came out on the porch to greet them.

As usual, Ali ran up the porch steps and straight into Gertrude's arms. As Eric stepped onto the porch, he inhaled the delicious smells coming from inside the small house.

He closed his eyes for a moment and was taken back to his Aunt Ida's house in North Georgia. Like Gertrude, she was an excellent cook. Nothing fancy, but the kind of home cooking becoming increasingly impossible to find these days. Simple. Fresh ingredients. Wholesome. Gertrude's voice brought him back to the present.

"I hope y'all are hungry. Come on in. Harlan's washing up, probably already sitting at the table, waiting. He's worse than an ole Plott Hound."

Eric laughed. They walked in, and Harlan was just coming out of the bathroom.

"That old woman don't know what she's talking about," he said, trying to act grumpy and letting everyone know there was nothing wrong with his hearing. The grouchy countenance was quickly transformed into a grin when he saw Ali. He promptly leaned down to give her a big hug. "I would've waited all night for you," he told her, making her giggle.

They all sat at the table, and after Harlan had said grace, they started passing the overflowing plates and bowls of food around.

Eric was always amazed at how much Ali ate here. Typically a picky eater, she helped herself to generous portions of most everything Gertrude had on the table. Looking down at his plate, he realized he didn't have much room to talk. *The pot calling the kettle black,* his aunt would say.

As they headed over to his house after dinner, Eric could see that Ali was tired and fading. After a full meal, including dessert, Eric was a bit lethargic himself.

Felix was expecting them when they walked in the door. He rubbed up against Ali, figuring she was an easier mark for treats than Eric. His feline intuition paid off as Ali reached for the treats and gave the cat a generous portion.

Darkness had settled over the mountains as they walked out on the deck to see the stars.

"Are we going hiking tomorrow?" Ali asked, stifling a yawn as she snuggled up next to Eric on the bench.

"If that's what you want to do."

She nodded. "Can Nicole come with us?"

He'd thought about it and even mentioned to Nicole that Ali was going to be here this weekend. Nicole seemed preoccupied and never gave him an answer. For all he knew, she had plans.

"I thought tomorrow it could just be the two of us."

He looked down and could see Ali wrinkling her face as she processed the information.

"Can she come Sunday?"

Eric relented. "We can call her and ask if you'd like."

"Now?"

He had to chuckle. Like her dad, Ali was persistent. He knew she wouldn't be satisfied until they called.

He picked up his phone and handed it to Ali. Like a pro, she pulled up Nicole's number and called.

A few seconds later, Ali frowned. She whispered to him, "It's her machine."

Eric smiled. Voicemail. "Okay, leave her a message."

"Hey Nicole," Ali said into the phone. "It's Alison. I'm at Daddy's, and we wanted to know if you could go hiking with us Sunday? Call us back."

Ali asked him to tell her a grown-up story, so Eric made up a tale about a mountain family that lived up the hill in Ferguson cabin. It was a story he'd told before, making up new details and weaving them amongst the previous version. Ali corrected him on several inconsistencies.

Thirty minutes later, she went into the bathroom to brush her teeth, and change into her pajamas. While he waited, he noticed Bear and Peter Rabbit on her dresser, remnants of a rapidly disappearing childhood. She needed a desk, he thought, and maybe some new curtains.

When she came back and got into bed, she noticed him looking at the stuffed animals. "I'm too big for stuffed animals."

Eric smiled. "I know, and it was sweet of you not to say anything to Uncle Wally. I don't think he realizes how grown you are."

Felix appeared and jumped up on the bed next to Ali. Whenever she was there, he would sleep with her. She reached out to pet him and he obliged, settling in next to her.

Eric leaned over and kissed her forehead. "Goodnight, Ali. I love you."

"I love you, too, Daddy."

He turned to walk away and Ali said, "Daddy?"

He stopped midway and turned around. "Yes?"

"Nicole didn't call us back."

He smiled. He'd forgotten about calling Nicole earlier, but Ali didn't forget anything. "She was probably just busy. She'll call tomorrow."

Ali returned his smile. "Okay. 'Night, Daddy."

"Night, sweetie."

20

Friday, Nicole knew Eric would be leaving early to go to Asheville to pick up Ali. Yesterday, he'd asked her about going hiking with the two of them, but she'd deferred, claiming she had too much to do.

The H4h virus had an incubation period of around 72 hours. She figured the duration at five days. Bookended with two weekends, she would have a total of nine days, which should be sufficient for infection and the subsequent remission.

She left the lab mid-afternoon and stopped by Ingles on her way home. Pushing the shopping cart around the store, she bought more than enough food to last a week.

When she got home, she weighed, took her blood pressure and temperature, documenting the results meticulously on her spreadsheet. She drew a blood sample and capped the test tube, labeling it with the date and time.

She poured herself a glass of wine and took a hot bath, luxuriating in the tub until her skin was wrinkled. She toweled off, put on her scrubs and went back in the kitchen.

She planned to start the trial Saturday morning. Looking at the clock and doing a quick calculation, she realized that would be twelve hours away. Timing was critical, and she felt relaxed after the bath and wine. That would be too much time to waste.

Nicole pulled out the vial she'd taken from the lab and held it up to the light. It contained a small amount of a clear liquid and had a handwritten label on it that read "H4h." While it looked harmless, she realized it contained millions of virus cells. It was a virus that had never known a human host.

She paused, then carefully stuck the syringe in the vial and withdrew 2 mLs. Then, she squirted the contents into a small aerosol bottle containing a sterile saline solution. After replacing the top, she shook it vigorously to mix the contents thoroughly. Without hesitating, she liberally sprayed three shots into each nostril, deeply inhaling after each one.

When she first constructed the trial protocol, she had considered injecting it. After much thought, she realized she also needed to confirm that aerosol delivery would work.

In a strict testing protocol, she would have never introduced multiple variables simultaneously. But, she didn't have the luxury of time to do everything by the book. She finished her wine, got her paperback, and went to bed. Before long, she fell fast asleep.

Saturday morning, she awoke at her usual time, feeling rested. She took her vitals and recorded them. No change. She picked up her phone and realized she'd missed a call last night. Eric had called and left a message.

She played the message and grinned when she heard Ali's voice inviting her to go hiking with them. She would've loved to go with them, but didn't want to be anywhere near the child now. She called them back and clamped her nose with her fingers when Eric answered.

"Well, hello, there. I was beginning to agree with Ali and think you were blowing us off," he said.

She replied in a nasal voice, exaggerating the congestion. "Sorry. I went to bed early, so missed your call. I think I'm coming down with a bad cold or the flu."

"Geez, you sound terrible."

"Just congested, but I don't feel like doing much."

"Can we bring you anything?"

"No," she answered, a little abruptly. Catching herself, she took a breath and continued, more slowly this time. "I stopped by Ingles on the way home, so I'm set. Besides, I don't want to risk Ali catching this bug. You, either, for that matter. I'll be fine."

"Hope you get to feeling better. Call if you need anything."

"I will. Y'all have a good time and don't worry about me. I just need to rest and drink plenty of fluids." She hung up the phone, feeling guilty for lying.

* * *

Eric set his phone down. Ali would be disappointed that Nicole wouldn't be joining them.

He sat out on the deck with his coffee, watching the morning light drift in through the peaks and valleys. He'd checked when he got up, and Ali was still fast asleep.

Halfway through the cup, he heard the kitchen door open. He turned to see Ali, still in her pajamas, rubbing the sleep from her eyes. Not saying a word, she padded over to him and climbed up in his lap.

"Good morning, sleepyhead," he said, holding her close to his chest.

She answered with a hug. He held her tight, enjoying the moment. The day was coming, too soon, when she'd no longer do this. There wouldn't be any warning. One day would be like this, the next, it would be gone forever. He dreaded it.

After a few minutes, Ali said she wanted some cereal and orange juice. He started to tell her that Nicole wasn't coming, but decided he'd wait until she was fully awake.

He got up from the chair, still holding Ali, grabbed the coffee cup with his free hand, and walked into the kitchen. One-handed, he poured Cheerios into a bowl. He added some milk and then took her and her breakfast over to the bar. She wriggled out of his arms onto the stool and started eating while he got juice for her and more coffee for him.

"What time is Nicole coming?" Ali asked.

He shook his head. "She called while you were still asleep. She's not feeling well."

"Can we go see her?"

"No, she doesn't want us to catch whatever bug she has, so it's probably better if we don't."

Ali digested the information and scowled. "Nicole always brings pimento cheese for sandwiches," she said. "What are we going to eat now?"

He paused for a minute as if he were giving it serious thought. "I've got some asparagus and broccoli."

Ali looked at him and rolled her eyes. "You're teasing, Daddy."

He laughed. It was getting harder to fool her.

After she finished her cereal, they went out on the deck.

"Remember when we used to play I Spy out here?" he asked. They had played that popular children's game dozens of times.

She nodded. She sat at the table and slowly rotated her head 180 degrees and back, careful now not to dwell on any one object. "I spy something green," she said.

Eric smiled and picked up the challenge. "Green? That's not fair. There are a million things out there that are green. You've got to give me another hint."

She looked directly at him, set her jaw, and shook her head.

He looked around, tracing the same path her eyes had taken, and named a half-dozen different items. Each guess was met with a shake of her head and "nope."

Finally, she asked, "Do you give?"

He mocked her head shake and answered, "Nope." He continued for another four or five guesses, then threw up his hands.

Ali smiled, clapped her hands, and pointed at the tree line less than fifty yards away. "That man in the green jacket."

He sat up, squinted, and looked to where Ali was pointing. Sure enough, a man in a camouflage jacket stood there, looking at them. While he blended in with the surroundings, he was not making any effort to avoid being seen.

That's strange, Eric thought. He has no hunting vest and doesn't appear to be carrying a gun. Yet, he was standing there watching them and didn't appear to care that they had spotted him.

"What's he doing, Daddy?"

"I'm not sure. Maybe he's lost," Eric said. He didn't want to alarm Ali, but something was off. "I'm going to get the binoculars, so I can see if it's somebody I know," he said as he rose. He went into the kitchen, grabbed the binoculars that he kept on the island, and went back outside. The man hadn't moved.

"I still see him," she said.

"I see him, too, but I'm old, and I can't see his face."

She laughed. "You're not old, Daddy."

He looked through the binoculars and focused them on the man's face. He was still staring in their direction.

Eric didn't recognize him. The man appeared to be in his thirties, medium height, with short brown hair. He looked to be in good shape. As Eric studied his face, trying to place him, the man smiled and waved.

Eric lowered the binoculars. The man appeared to want Eric to know that he was watching them. When Eric raised the binoculars back up and looked, the man was gone.

"He left, Daddy."

Eric set the binoculars on the table. "I see that."

They cobbled together some peanut butter and jelly sandwiches, chips, and a couple of apples for lunch. As they hiked up to Hemphill Bald, Eric was on edge. He was still thinking about the man standing at the edge of the woods. *Was he being a smartass or was he specifically sending a message?*

He'd never felt unsafe hiking in the park, unconcerned about people or bears. Home to over 1,800 black bears, the park gets ten million visitors a year. Yet, there has been only one fatal bear attack. Although he'd hiked dozens of trails and hundreds of miles in the Park, Eric had seen bears only twice. Neither time did he feel threatened.

Too many times to count, he had hiked for hours without ever seeing another person. Today, he was on full alert, listening for any sound that someone was following them. They saw no one on the way up to Hemphill Bald and had a nice lunch overlooking the valley. On the way back to the house, they passed a young couple on the trail. In a glance, Eric could tell that it was not the same person he had seen in the binoculars.

Later that night, after Ali had crashed and gone to sleep, Eric's phone buzzed. He figured it was Nicole, but was surprised to see that it was Kate.

He debated answering, then pressed the button to take her call.

"Hello?"

"Hey, it's me."

"What's up?" he replied, his voice neutral.

"Is she asleep?"

He loosened up slightly. "Yes, out like a light. You know Ali—two speeds, wide-open and asleep."

Kate laughed. "That's our daughter."

Eric was surprised at her use of the adjective "our." It had been a while since he'd heard Kate acknowledge Ali as "their" daughter, instead of "her" daughter. Maybe she'd had a second glass of wine this evening.

"Is everything okay, Eric?"

He considered her comment carefully. Before he could reply, she continued.

"I mean, you bit my head off when you picked her up."

"You're telling me you don't know?"

"Know what?"

"Tera Pharmagenics is trying to sell Panther Cove."

Kate gasped. "Oh, Eric. No, I had no idea. Why would I?" Her surprise was authentic and difficult for her to fake. Eric had always told her never to play poker for money.

He started to tell her to ask her husband but bit his tongue. "You usually know more about what's going on at the lab than I do. I just assumed you knew. Last time I had Ali, she told me that you said 'I might be moving.' That's why I reacted as I did."

"I swear, I didn't know. And to set the record straight, Ali asked me if you would ever move. I told her that I didn't think so, but sometimes we don't always get to do what we want and that anybody might move, including you *or* us. That was exactly what I told her, nothing more."

"If you say so." Before she could react, he added, "Sorry. I didn't mean to sound so sarcastic. This is all hard, okay?"

"What are you going to do?"

He spent the next fifteen minutes telling her about what happened. "I know I can get a job in Silicon Valley, but I don't think I can move that far away from Ali. I've got another idea to try to salvage Panther Cove, so right now, I just don't know what's going to happen."

They talked for a few more minutes, then hung up. He felt better believing Kate hadn't known.

21

Monday morning, Nicole awoke with a slight tickle in her throat. Her sinuses seemed to be a bit congested. Excited, she took her vitals. Her temp was up slightly. She called Carmen and told her that she had the flu and wouldn't be in for a few days.

By the afternoon, she was feeling horrible. All the flu symptoms were there, in spades. She pricked her finger and squeezed out a tiny drop of blood which she put on one of the custom test strips she'd made at the lab.

After ten seconds, a dark blue line appeared on the end of the strip, indicating a positive result. She smiled. From experiments she'd run, the rapid test strip had an accuracy of 95%. That was sufficient for her purposes, indicating the presence of the H4h virus. She was the first human infected with the strain.

Nicole took the vial labeled Fluzenta and with a syringe, withdrew 5 mL. She had to guess at the dosage and after numerous mathematical simulations had arrived at this amount based on the concentration and her body weight.

She held the syringe needle up and thumped it several times with her left hand, getting the air bubbles up to the top. She pressed the plunger until liquid squirted out. She took a breath, then stuck the needle in her left upper arm and injected the contents into her muscle.

In the clinical trials for Fluzenta, they had found that the most effective dosage was three mL intramuscular, twice a day for three days. Of course, that had been with H5. Nobody knew the correct dosage for H4h. Based on her simulations, she'd bumped it up to 5 mL, preferring to err on the side of caution.

She stretched out on the sofa and turned on the television, just to have some background noise. She was feverish and felt horrible, like the worst flu she'd ever experienced.

Eric called wanting to know how she was feeling. This time, she didn't have to clamp her nose shut while talking on the phone. The congestion was for real.

"I've got the flu," she told Eric. "And I feel like crap. Nothing to do but ride it out. How was your weekend with Ali?"

"Good. We missed you," he said. "You sound horrible. Are you staying hydrated?"

She gave him a weak, hoarse laugh. "I have to get up and pee like every hour. Damn Gatorade."

He chuckled. "Rest and fluids, that's the best things you can do. Call me if you need anything."

The next morning, Nicole awoke feeling worse. She'd had a restless night, tossing and turning the entire time. Even though she still had symptoms, she took her vitals and did another test strip. No surprise, it was still positive. Her fever was up.

She tried reading, hoping to distract herself, but the thought kept creeping back in. *What if the Fluzenta didn't work?* After an hour and reading only six pages, she gave herself another injection and went back to bed.

Wednesday, or day two of the active infection, she still felt no better. She was congested and had gone through another box of tissues. She looked into a mirror. Her nose was red and dripping. Her eyes were puffy, and she looked horrible.

When she embarked on this path, she decided that she would call Eric if she showed no signs of improvement by day three. It was exhausting just to get up and go to the bathroom. She'd give it one more day.

Thursday morning, she woke up feeling chilled to the bone. She'd turned the heat up and piled every blanket she owned over her. She was still shivering.

She'd failed. Not only had her experiment backfired, but she was also deathly ill, with a virus for which she now knew had no cure. She picked up a quarter and flipped it over and over in her hand. Heads or Tails? Fifty percent mortality rate. On which side would her coin land?

Reluctantly, she picked up her phone and pressed Eric's number. The call went straight to voice mail. She hung up, not leaving a message. She had fucked up beyond belief. *Now what?*

Her phone in hand, she lay back down on the sofa. Within minutes, she fell asleep.

The vibrating phone on the sofa woke her. Dazed, she fumbled around trying to find it. By the time she did, the buzzing had stopped. Eric.

Nicole looked at the time on her phone. 7:33 p.m. She looked out the window, and it was dark. She'd been asleep for almost twelve hours.

Slowly, she sat up and noticed she was sweating. Her fever had broken, although she still felt weak. Unsteady, she leaned over and grabbed the thermometer, and inserted it under her tongue. When it beeped, she pulled it out and read the results. 100.4, a drop of almost 2 degrees since that morning. She allowed herself a smile, a sense of relief overwhelming her.

The Fluzenta was working. She wasn't going to die.

She took a deep breath and looked at her phone, wondering what to do about Eric. She didn't want to talk with him yet, but knew him well enough to know that he'd call back if she didn't acknowledge his call. She texted him a message.

> Asleep. Sorry. Fever broke and feeling better. Call you in the morning.

In a few minutes, she received a text back.

> Good. Beginning to worry about you. Sweet dreams.

Now she knew not only was H4h capable of infecting humans, but she had also confirmed that Fluzenta worked in treating it.

She called Frank Liles. It was time to implement phase II.

22

It had taken Nicole the rest of the week to regain her strength. That was one nasty flu bug. Now, she needed to get the second phase started.

Nicole had researched different ways to spread an airborne virus. The ideal situation was a restricted area with a dense population confined for an extended period.

She considered subways and buses, but the constant influx of fresh air made that problematic. Another good choice was a crowded, interior room, like a bar or classroom. Unfortunately, the problem was how to release it unobtrusively. She couldn't exactly go around a packed bar and spritz everyone with a small sprayer.

The incidence rate or the percentage of a given, exposed population that would develop the disease was also an issue. No disease was 100 percent, and since she was the only human H4h case, there was no good data on estimating the incidence rate. All she could go by was the rate in avian populations, which varied according to species. Her best guess was thirty percent in a highly-effective environment.

After much deliberation, she realized the cabin of a commercial airliner on a long flight was perfect. She wasn't happy with exposing that many people, but took comfort in knowing there was a proven cure.

The only other drawback she could see was that commercial aircraft, while utilizing a mix of recirculated air, also used HEPA filters. High-efficiency particulate air filters, like those used in hospital operating suites, were also used to filter recirculated air in passenger planes. True HEPA filters have a microbial efficiency of 99.97 percent, removing most viruses and bacteria.

However, she also knew the efficiency of any filtration system was only as good as the weakest link. A poorly maintained system was nowhere near the textbook value.

Furthermore, Type A viruses, like H4h, were around 0.1 microns in diameter. The highest rated HEPA filters typically filtered particles as small as about 0.3 microns in size. Point-three microns was three times the size of the avian virus.

She decided to book a flight from Atlanta to Los Angeles and back for the weekend, ostensibly to see her parents who lived in Santa Barbara. Atlanta was the world's busiest airport, averaging over a quarter-million passengers per day and within a two-hour flight of 80% of the U.S. population. Los Angeles was one of the largest international airports in the United States. The combination was ideal for a new product launch.

Since she had been sick with the H4h virus, she had immunity against further infections from it. She retrieved the aircraft models for her flights and after a little Internet research, found out the locations of the cabin air returns.

On both layouts, the returns were on the outside wall near the floor. Since the seat configurations could vary slightly for different airlines, she had to make an educated guess as to which seat would be closest to the intake vent.

Saturday morning, she settled into her window seat, conveniently located next to a window near one of the cabin air returns. She'd brought one small spray bottle in her pocketbook, figuring it wouldn't garner much attention going through security. If anyone asked, she would say that she had repackaged an over-the-counter nasal spray for travel.

She was careful to make sure she complied with the quantity requirements for liquids and packed it in a clear plastic bag for the security checkpoint. The TSA employees didn't give it a second look.

After the flight had reached cruising altitude, she leaned over and reached into her pocketbook, careful to keep it between her and the person seated next to her. She removed the spray bottle and quickly spritzed the contents into the return louver while continuing to dig around in her purse with her left hand as if she was looking for something. After she'd sprayed as much as she dared, she slipped the nearly empty bottle back into her purse. She straightened up, shaking her head, and muttering to herself. "I guess I left it in Atlanta," she said for her seatmate's benefit.

She'd packed another bottle in her suitcase that she'd checked. Although she planned to come back the next day, she felt that a checked bag would make her less obvious. Plus, if the one didn't work, she'd have a backup. It would be for the flight back to Atlanta tomorrow.

When she got to LAX at noon, she called her parents, who were waiting in the cell phone lot, a special area for those waiting to pick up arriving passengers. She was tired, and the trip had taken a lot out of her.

She picked up her suitcase at baggage claim and walked out to the curb to wait for her parents. She spotted the white Mercedes sedan and waved them over.

Her mom was driving. She pulled up to the second lane from the curb, and her dad got out to greet her.

"Hey sweetheart," he said, enveloping her with a giant hug. Carlton Peters was tall and sported a head full of white hair. *He cut quite a dashing figure,* Nicole thought. She was glad to see that he was keeping his weight under control and looked pretty fit for someone in their early 70's.

"Hi, Dad. Good to see you. Thanks for coming to pick me up."

He picked up her bag to put it in the trunk. "You travel light," he said. "But since you're only staying for the weekend . . ." his voice trailed off, the disappointment unmistaken.

"I know. I wish I could stay longer, but you know how work is."

He closed the trunk and opened the front passenger door for her so she could sit next to her mom.

Winnie Peters leaned over, hugged her daughter, and kissed each cheek. "I'm afraid to get out here. You know how these airport cops are. I think they get a commission."

"I'm glad to see you both," Nicole said. She nodded her head toward the back seat where her father sat. "Dad has already dinged me for not staying longer. But I missed you guys and wanted to come, even if it is a short trip."

"Are you okay?" her mother asked. "You look pale."

Nicole smiled and nodded. "I had the flu last week, but I'm fine now. Just not quite a hundred percent yet."

"Well, we figured we'd go to the house, give you a chance to freshen up, and have a little lunch out by the pool. This evening, we've got dinner reservations at the Lark for 6:30," Carlton said.

"That sounds great, Dad."

They spent the afternoon relaxing by the pool. Nicole enjoyed catching up with her parents, and after eating a light lunch, she felt better. They, of course, wanted to know all about her work. As an only child, she was comfortable being the center of attention. She shared as much as she could, putting a positive spin on the recent events.

As the cocktail hour approached, Nicole was excited. The Lark was her favorite restaurant in Santa Barbara. Though she hadn't requested it, she was glad her father had remembered.

The restaurant was crowded, as always, and even with reservations, they had to wait twenty minutes before their table was ready. Dinner was fabulous. Nicole realized how much she missed southern California. Asheville was nice, but it wasn't Santa Barbara.

She was glad they had an early dinner. By the time they got back to the house, she was exhausted. She wanted to immediately retire to her room and go to sleep, but she knew her father would insist on an after-dinner glass of port. To deny him would be cruel, since she would be leaving after breakfast in the morning.

She smiled, and agreed to a nightcap. He was delighted. Fighting to keep her eyes open, she nursed hers until her parents finished theirs.

The next morning, she awoke refreshed after a good night's sleep. After breakfast, she packed her small bag. She took the remaining spray bottle and carefully placed it in her purse.

Her parents dropped her off at the ticket counter entrance. Willing to risk the wrath of the airport police, both of them got out of the car to see their daughter off.

At the security checkpoint inside LAX, she noticed her purse didn't make it all the way out of the x-ray machine. The operator backed it up, studied her screen, and then said something to a male TSA employee standing next to her.

The conveyor discharged her bag, and before Nicole could get it, the TSA rep grabbed it and held it up.

"Does this bag belong to you?" he asked.

Nicole tried to keep calm. She was sure there was no reason for their suspicion but was still unnerved by the hitch.

"Yes."

"Would you step over here, please?" It was an order, not a request.

She followed him over to a machine at the end of the conveyor, where he explained they were going to swab it for explosives. She watched intently as he went about his task.

She'd seen such machines before, but didn't think there was anything in the bottle that might trigger a warning. She wasn't sure and chided herself for not considering the possibility.

After a minute, the machine beeped. The man looked at the screen, nodded and then handed her the purse.

"Have a nice day, ma'am."

At the gate, she texted Frank.

> Good visit. Delivered gift Sat. Back at work tomorrow.

* * *

Monday morning, Nicole was back at the lab. The past week was a blur. Coupled with a cross-country flight Saturday and again yesterday, she was exhausted. The good news was that she felt better and was regaining her strength.

"How was your visit? Your parents doing okay?" Eric asked.

"It was great, just too short." She'd told Eric that she'd cut her trip short since she'd missed the better part of the week due to the flu. He'd tried to talk her into rescheduling, but she didn't want to delay it. "I feel like I've been gone forever."

"You were gone?" Wally said, smirking.

She gave him the finger, but smiled. It was good to be back.

She turned to Eric. "What's going on with the veterinary proposal?" She knew Frank had squashed it, but couldn't let on that she knew.

Eric frowned. "Not much progress, unfortunately. I just don't get it. K.T. seemed so excited at first, and now she won't even return my calls. Apparently, the only thing moving forward is the sale of this facility."

Nicole smiled. "Hey, you know how long these things take. That's good, as far as selling the lab goes. And, didn't you say that Chip Miller wasn't too keen on it?"

She was in a good mood. If disbursing the virus on Saturday had worked, then the first cases should start showing up soon. There would be no veterinary license and no sale of Panther Cover.

Fluzenta and Tera Pharmagenics would be safe.

23

Friday, when Eric walked past Carmen's desk, she was on the phone but held up her hand to stop him. She covered the mouthpiece and said, "A Dr. Terrance Lumpkin from CDC called. He needs to speak to you as soon as possible. It's urgent." She handed him a stack of messages and returned to her call.

He looked down and saw Lumpkin's message on top. Eric went into his office, smiling. Terry was the head of the National Center for Emerging and Zoonotic Infectious Diseases at the CDC in Atlanta. The tall, African-American and former linebacker at Georgia Tech was one of the smartest people Eric had ever known. They had become friends when they were both in med school at Emory. After med school, Eric went on to do his residency at Brooke Army Medical Center in San Antonio and fulfill his military commitment. Terry stayed at Emory and eventually went to work at the CDC.

Eric dialed the number on Terry's message, and he answered on the second ring.

"Hi, Eric. Thanks for getting back to me so soon."

"No problem. How are you?"

Terry let out a guttural laugh. "Wishing we were back at the Mellow Mushroom on Spring Street, drinking beer, eating pizza, and flirting with the girls."

Eric smiled. "That was a while ago. I've still not seen anyone eat as much pizza as you could."

Another laugh. "Yeah, and it's caught up. I'm getting old, fat, and bald."

Eric shook his head and chuckled. The last time he'd seen Terry, he still looked like he could suit up and crack some heads on a football field. He was betting that his friend was still in excellent shape.

"Hey," Terry said, his voice taking a more serious note. "The reason I called is I wanted to chat with you about your baby—Fluzenta. Got a few minutes?"

"Sure." Eric's antennae went up as he waited for his friend to continue.

"I heard the FDA torpedoed it."

Eric bristled slightly at Frank's comment. "Yeah, but that's old news. Personally, I think it was bullshit, but they make the rules. Why?"

"We've known each other a long time, Eric. My attorneys would shit themselves if they knew what I was about to tell you. I know I can trust you to keep this under your hat, so I'll dispense with the usual bureaucratic bullshit and get right to the point."

He told him that the CDC was on full alert. There had been three confirmed cases of the H4N4 virus in the past week.

"Only three? I'm surprised there's not more. H4 is fairly prevalent in the avian population. What's that got to do with Fluzenta?"

"These three cases weren't found in birds, Eric." Terry paused before continuing. "They were found in humans."

"Humans? Are you sure?" As soon as the words left his mouth, he realized how condescending he sounded. Here he was, talking to a director at the CDC, asking if he was sure.

Terry didn't appear to notice or care. "Completely. We double-checked everything. Confirmed in all three cases."

To Eric's knowledge, H4N4 had not been found in humans, so three cases were cause for concern. He could see why Terry was upset. "I haven't seen anything on the news about this."

"That's because we've managed to keep a lid on it so far. Which is why I'm talking to you in strictest confidence."

"This is unbelievable, Terry. Where were they?"

Terry paused. "They were all here."

"Here? Here as in the United States?"

"Not only in the U.S., but two of the patients are next door at Emory University Hospital. The third just died at Cedars-Sinai Medical Center in Los Angeles."

"Los Angeles? Atlanta? What's the link between Cedars-LA and Emory?"

"RESPTC–Regional Ebola and Special Pathogens Treatment Centers. Those two hospitals are two of the ten designated RESPTCs in the U.S."

"My God, Terry. Where did this come from?"

"We don't know, yet. All three were at the same conference in Los Angeles, an American Bar Association meeting. The two here in Atlanta are local attorneys and fell ill on their way home two days ago. The third, who died this morning, was from LA."

Eric slumped back in his chair. Three human cases of H4N4 with one dead already. He had a sick feeling that this was the tip of an iceberg.

"How can we help, Terry?"

"If I remember correctly, some of your earlier work with Fluzenta related to H4, not H5."

Eric thought and nodded. That had been years ago, in the early stages of developing Fluzenta. "True, we did some of our first work with H4N4 because it was relatively low-risk. Later, we shifted the focus to H5 because H4 hadn't made the jump to humans. H5 had. We felt that we were too far out in front by concentrating on H4. We haven't done anything with H4 in probably five, six years."

"I know, I pulled up the research. Fluzenta was very successful with H4. You probably know more about H4 than anyone else."

"Yes, but that was a long time ago. And, it was with the avian strain. We have no idea how effective it would be with a form that presents in humans. What are you getting at?"

"We want to give Fluzenta to the two patients in Emory."

"What?"

"We're out of options, Eric. We've done everything we can, and nothing is working. I've compared notes with the medical director at Cedars to see if we've missed anything and we haven't. Fluzenta represents our only hope."

"Fluzenta was developed to work with multiple strains, but primarily in the H5 line. We don't know enough about this particular H4 subtype to know if it would be safe, let alone effective."

"These two people are dying, Eric. They have nothing to lose and we are out of options."

Eric shook his head. Obviously, he was willing to do anything he could to help the patients. At the same time, there were significant hurdles in doing so. First, there had been no human trials with Fluzenta administered for H4N4. The only human trials had involved the H5N1 virus. All their earlier research with H4 had been done on birds. The FDA would have to grant accelerated approval.

Second, the patients, or their surrogates, would have to sign a waiver to use an experimental drug. Patients can petition the FDA to allow the use of experimental drugs under certain circumstances. The fact that one patient had already died and that the CDC would be initiating the request would go a long way toward making that happen.

As if reading Eric's mind, Terry said, "We've already gotten the spouses' signatures on the necessary legal documents. Everybody is aware that Fluzenta has not been tried on humans with H4, so they're aware of the risks. FDA has given us the green light on these two patients. They've also promised to fast-track expedited approval of Fluzenta if it works."

Damn, Eric thought. Terry's been busy. He wondered if the CDC was aware of the business concerns surrounding Tera Pharmagenics. For all he knew, Frank was signing the closing papers on Panther Cove even as they spoke. Though technically illegal, he had to disclose this since Lumpkin had taken him into his confidence on the H4 outbreak.

"Terry, I need to share something else with you. Keep in mind that I'm an officer of Tera Pharmagenics and this is insider information, so this falls into the same category as what you've told me. Our attorneys would also stroke out."

He told Terry about the investors' plan to sell Panther Cove and also solicit offers for Tera Pharmagenics and/or Fluzenta. "They are folding up the tent as we speak."

"Not a problem. We can take care of that. How much of the drug do you have available, now?"

Eric thought about it for a minute. "I'd have to check, but probably enough for a hundred or so doses."

"How soon can you get it to me?"

"As soon as you get the paperwork done, I can drive it down there." He looked at his watch. It was three hours to Atlanta, but he'd be getting there at rush hour. That meant adding an hour, at least. "Four hours, once we get it packed."

"Go ahead and start getting it ready. Keep your phone close by." Terry hung up.

Eric was in shock. This was a development he would've never predicted.

An hour later, Frank Liles called.

"Jesus Christ," Frank said when Eric answered the phone. "You've got some very powerful friends in really high places," Frank said.

"I assume you're talking about Terry Lumpkin. News travels fast. He and I go way back."

"Well, he's got big-time clout, I'll say that. How soon can you and your team be ready to leave for Atlanta?"

"Well, at Terry's direction, we've already started packing the Fluzenta. As soon as the paperwork—"

"You don't understand, Eric. This is a done deal. Finish packing, saddle up your team, and be ready to go in two hours. They're sending a helicopter to pick you up at the lab."

Eric hung up and alerted Wally and Nicole. He told them to pack for overnight. Two hours later, they were standing out near the helipad by the parking lot in front of the lab. Each of them had packed a small duffel bag and Wally had a hard-shell case containing ninety doses of Fluzenta.

They heard an aircraft getting close and looked up to see a helicopter checking out the landing zone. It made a complete circle, then the pilot turned into the slight breeze blowing from the west. Quickly and softly, he touched down on the concrete pad with ease. The co-pilot jumped out on the opposite side and stooped down as he made his way past the front of the craft and ran toward them.

"I'm Alan, the co-pilot," he said, raising his voice to be heard above the din of the aircraft still operating behind him. "I'll be escorting you out to the bird and getting you secured for takeoff."

He looked at each of them, then pointed to Wally. "Sir, I'd like you to sit in the middle seat, please." He pointed to Nicole and Eric. "One of you on the left, the other on the right."

Eric pointed to the case Wally held. "That's the Fluzenta."

Alan nodded and reached out for the case. "I'll take that and load up your gear. Stay close to me and keep your head down. As soon as you get in, buckle your seat belt and shoulder harness, and then put on the headphones hanging next to your seat. Everyone OK?" He held up his thumb.

Everyone responded with a thumbs-up, and they followed him out to the aircraft.

Once loaded, Alan shut their door and climbed in next to the pilot. After he had donned his headset, he turned his head around and spoke.

"Everyone hear me OK? Please respond verbally so I know your mic is working." They all nodded and could hear each other's voices as they answered.

"Good. Tigger is your pilot, but he's going to be pretty busy flying, so I'll do most of the talking."

The pilot gave a flick of his hand to acknowledge he was listening to the conversation.

Alan asked, "Everyone buckled in and ready?"

Everyone said "Yes."

"It'll be about an hour to Atlanta. Weather is fine, so sit back and relax. Bags are in the pockets in front of you, but we should have a smooth flight. Enjoy the ride and let me know if you need anything."

Alan turned his attention to the instrument panel and started talking to Tigger. The two were obviously going through some type of takeoff checklist. In less than a minute, Eric felt the vibration and noise increase as the engine revved up, spinning the blades above them even faster.

The aircraft lifted straight up, then tilted forward and started moving the same direction while climbing. Tigger banked toward the south, and they settled in for the trip.

They flew directly to the helipad at CDC, a first for Eric. *He could get accustomed to this mode of travel,* he thought, looking down at the cars like ants on the highways below.

They disembarked, with Alan handing Eric the metal case containing the Fluzenta. He led the group over to the edge of the helipad, where a woman in scrubs and a white lab coat awaited them.

"I'm Monica," she said. "I'll be escorting you to Dr. Lumpkin's office."

She took them inside the building and ensconced them comfortably in Terry's office, stating that he would be with them shortly.

"So, is the helicopter going to take us back home?" Wally asked.

Eric laughed. "Good question. I certainly hope so."

Nicole just looked at them and shook her head. "Boys."

Shortly, Terry walked in with Monica and two other staffers in white coats, one male, one female. He introduced Monica as the head of the RESPTC unit at Emory. The other two were scientists at CDC who he'd asked to sit in on the meeting.

"I'd like to thank our guests from Tera Pharmagenics for coming down on such short notice," Terry said. He nodded toward Monica and asked her to give a quick update on the three reported cases of H4.

She pulled up copies of the patients' medical records on the wall screen opposite the conference table. The screen was filled with an electronic medical record, displaying patient history, lab values, vital signs, and detailed physical information.

"Sandra Peck, who we think may be the index patient, was a female, age 47, in good health. She lived in Los Angeles. Tuesday, she came down with the symptoms and was admitted to Cedars in Los Angeles. Unfortunately, she died this morning."

Eric shook his head. Today was Friday. Sandra exhibited symptoms this past Tuesday. That was fast.

Monica gave the Tera Pharmagenics team a few minutes to read the slide, then clicked a button for the next screen.

"Patient Two, Phillip Brown, was a male, age 53, from Atlanta. According to witnesses, he exhibited symptoms on the flight from Los Angeles to Atlanta Wednesday. The first responders at the airport thought it was suspicious and alerted us. He was brought directly here."

Eric recognized Phillip Brown's data exhibited similar values and trends as Sandra Peck's. Monica moved to the third slide.

"Patient Three, Donna Ledford, a female, age 42, was also from Atlanta and on the same flight as Mr. Brown. Her symptoms surfaced on Thursday, a day later than his. Fortunately, we had alerted area first responders and they were able to get her here immediately. This morning, Dr. Lumpkin called Dr. Carter, and here we are. Questions?"

"What's their current status?" Eric asked.

Monica shook her head. "Critical. The records for Mr. Brown and Ms. Ledford are real-time. As you can see, their organs are shutting down. We're basically trying to keep them hydrated and comfortable, but their conditions continue to deteriorate. We're in almost constant contact with Cedars in LA and following their protocols."

"We believe the method of infection was airborne," Terry said, "but we still don't know how. We've got another team working on the epidemiology, but right now our focus here is trying to help the two patients next door. We're prepared to initiate Fluzenta therapy immediately."

The conversation shifted to medication administration. Monica asked what dosage and frequency were recommended.

"In our cohort groups, we used 3 mL twice a day," Wally said.

"I think we should increase it," Nicole said. "I would suggest 5mL twice a day."

Eric stared at her, surprised. In their haste to get to Atlanta, they'd not had a chance to discuss dosage amongst themselves. He'd assumed that they would go with what they'd used in the clinical trials.

"That's a significant variation from our trials," he stated. "Why the difference?"

Nicole returned his stare. "Are they aware of our veterinary . . . proposal?"

Eric shook his head. In a rush, he'd failed to mention it to Terry. He turned to the group. "Since the FDA turned down our application for Fluzenta, we're exploring a veterinary licensing agreement for that market." He looked at Nicole. "Go ahead, you were saying?"

"As preparation for the veterinary option, I've been going back through our early H4 research and updating the files. My review indicates that a higher dosage was more effective in the avian population for H4N4. Our clinical trials on humans were based on H5, not H4. Based on those factors, I'm suggesting we go with the higher amounts. I'd rather err on the high side, given the circumstances."

Monica and Terry both nodded in agreement. After further deliberation, the group agreed upon a dosage of 5mL mg twice daily for three days.

As they prepared to adjourn, Terry said to Eric, "I hope you don't mind, but I've arranged for you and your team to stay across the street at the Emory Conference Center Hotel, at least overnight. It's nothing fancy, but only a ten-minute walk from here. I'd rather have you close by if we need to make any adjustments."

"That's fine. We came prepared to stay a few days. It'll take that before we know."

"How long before you think we can start seeing any change?" Monica asked.

Nicole shrugged. "Twenty-four to forty-eight hours."

Eric nodded. "Hopefully, we'll see some signs that it's working within twenty-four hours. Hard to tell. Remember, we haven't done any trials with humans having H4, so we're in uncharted territory."

"I understand. Let's hope it works," Terry said.

* * *

Thirty-six hours later, Phillip Brown's fever broke. Vital signs stabilized, then started trending slightly upward, reversing their course. Eight hours later, Donna Ledford followed a similar pattern. The prognosis for both was a complete recovery with no apparent lasting effects.

Two days later, the team assembled in the same conference room for their daily status meeting. This time, everyone was in a considerably better mood.

"Good news first. The two patients are continuing to do well and expected to fully recover. We're asking the FDA to expedite approval of Fluzenta to be used as a vaccine for Hapeville," Terry said. Apparently, the human variant of the H4 virus had been given the moniker Hapeville, after the suburb of Atlanta that was home to Hartsfield-Jackson Atlanta International Airport.

"We're already on it. I've been talking with our people in California and they're ready to move forward," Eric said. He looked at Terry. "You implied there was bad news."

Terry nodded. "Eighteen more confirmed cases have surfaced. So far, sixteen of the eighteen have been traced back to the meeting in LA. The other two, we haven't been able to pin down, yet. Our epidemiologists are still sifting through all the data, trying to make sense out of it. Right now, we simply don't know."

24

Terry had arranged for a helicopter to take them back to the lab so they would get home that afternoon. There was an air of subdued ebullience on the flight back to Waynesville. While the group was excited about the news on Fluzenta, it was clouded by the specter of a flu pandemic.

As soon as the aircraft landed at the Panther Cove helipad, rotors still turning, the co-pilot jumped out and opened the door. He helped them step out, handed them their bags, and escorted them a safe distance away before returning. The three stood and waved goodbyes as the chopper lifted off and headed south.

"Frank's flying in late tonight. He wants to get together first thing in the morning with us for a debriefing," Eric said as they walked back toward the building.

"I guess he wants to be the one who announces to the troops that Tera Pharmagenics is expanding production and the rumors that Panther Cove is going to be sold are entirely false," Wally said, the sarcasm unmistakable.

Nicole piped up. "The result is what counts. Let him take credit, who cares?"

They stepped into the lobby of the mostly deserted lab. "I'm famished," Eric said. "We can talk over dinner at La Ferme. I want us to go over a few things before tomorrow. If you need anything here, grab it quickly. I'll meet you there in thirty minutes."

"I was kinda hoping for pizza," Wally said, frowning.

Eric shook his head. "Pizza and beer are good, but you'll have to make do tonight. We've got too much work to do. They've got a separate dining room so we can have some privacy. Don't be late."

Eric split off to go to his office while the other two went upstairs. Carmen was gone but left him a note on his desk welcoming him home.

What a difference a week makes, he thought. When he'd left, the sky was falling. It was gloom and doom. Now, they were riding the wave.

There was a lot to be done to ramp up production of Fluzenta. While he would prefer to do the manufacturing here, he knew it would be much quicker to do it in California. Time was of the essence.

New cases of Hapeville were coming in daily. Tera Pharmagenics had to start producing as much Fluzenta as they could as soon as possible.

He picked up the stack Carmen had left him, stuffed it into his backpack, and left to drive to Waynesville.

La Ferme was owned by his friend, Francois Duchamp. Francois had operated a highly rated brasserie in Atlanta for years, which is where Eric had met him, and retired to Waynesville.

Unable to stay away from the food business, he'd opened La Ferme, an intimate country-French bistro on

Main Street. Francois had a small room upstairs that he kept available for his closest friends.

As usual, Francois was working. From the bar, he spotted Eric and waved him over.

"Salut, mon ami," Francois said as Eric approached.

"Salut," Eric said. He didn't know much French, but always had the courtesy to greet Francois in his native language.

They exchanged the traditional French greeting of a kiss on each cheek, invoking the stares from a few of the newbies in the dining room. Waynesville was still firmly rooted in the Deep South, and men kissing was unusual.

"Your friends are already upstairs. Let me get you an aperitif." Francois reached over, picked up an opened bottle of Cerdon, and filled two champagne flutes.

Francois had introduced Eric to the refreshing pink sparkling wine popular with the French. They toasted, then politely chatted for a few minutes as they finished their drinks. Eating and drinking were a social event for the French, a custom Eric appreciated. It reminded him of Sunday dinners growing up. Even though he was anxious to get upstairs, it would have been impolite not to share a glass with his friend.

"Ah, you must get upstairs, and I must get back to work," Francois said graciously as they drained their glasses. "I'll talk to you later."

Eric went through the unmarked door next to the bar and climbed the steps to the second floor. Wally and Nicole were sharing some appetizers with half of a bottle of red wine on the table.

"What took you so long?" Nicole asked.

"You know I had to stop and have a drink with Francois. It would've been rude not to."

Wally pointed to his wine. "No problem, as you can see, we didn't wait for you."

Eric laughed. "I would've expected no less."

He pulled up a chair and sat while Wally poured him a glass of wine. "We're going to be swamped starting tomorrow, so enjoy," Eric said as he held up the glass.

Over dinner, they talked about shifting to production mode. Wally was nominated to be the liaison with Cupertino. Eric was concerned about sending him back and forth to California alone, given his lack of social skills. Nicole convinced him that not only did Wally have the experience, but his blunt manner was what was needed at this juncture.

Nicole would remain at Panther Cove, compiling the requisite research and safety data for the FDA. Eric would deal with the inevitable political issues and be the front person for the project.

They worked until a little after ten, which is when Francois closed. He appeared upstairs, not to usher them out, but to see if they needed anything else.

Not wanting to take advantage of his host's hospitality, Eric adjourned the meeting, telling Wally and Nicole he'd see them at the lab in the morning at 7:30.

When he got home, Felix was waiting for him.

"Did Aunt Gertrude take good care of you?" he asked, as the cat rubbed up against his leg, working him for a snack. Eric obliged, then unpacked. Despite the schedule of the last few days, he was wide awake.

He picked up his phone and called Rae via FaceTime. He wanted to see her tonight. It took a few extra seconds to connect, as usual, then her smiling face appeared on his phone.

"Good evening, Dr. Carter. I was thinking about you. I started to call, but figured you were still busy giving interviews."

He laughed. "Zero to hero, that's me." He filled her in on his version of the events. "I'm exhausted but wired."

"You're just processing and can't shut it off. If I were there, I think I could get your mind on other things."

He grinned, forgetting for a moment that she could see his face on her phone.

"Oh, I like that smile," she said.

"I miss you."

"I miss you, too. I've got to be in Atlanta next week. Any chance of you coming down so I can make good on my promise?"

"I've got a better idea. Why don't you stay over for the weekend and come up here? I've got Ali that weekend."

There was a hesitation as she realized what he was saying.

"I'd love to, but are you sure?" She paused, then said, "I could get a room if that's going to be a problem."

He could see the expectancy on her face, even on the small screen. "It'd be a good time for you to meet her. And yes, I want you to stay here. Of course, the downside is you won't be able to show up dressed as you did before."

Rae laughed, the relief evident. "No, but maybe I can come early. Pun intended."

"I like the way you think."

Early the next day, Eric met Frank for breakfast before going to the lab. He filled him in on the dinner meeting the night before, covering the major tasks and assignments. He saved Wally's role for last.

Frank shook his head after hearing Eric's plan. "I don't want Wally as the liaison. Why don't you put Nicole in that role? She has much better people skills."

He tried to reason with Frank, but his boss was reluctant. "I know you don't like Wally, but he's the best one for that. He's got more experience, and we need someone that is . . . direct."

"*Direct,* hell. He's a bull in a fucking china shop."

Eric nodded. "And, that's exactly what we need. He's good, and you know it. Even Nicole acknowledged Wally would be best for the liaison role." Eric folded his arms across his chest, determined not to budge on this. "This is too critical, Frank. We've got another chance, and we need to give it our best. It's got to be him."

Frank set his jaw, started to say something, then scowled. "Whatever."

Satisfied the lineup was set, Eric asked, "What's going on with Chip?"

Frank broke into a grin. "Oh, now he's our biggest cheerleader, don't you know? He told Bearant the deal was off, that Tera Pharmagenics was here to stay, and we weren't interested in selling Panther Cove. Amazing what a huge order from Uncle Sam will do."

Eric laughed. "I suppose you will want to announce the news to all of the employees here. It would mean a lot coming directly from you."

Frank nodded. "I still want to meet with you, Nicole, and Wally first. It won't take long, I just want to thank you all personally." His countenance turned serious. "Thank you, Eric. I appreciate what you and your team did. You saved this company . . . and my ass. I owe you."

"We got lucky. We brought Fluzenta to market, which will save lives. That's the most important thing."

25

Friday afternoon, Eric headed over to Asheville to pick up Ali. He and Rae had decided it would be better if Ali were at the house first. That would give Eric a chance to set the stage before she arrived Saturday morning.

He was disappointed that he wouldn't get to see Rae make another entrance like she did last time, but agreed it would be better this way. He was excited and nervous about Rae and Ali meeting. On the drive over, he'd thought about the best way to present it to his daughter.

He didn't want to be deceptive, but he was unsure of how much to say. He decided on leaving it that he and Rae were good friends and go from there.

On the way to Waynesville, Ali wanted to know what they were doing this weekend. As usual, she wanted to fill up her schedule, making the most of her time with her dad.

"I thought we could just sit on the porch with Felix," he said, trying to keep the smirk off his face. In his peripheral vision, he saw Ali staring at him.

"You're teasing," she said. She rattled off her usual: Felix, supper with Gramma and Harlan, hiking. She added that she wanted to see the elk this time, since they'd not seen them on her last visit.

"Can Nicole come hiking with us?"

He had been expecting that question and wanted to defer discussing it at this time. "I thought maybe tonight we could go by Frog Level—"

"And see Mr. Pete? And Uncle Clark? And get pizza?" Mr. Pete was Clark's lovable rescue dog with dirty blonde fur and a goofy grin, more standard poodle than anything else. Mr. Pete had won the lottery when he picked Clark.

As a child is sometimes wont to do, Ali had always called Clark "uncle." He was her godfather, and as far as she was concerned, he was her uncle, too.

Eric had to laugh, relieved that she dropped the question about Nicole, at least for the time being. "Yes," he answered. "Yes, to all three."

When they walked in, Clark spotted Ali as she ran toward him. "Well, well. Look who's here." He looked down at his feet. "You better wake up, Mr. Pete. We've got company."

"Yippee. Hey, Uncle Clark," she said as she ran around behind the bar and gave him a quick hug. She immediately turned her attention to the blond dog standing next to him, wagging his tail.

"Evening, Eric," Clark said as he drew a Nutty Brunette and slid it over to Eric. "I don't think she's as excited to see me as she was before Mr. Pete came to live with us."

"Welcome to the club. She's been on pins and needles since I told her we were coming here tonight." He took a sip of beer as Maryann walked over.

"I'm guessing you'll be ordering pizza tonight," she asked, nodding toward Ali, who was playing with Mr. Pete. The perky blonde server was Ali's favorite. "The usual?"

Eric nodded. "Of course."

"Outside or in?"

"It's a nice night, let's sit outside. Thanks, Maryann."

"No problem, I'll save you a table by the creek," she said as she walked away to wait on another table.

"You're looking to be in lots better spirits than last time you were in here," Clark said.

Eric nodded. "Feast to famine and back to feast again, all in the space of a week." He was reminded of the song "Six Feet Away" by the SteelDrivers. The theme was that anyone is only a short distance away from disaster.

"I'm glad it worked out," Clark said.

"Me, too." He glanced over at Ali, who was still busy with Mr. Pete, then turned back to Clark. "I've got company coming in tomorrow."

Clark raised his eyebrows. "Anybody I know?"

Eric nodded. "You've met her before. Rae?"

"The brunette. I thought you two made a good couple."

"I'm bringing her to meet Ali. Got any advice?"

Clark looked over at the little girl talking to the dog. He nodded and turned his attention back to Eric. "She'll be fine. Just take it slow."

"That's the plan. Rae's coming in tomorrow and staying the night, but we're keeping it simple right now."

"Must be getting serious?"

Eric shrugged. "Maybe. I'm taking it slow, too."

When their pizza came, Eric and Ali moved out to the table out back by the creek. She had begged Uncle Clark to let Mr. Pete come out with her, but he convinced her to let him stay inside with him, insisting that he needed company. He assured her that after she finished her supper, she could come back in and visit with him some more.

Sitting out on the table, eating cheese pizza, Ali was still animated. Now, she wanted the schedule for tomorrow.

"Well, we'll get up before the sun comes up and you can fix me breakfast."

Ali laughed. "You're silly." She poked a finger into his chest. "You fix breakfast for me, you know that. Pancakes, please."

"Okay, that I can do. Then, I thought we'd pack a lunch and go hiking."

"Good. Can Nicole come?"

He knew that Ali would return to that subject at some point. Now was as good a time as any. He needed to extricate himself, quickly and painlessly. "No, I think she's busy this weekend. But . . . I've invited a friend to come stay with us this weekend."

Ali scowled and looked at him suspiciously. "Who?"

Eric took a deep breath. "Her name is Rae. You probably don't remember, but you met her at my company's picnic last year." The scowl remained.

Ali crossed her thin arms over her chest. "I want Nicole to go."

Shit, Eric thought. *Now what do I do?* This was not going according to plan. He was already on his heels and didn't want to make things worse. He tried to remain nonchalant. *Don't force things.*

"Daddy has lots of friends, sweetie. Like Uncle Clark, Nicole, Uncle Wally . . ." The mention of Clark and Wally erased the frown and prompted a smile from Ali.

"Why can't Uncle Wally go?" she asked.

He couldn't figure out whether her objection was based on the fact that Rae wasn't Nicole or that somehow, she perceived Rae as a threat. He was flying blind here, with no compass.

"Rae's a friend, too. Since she's going to be in town, I invited her to meet you and stay with us." Ali's expression remained neutral. "In the spare bedroom," he added. "And she likes to hike, too. I thought you might like to show her our cabin."

Her posture relaxed slightly, and Eric hoped that had satisfied her for the moment.

"What time is she coming?"

Eric exhaled, hoping he was off the hook. "Around ten. We can pack a lunch and then go hiking."

"Is she nice?"

He smiled. "Very. I think you will like her."

The next morning, they awoke, and Eric prepared Ali's pancakes for breakfast. There was no mention of Rae. Eric figured Ali had forgotten, which was unlikely, or accepted it, which was more unlikely. Like an expectant father, he kept watching the clock.

They were out on the deck, when Eric heard the car. A moment later, Ali heard it and turned to look at Eric. Her expression didn't telegraph anything.

Showtime, he thought. "That must be Rae. Let's walk out and greet her, okay?"

Ali gave him a slight nod and waited for him to make the first move. They walked around the corner of the house, Ali a step behind, and down the stairs toward the rental car parked next to the carport.

Rae stepped out of the car, dressed more demurely than the last visit. She wore tan hiking shorts, low-cut trail shoes, and a yellow sports shirt.

"Hello," she said. She was careful not to display any affection toward Eric and instead, leaned over and addressed Ali. "You must be Ali?" She extended her hand and said, "I'm Rae. It's so nice to meet you. Your dad's told me a lot about you."

In spite of herself, Ali smiled and glanced over at her dad with an approving look.

"I hope I didn't disturb your breakfast," Rae said.

Ali shook her head. "Do you want to meet Felix?"

"I'd love to." She flashed Eric a smile as she walked past, following Ali into the house.

Eric followed them inside, where Ali took Rae over to Felix, asleep on the bookcase. She told Rae all about Felix and his cat habits. Rae patiently waited until Ali said, "You can pet him if you want."

Rae reached over and lightly scratched Felix behind the ears. He approved, closing his eyes and purring loudly. Ali was delighted. Eric started to ask Rae if she wanted a cup of coffee but realized she was entirely focused on Ali.

He followed them around the house as Ali played hostess. She showed Rae his bedroom, and then stopped at the door of the guest bedroom. "This is your room,"

Ali said, glancing at Eric to make sure she was right. He just nodded and smiled.

The last stop was Ali's room. Eric leaned up against the door jamb while Ali proceeded to show Rae everything in the room. He realized that Rae knew considerably more about dealing with eight-year-old girls than he did. For the first time since he broached the subject yesterday evening with Ali, he was able to relax.

So far, so good.

26

They finally made it to the kitchen where Eric was able to ask Rae if she'd like a cup of coffee. As soon as he poured her a cup and refilled his, Ali suggested they go out on the back porch.

"When I was little, we used to play I Spy out here," Ali said as they sat, Ali taking the seat between Eric and Rae. It was clear she was keeping them separate.

"I used to love to play that when I was a little girl," Rae said.

Ali smiled. "Do you want to play?"

Eric looked at his daughter, then at Rae. He was surprised that Ali wanted to play. Then, he realized that Ali was challenging Rae. It was not a polite move after all. It was a test.

"Sure," Rae said, taking a sip of her coffee.

"You go first," Ali said, "then me, then Daddy."

Rae furrowed her brow and squinted her eyes, scanning the near horizon. Ali was tracking her to try and guess what she would pick. After a slow scan left to right and back, Rae said, "I spy something yellow."

Eric looked outward, trying to discern what Rae might have settled on. There were many yellow leaves, but somehow, he didn't think that was what she had called. Neither did Ali.

Ali turned to her dad with a self-satisfying grin, then back toward Rae. She then pointed to her right and said, "That yellow house."

"Very good," Rae said. "I thought that would be a hard one."

Eric squinted and could barely see the house in the distance, even though he was looking for it. "That's not fair," he said. "I didn't even get a chance."

"Too bad," Ali and Rae said almost simultaneously. Then they started laughing like schoolgirls.

They played for another thirty minutes, with the two girls seeming to have some sort of psychic connection that Eric didn't share. He looked at his watch and announced that they probably should make lunch if they were planning on eating at the cabin.

"Can you make pimento cheese?" Ali asked Rae at the kitchen island.

Rae shook her head. "No, sorry, Ali. That's not one of my specialties."

Eric held his breath, knowing what was coming next.

"Nicole makes it when we go hiking."

Rae shot Eric a brief glance, then reverted to form before Ali could notice.

"That's okay," Ali said. "Can you make a turkey sandwich?"

Rae smiled, and it was genuine. "That I can do. What would you like on it?"

They eventually got sandwiches made and headed out to the trail. They stopped at the fence, and Eric asked which way they were going.

Ali pointed to their left and explained to Rae that it led to a tall mountain with a picnic table. She pointed to the right and said that went to her cabin.

"Which way would you like to go today?" Rae asked.

Eric shook his head. Rae was more perceptive than he'd thought. Maybe it was a female thing, but she made it look easy.

Ali pondered it for a few seconds, then looked up at him. "I think we should take her to our cabin."

"I think that would be a great idea."

They got to Ferguson Cabin and had lunch. Ali played the perfect guide, explaining things to Rae. Eric had to smile. A lot of what she'd told Rae was what he'd told Ali on previous trips. It had obviously found a home in Ali's memory.

After eating, they walked up the hill to the Learning Center. Ali insisted on taking the woods trail. Again, Eric was convinced that Ali was measuring Rae.

When they got back to the house, Ali asked Eric if they were having supper at Gramma and Harlan's.

"Yes, we are, but I need to call Gramma and let her know we're coming." He explained to Rae who Gramma and Harlan were, although she already knew.

"Gramma is the best cook, isn't she, Daddy?"

"Yes, she is. Her cooking reminds me of my Aunt Ida, who raised me," Eric answered.

"Do you call it supper or dinner?" Ali asked Rae. *Another test,* Eric thought. Rae was on her own with this one. He couldn't ever remember discussing that with her.

Again, with undivided attention, Rae looked into Ali's eyes. "Well, a lot of people I work with call it dinner, so sometimes I say that. But when I was growing up, my mother and father always called it supper, and so did I."

Ali beamed. She turned around to Eric, and her eyes gave him the thumbs up. Rae had passed.

When it came time to shower and get ready to go over to Gramma's, Ali insisted on going first and dragging Rae along with her. They took so long that Eric had to rush to get ready in time.

Gramma and Harlan took a liking to Rae as well. After they had finished, Gertrude tried to shoo everyone out to the porch. Rae wasn't so easily deterred. She enlisted Ali's help.

"Let's help your Gramma clean up. After that wonderful supper, I need to do something besides sit."

Ali clapped her hands together, excited to be included in this rite of passage. So, Harlan and Eric went out to the porch as directed. Eric started to sit in one of the rocking chairs, but Harlan motioned him out to the yard. "Come out to the barn with me for a minute, I want to show you something."

Eric smiled, knowing what it was Harlan wanted to show him. Inside the barn, Harlan shuffled over to his workshop in the far-right corner. When he turned around, he was holding a Mason jar half full of a clear liquid.

"I thought we might have a little nip before dessert," he said as he twisted the lid off. "You know she won't let me bring it in the house."

Eric nodded and smiled. Harlan always gave him the same explanation.

Harlan took a swallow, then wiped the edge of the jar off with his sleeve before handing it to Eric. "This is sipping 'shine, so go easy."

Eric took a sip and it burned all the way down his throat, making his eyes water as always. It had to be 150 proof, which meant 75 percent alcohol. He held it up and looked at it. The liquid was clearer than glass, an almost surreal clarity to it. He handed it back to Harlan, who put the lid on.

"Tell me, are you making this stuff?" Eric asked.

Harlan grinned as he shook his head. "I've told you—a friend of mine makes it, so I know it's safe. There are still people making bad liquor up here, so you have to be careful."

They walked back to the porch and sat in the rockers. Rae came out of the house in a few minutes with four coffee cups in one hand and the coffee pot in the other. She sat them on the table and disappeared back inside. Ali came out carrying cream and sugar, along with spoons and forks.

Gertrude came out carrying two plates, each containing a slab of lemon meringue pie. She handed one to Eric, then gave the other to Harlan. Her glare lingered on Harlan for an extra second, and Eric realized that she knew exactly where they'd been. He felt like a kid who'd been caught with his hand in the cookie jar. This was a ritual that didn't fool anyone.

Later that evening, after Ali was in bed and sound asleep, Eric poured two glasses of wine. He handed one to Rae, grabbed a blanket, and led Rae out to the porch. They sat on the bench, looking out over the valley. Rae snuggled up to him and pulled the blanket up over them both.

After they had taken a sip of wine, Rae said, "Does that taste better than Harlan's whiskey?"

Surprised, he asked, "How did you—"

"You don't think Gertrude knows?" Rae chuckled. "She's sharp as a tack, and she knew exactly what you boys were doing. I quote, 'That old man thinks I don't know he's taking Eric out to the barn for a drink of whiskey.'"

They both laughed. Eric said, "I always figured she knew, but she's never mentioned a word to me."

Rae squeezed his leg underneath the blanket. "Thank you for a wonderful evening."

He moved his hand further up her leg. "We could have some fun underneath this blanket."

She put her hand over his and moved it back down a few inches. "I want you, too. But, it's not worth the risk. I feel like I got off to a good start with Ali and I'm not willing to take a chance on betraying her trust."

Disappointed, he didn't reply right away. Rae stretched up and kissed him.

"I'll stay over Sunday night. After we take Ali home, I'll make it up to you, I promise."

27

The next few weeks were a blur. As expected, Tera Pharmagenics canceled the sale of the Panther Cove facility. Convinced the FDA would quickly approve Fluzenta, the company was busy gearing up to roll out the blockbuster drug to an eager worldwide market.

Over a hundred cases of Hapeville had been reported. Every patient had been given Fluzenta and all but three had recovered. The three who didn't make it had waited too late to seek help. Although the drug was proving effective after a patient was infected, everyone believed that a vaccine would be even better.

Eric knew that once the virus was isolated and identified, the jump to a vaccine was not that difficult. Attenuated, or live vaccines, were relatively easy to create since they used a weakened version of the live virus. While they offered a stronger response, they did have several drawbacks. First, there was a remote chance that the virus could revert causing an infection. Also, handling and the possibility of reactions were considerably more problematic.

On the other hand, inactivated vaccines were created by killing the virus. Thus, they couldn't infect someone with the flu. In addition to being easier to store and transport, they were less likely to cause a reaction. The biggest drawback was that they generated a weaker response from the body's immune system, so the effectiveness was an issue.

DNA vaccines, the latest in immunization, were the Holy Grail. They used the body's own cells to attack the virus. Once you had the map of the unwanted virus, they were not that difficult to manufacture. The challenge was getting the virus decoded.

"Dr. Zheng is on Line Two," Carmen's voice on his intercom announced, breaking his train of thought on vaccines.

Eric picked up the handset and pressed the button for Line Two. "Hi Lin, how are you?"

"Well, thank you. Since I had the dubious honor of calling you before with bad news, I thought it was only appropriate that I called you this time with good news. The committee just approved Fluzenta. The press release will be out within the hour."

Eric pumped his fist. *Finally,* he thought. The last hurdle.

He hung up and immediately called Frank's cell phone. As usual, it went straight to voice mail. He called Gwen, Frank's assistant, and asked her to track Frank down and have him call as soon as possible.

Fifteen minutes later, his cell phone buzzed.

"I'm in the middle of a meeting. What's so—"

"Fluzenta was approved," Eric said, interrupting him.

"What? Really? That's awesome. Perfect timing. I'm in a meeting with Chip. I'll call you later."

Eric hung up and walked up to the lab to tell Wally and Nicole. After exchanging hugs, he went back downstairs to Carmen. "It's official," he said, beaming.

Carmen squealed, jumped up, and hugged him. "I'm so happy for you," she said, tears in her eyes. "You deserve this."

He took a deep breath and looked at his watch. "Any way you can patch me into the office intercom system in thirty minutes?"

Still grinning, she said, "Absolutely. I'll let you know when it's ready."

He went to his desk and called Rae.

"Well, hello, handsome. Didn't expect to hear from you in the middle of the day."

"They approved Fluzenta," he said, unable to contain his excitement.

"Awesome," Rae screamed. "I am so proud of you."

They chatted for a few minutes, then Rae said she needed to go. "We'll talk later."

Twenty minutes later, Carmen walked into his office and said, "Line Three when you're ready. Just pick it up and punch the Talk button." She stood there waiting.

Calmly, he picked up the handset, cleared his voice, and then punched Talk.

"Your attention, please. This is Eric Carter." He paused for a few seconds to let the building quiet down before continuing. "I wanted everyone here at Panther Cove to hear the news firsthand. The FDA has just approved Fluzenta for production. Thank you all for your hard work."

Later that afternoon, Wally and Nicole were in Eric's office for a status meeting.

"I wish you could have been up on the second floor when you made that announcement," Nicole said. "You would've thought we won the World Series."

"We did," Wally said. "The fucking jackpot."

After the meeting was over, Nicole lagged. As soon as Wally left, she got up, closed the door, and came to Eric's desk. She stood with arms folded across her chest. "Have you been avoiding me?"

He started to answer "no," but in truth, he had. He didn't want to get into it now, but since she brought it up, he plunged in.

"Probably," he said, hedging. "I told you that we can't . . ."

"I understand that part, and I agree. But why can't we continue to be friends? Going fishing and hiking? I miss that, and I miss Ali."

He shook his head. "I do too, but it's hard to put the Genie back in the bottle." The truth was that he couldn't get that night out of his mind. Every time he saw her, he was reminded of it.

He felt guilty enough, but when he was with Rae, he felt even worse. Although they weren't in a formal relationship, it was turning into that quickly. Avoidance was the best route, but Nicole wasn't going to accept that.

"I just think we need to cool things for a while." He saw the hurt look on her face, then added, "Not forever, just until I can get my head straightened out."

"You told me you didn't regret it."

He shook his head. "I didn't—I don't, I . . . damn, Nicole, this is complicated. And we can't."

A thin smile crossed her face, and she relaxed her arms. She put the heels of her hands on his desk and leaned toward him. "It won't happen again, I promise. I just miss you, and I don't want to lose our friendship."

She paused and let the words sink in. "Let's start with something safe, like going fishing in J Creek, there at Hemphill. In the middle of the afternoon. I'll prove that we can just be friends."

He exhaled, considering what she proposed.

"I promise not to attack you," she said, smiling.

Her smile was infectious, and he couldn't keep from reflecting it. "Alright."

She stood upright and put her hands on her hips. "When?"

Eric had to laugh. "You are relentless, you know that?"

She flashed him an exaggerated grin. "That's one of the reasons you like me, remember?"

They agreed to go fishing the next afternoon.

For the next twenty-four hours, Eric tried to convince himself that they could put the Genie back into the lamp. He got to their spot first. By the time he'd put on his waders and assembled his fly rod, Nicole's blue Volkswagen Bug pulled up and parked behind his Jeep.

She got out and shouted, "Let me slip my waders on, and I'll catch up with you."

He nodded, turned, and made his way down the bank into the stream. His first few casts were unproductive. He moved upstream a few yards, spotting a nice eddy just above him, off to the left. He dropped the fly just above it, and when it drifted down, a trout devoured it.

He pointed the rod tip upstream, setting the hook, then stripped in line with his free hand. It was a rainbow, not huge, but decent. Would have been dinner if he'd wanted to keep it. He netted the fish, took the hook out, and released him back into the stream.

"That was quick," Nicole said, coming up on his right.

"I think there's more where that one came from. Why don't you work the right side and I'll work the left? We can switch when I get too far ahead of you."

"Ha," she said. "That's not happening."

They both laughed, and he was pleased to see them drop back into their familiar routine. He had to admit, it was nice, and he had missed her company.

They fished for a couple of hours as dusk started to settle in the mountains.

"I think you owe me dinner," Nicole said. "By my count, I caught nine and you had seven. And, I had the largest one."

Eric stiffened, wondering where this was going. It was their standing wager, but he hadn't thought about it until now.

She said, "Don't worry, I'll take a raincheck. I had fun. It was nice being out on the water with you again." As she turned to walk toward her car, over her shoulder she said, "See you at the lab in the morning."

"Me, too." It was all he could manage to say as he watched her walk all the way back to her car. As she got in, she gave him a little wave over her shoulder.

Eric returned the gesture as she started her car and drove away.

He was relieved that she didn't pursue dinner. Maybe she was right that they could be friends again.

28

Nicole smiled as she pulled out onto Hemphill Road. She liked the look in Eric's eyes. He'd been expecting an invitation from her and was disappointed when she didn't bite.

Now that Tera Pharmagenics was on track, she planned to turn her attention back to him. Her aggressiveness had seemed to push him away, but she chalked that up to his being distracted with the obstacles related to Fluzenta. Now that it had been greenlighted, she intended to remind him in subtle ways what he was missing.

She wondered about his relationship with Rae, that bitchy accountant from the West Coast. When Wally had mentioned that Eric and Rae had gone out to dinner in Asheville, Nicole had pressed him for details. All he would say is that a friend of his saw them at a cozy table for two at Zambra, a romantic restaurant on Walnut Street.

She never suspected Eric was seeing Rae, thinking they were just co-workers. Apparently, Nicole had underestimated her. The good news was that as far as Nicole knew, he'd yet to introduce Rae to Ali.

When she got home, she called Frank Liles. "You didn't return my call," Nicole said into the phone when he answered.

"I've been busy, as you can imagine. It's been crazy, what with the demand for Fluzenta. We can't ship it out quick enough. Thanks to you, I might add."

She smiled. *You're damn right,* she thought. "I was just curious, what's going on with Eric and Rae?"

There was a hesitation before Frank answered. "What do you mean?"

Nicole kept her voice light. "Someone here at the lab saw them out to dinner in Asheville. The employee seemed to think it was more than business, if you know what I mean. They asked me about it, and I said I'd check into it."

Frank hesitated again, which gave Nicole her answer. "I, uh, I think they may be seeing each other, socially. I mean, they don't work in the same area, so as long as they're discreet . . ."

"Oh, I don't care. They're both consenting adults, like you say. I'm just concerned about how it may look if word gets out. Especially with all the public attention we're getting now."

She heard him exhale on the other end of the phone. "You bring up a good point. I'll talk to him about it."

* * *

Later that evening, Eric was sitting out on his deck when his phone buzzed. It was Rae.

"Hi. What are you doing?" Her voice was tight and businesslike.

"Sitting out on the deck, catching up on my reading. You?"

"Have you talked to Frank, like in the past day or so?"

"No. He called this afternoon, and I haven't had a chance to call him back. Why?"

"He called me to warn me about seeing you."

"What?"

"You heard me." Rae went on to explain that apparently an employee had seen the two of them out to dinner in Asheville. Frank was concerned about the kind of message that might send to the staff and to outsiders.

"We went out to dinner together, for Christ's sake. What's the big deal about that?"

"According to Frank, it appeared to look like 'more than business.'"

Eric's thoughts rewound back to their dinner date. They'd had a nice dinner at Zambra, seated in the alley space with a bottle of wine. He recalled that they sat next to each other at the small table, more a matter of convenience in the tight area. He tried to remember any overt displays of affection, although he hadn't been paying attention.

"What did we do?" he asked.

Rae snorted. "I don't remember doing anything. At least at the restaurant."

Eric felt his face blush as he thought of the after-dinner activities in the privacy of Rae's room when they got back to the Grove Park Inn. It was reminiscent of her visit to his house. "Did he say where this came from?"

"No. He suggested to me that it would be in both of our best interests to 'tone things down a bit.' He inferred that with the recent public attention to Tera Pharmagenics, it might cause problems for two officers to be romantically involved."

"Bullshit. Let me try to call him and I'll call you right back."

He disconnected and called Frank. It went straight to voice mail. He didn't bother to leave a message and called Rae back.

"My call went to voicemail. I'll talk to Frank tomorrow and get to the bottom of this."

They chatted for a while, then said goodnight. After he had hung up, he thought back to that night in Asheville. He tried to remember seeing anyone he knew at the restaurant. He knew most of the employees at the lab, although he had to admit he hadn't been that observant at the restaurant.

Rae had worn a striking outfit that evening. She had on a thin, cream-colored silk top with a black shawl. Outside, she'd rearranged it so he had a good view. In the cool night air, her nipples were clearly visible. While not as risqué as what she'd worn at his house, it was far from chaste.

Shaking his head, he dismissed the complaint as a nosey employee with nothing better to do. Frank was overreacting, and Eric intended to tell him so.

The next morning at the office, Frank called. He claimed to be touching base on Fluzenta production, but Eric knew better.

"What's this bullshit about Rae and me seeing each other?" Eric asked.

"I'm just concerned—"

"We have always been discreet, Frank, and you know it. Besides, there's no reporting relationship, so no violation of company policy."

Frank backpedaled. "I know that. I'm just passing this along. With both of you being officers and with all the recent scrutiny of Tera Pharmagenics, I don't want to give anyone ammunition. You know how that sort of thing can spin out of control."

"Where'd this come from?"

Frank stammered. "I'd rather not say. It's not that big of a deal."

"Well, it was important enough that you felt the need to call Rae and me about it."

"I was just giving you both a heads-up. We're under the microscope these days, and we all need to be careful."

Eric was tempted to bring up the text message from Frank to Nicole. "Good advice. For us all, right?" He wondered if Frank caught the innuendo.

There was a pause, then Frank changed the subject and said, "By the way, I'm hearing good reports on your guy Wally. Production is ramping up smoothly. We should be at max capacity by the end of the month."

After he'd finished the call with Frank, Eric started thinking again about a trip to London with Ali. Over Christmas break would be perfect for her school schedule and a wonderful time to visit the city. It would be expensive, but with his newly-expected bonus, that wouldn't be an issue.

Ever since Kate's marriage to Bryson, Ali had always spent Christmas with Kate and Bryson's family. Eric had acquiesced to Kate on that holiday, even though their agreement specified alternating years.

Maybe this year he could talk Kate into letting her go to London over Christmas.

Later, Eric was immersed in paperwork when he heard a knock on his office door. He looked up to see Wally standing there, holding his laptop.

"Hey Boss, got a minute. I want to show you something."

Eric nodded. "Come in." Wally closed the door behind him, walked over to the conference table, and sat. He opened the laptop computer and started tapping on the keys.

His curiosity peaked, Eric got up and joined him. "What's up?"

"Give me a second."

In a few minutes, Wally slid his laptop around in front of Eric. Eric studied the two pictures on the screen.

"The one on the left is Hapeville," Wally said. "I got this from CDC. The one on the right is H4N4 or what I call 'pure' H4 that I got from our files here at the lab. Look at the proteins I circled in red."

Eric looked closer at the area Wally had marked. The Hapeville virus was missing a protein that was clearly present in the H4N4 virus. He looked up at Wally. "Hapeville is missing a protein. If that's so, that means . . . what? It's a variant? That's to be expected, right? H4N4 has only been seen in birds so far." Most viruses acquired slight variations when they jumped species.

Wally nodded. "It appears to be a variant, for sure. What bothers me is that variation. Don't you think that's unusual?"

Eric looked back at the screen and studied it again. It was odd. "I'd agree. How, then, did the change occur?"

His scientist wore a serious expression. "I don't think it occurred naturally."

"What?" Eric couldn't believe what Wally was saying. "Are you suggesting Hapeville is man-made?"

Wally shrugged. "I don't know. I'm just saying it looks suspicious. Natural mutations aren't usually that significant. They're more subtle, and that's not the area where they usually occur."

Eric looked back at the two pictures and then shook his head. "Why would anybody modify the H4N4 virus?"

Wally slid the laptop back. He paused for a moment before continuing. "First of all, I'm not sure it is man-made. To answer your question, I have no idea why anybody would do it."

"What did Nicole say?"

Wally shook his head. "I haven't shown it to her. She wasn't at her desk, so I came straight to you."

Eric nodded. "Send me these files and don't mention this to anyone. I'll track Nicole down and tell her."

After Wally left, Carmen stuck her head inside his door. "Don't forget, you're supposed to pick up Ali in forty-five minutes."

"Shit," Eric said, looking at his watch. The time had slipped up on him. He grabbed a stack of papers off his desk and bolted out of the office.

29

"Sounds like things are looking up at Tera Pharmagenics," Kate said.

Eric was at Kate's house, seated on the sofa in the living room. He and Ali had just returned from an early dinner and ice cream. Ali had gone upstairs to her room to get her iPad to show him something.

He wanted to say that he was sorry Bryson didn't make the sale on Panther Cove, but bit his tongue. "Sometimes, being in the right place at the right time is worth more than hard work. I'm just glad I still have a job here in North Carolina, so I can be close to Ali."

Eric shifted in his seat and leaned toward Kate, who was sitting in a chair next to him. "Speaking of Ali, I'd like to ask a favor." He'd rehearsed his lines on the way over to Asheville.

She eyed him warily and nodded.

"I know Ali usually spends Christmas with you and Bryson, but this year, I'd like to surprise her and take her to London for Christmas. I want to make up for having to cancel our trip earlier this fall."

He'd decided not to mention the fact that their agreement gave him that right every other year, trying to keep the peace up front and hoping she'd be reasonable.

Kate exhaled, clearly caught off guard by his request. She opened her mouth to say something, then reconsidered and paused for a few seconds. "What specific dates were you thinking about?"

He smiled, thankful for her question instead of stonewalling. He was prepared and gave her the dates along with his planned travel itinerary. Before she could answer, they heard footsteps upstairs.

Kate glanced toward the stairs, then back to Eric. "Give me a call this evening when you get home," she whispered.

He cocked his head, immediately suspicious. "Why? What is it?"

Before Kate could answer, the squeal of an eight-year-old punctuated the silence. Ali ran into the room straight over to her dad's outstretched arms. Looking over his daughter's head, he saw Kate mouth the words *call me later.* He wondered what was going on.

"Thanks for the pizza and ice cream, Daddy. I wish I didn't have to go to school tomorrow."

Turning his full attention to Ali, Eric nodded. "You're welcome. I know, I wish you didn't have to go to school either. But, you'll be with me this weekend."

"Can we have supper with Gramma?"

"We've been invited, if you'd like."

She stepped back and put her hands on her hips. "Duh," she said, with an attitude.

"Careful," he said. He was already dreading the teenage years.

As he stood, he nodded toward Kate. "I should get going." He looked at Ali. "You need to get started on homework."

She smiled and nodded. "See you Friday."

After he got home, he poured himself a glass of wine, grabbed his phone off the island, and walked out on the deck. It was a clear, cool night and he was glad he'd slipped on his jacket before coming outside.

The moon was almost directly overhead, lighting up the entire mountaintop. He eased into a chair, took a sip of wine, and pondered Kate's actions.

He was confused. Her initial reaction to the London trip seemed favorable, asking him for dates. When he gave her the information, she didn't react negatively. He knew Kate well enough to read her emotions. It was only when she heard Ali's footsteps that she seemed to panic and asked him to call her later.

An owl hooted at the tree line. He couldn't think of anything he'd missed. Another owl answered, and he listened as they went back and forth for a few minutes. Then, it was still and quiet. He'd waited until he was sure Ali was asleep. He pressed Kate's cell phone number.

She picked up on the second ring. "Hi," she answered, her voice seeming a tad slurred.

"Is she asleep?" he asked.

"Like a rock. Are you home?"

"Been home. I was just waiting until I thought Ali would be asleep. What's going on, Kate?" he asked, impatient to get to the bottom of whatever big secret she was harboring.

She hesitated a moment before answering. "The dates you gave me for Christmas are fine. I know she would love that."

He didn't like where this was headed. His intuition told him bad news was following.

"Thank you. I'll tell her this weekend." He waited for Kate to continue.

"There's something else. I wanted to tell you in person, but I didn't want to talk in front of Ali. And I didn't want to wait."

He wanted to scream, *What else, Kate? I know there's more.* He waited her out until she finally said, barely louder than a whisper, "We're leaving Asheville."

He drew a sharp breath, as if he'd been gut-punched. "What do you mean, Kate? Leaving Asheville?"

"Bryson's dad is starting this huge project in Orlando. He wants Bryson to run it."

Eric shook his head. He couldn't believe this was happening. This was the last thing he expected. "Why can't he run it from here?"

"You probably don't believe me, but I suggested that."

"Kate, you can't do this," he said, pleading. "You're taking Ali from me."

"It's not forever. I don't want to leave Asheville. Bryson promised we'd move back soon as he's done. His family is here, and he doesn't want to leave either."

"Then don't."

"It's not that easy. His dad is getting older, and he wants Bryson to take over the business."

"How long?"

Kate hesitated, then murmured, "Three years."

Eric exploded, unable to hold back his anger any longer. "Three years? You're taking my daughter away from me for three fucking years?"

"It's not like that, Eric, please. We're staying here until the end of the school year, so it won't even be for an entire three years. Her friends and mine are here. Asheville is home. We'll be back often, I promise."

He unloaded on Kate, and before long, she was sobbing, saying she was sorry. Eric slammed the phone down, picked it up, and disconnected the call without another word.

In a few minutes, the phone quietly buzzed again. He picked it up and looked at the screen. Kate. He set it back on the table and watched it until it stopped. He had nothing left to say to her.

He sat there in shock, unable to think clearly. He tried to remember what was in the settlement agreement. He thought, and hoped he remembered correctly that there was some type of restriction on either parent relocating. He'd never worried about it before because he knew he wasn't moving and didn't think Bryson would ever leave Asheville.

He got up and took his empty wine glass inside, swapping it for a whiskey glass and the bottle of Macallan. Back outside, he poured a couple of fingers worth into the glass and drank half of it, letting the warm, caramel-colored liquid numb his mouth and throat. After that faded, he finished it, sitting back in his chair.

The sounds of the night were interrupted as his phone buzzed again. Without looking, he picked it up and punched Answer. "What?" he snapped, expecting Kate.

"Whoa," a friendly female voice said. "Who pissed you off?"

Momentarily confused, he didn't speak, then realized it was Nicole. "Sorry," he mumbled. "I thought it was—"

"Kate, maybe?" she said, finishing his sentence.

He snorted. "Your perception is impeccable."

"Everything okay?"

He hesitated, and poured another inch of Scotch into his glass. "No, as a matter of fact, it's not."

"What's the matter?"

"Kate just told me that they're moving to Orlando. For three years."

"No. Can she do that?"

Eric took a sip and said, "I'm not sure, but probably."

"That's bullshit. Pour me a glass of wine and I'll be there in ten minutes."

He protested, but she wouldn't take no for an answer and hung up. Fifteen minutes later, he heard her car coming up the drive. When he heard her footsteps on the deck, he turned his head but remained seated.

She walked over to the table where the bottle of Scotch sat along with his empty glass. "I take it the wine bar is closed."

When he didn't answer, she poured a healthy dose into the glass, then took a deep swallow. She stepped over to the bench and sat next to him. "Talk to me," she said, holding the glass out to him.

He took another drink and told her about his conversation with Kate.

"No wonder you were so upset," she said. "What are you going to do?"

He shook his head. "I'm going to call Vic tomorrow." Vic was his attorney and an old friend. "Probably nothing much I can do."

"I'm sorry. Does Ali know yet?"

"I don't think so, but I'm not sure. I hung up on Kate."

"She pushes your buttons, doesn't she?"

"Oh, yes. She always has."

She looked up at him. "I could fix you breakfast?"

He saw the reflection of moonlight in her eyes. It was a tempting offer. Finally, he slowly shook his head. "I don't think that's . . ."

She stood, walked over behind him, and put her arms around his neck, nuzzling his face. He closed his eyes, her scent more intoxicating than the booze he'd consumed. He willed himself to resist, and put his hands on her arms, intending to pull them away from him.

He felt her warm breath in his ear, and his will was fading.

"Nicole . . ."

"Let's go inside," she whispered in his ear. "Now." She held out her hand.

He hesitated, then took her hand and let her lead him quietly inside.

* * *

Eric awoke the next morning with Felix sitting next to him, his whiskers inches away from Eric's face.

"Felix . . ." Eric's voice trailed off, not knowing what to say, not that it mattered since he was talking to a cat. He reached over, relieved to confirm that Nicole wasn't in bed with him. *My God,* he thought, *what had he done?*

Some details came back to him slowly, along with functioning synapses. As he sat on the edge of the bed, he was surprised that the throbbing in his head wasn't as severe as he might have expected. Nicole probably saved him from doing further damage, at least in that regard.

He looked around the room, half expecting to see articles of clothing or some other evidence of Nicole's being there last night. Nothing. Satisfied the bedroom was safe, he managed to walk into the bathroom.

A single, empty, Scotch glass sat on the counter next to the sink. No other clues that anyone else had been there were visible.

He was puzzled as he made his way into the kitchen, smelling fresh coffee. He gave Felix his treats and noticed a pot of freshly-brewed coffee on the counter. He looked out on the deck and saw Nicole sitting there, wearing his sweats, drinking a cup of coffee.

He was angry at himself for succumbing to his carnal desires last night. As tempting as it was to blame the Macallan, he knew that the whiskey was only guilty of lowering the barrier on his inhibitions. He had wanted Nicole.

He poured himself a cup of coffee and walked outside. She turned, smiling, and said, "Good morning."

"Morning," he replied, as he sat down across the table from her. Neither of them said anything for a few minutes, sipping their coffee and listening to the mountains waking up as the critters stirred.

She reached out and gently placed her hand on his arm. He felt a jolt surge through him as if he'd been touched by a wire carrying electricity.

"Feeling better this morning?" she asked.

He looked at her, not knowing how to answer. He felt better and worse, all at the same time.

"I feel like you're about to give me 'the lecture.'" Her fingers surrounded the phrase with air quotes. His mouth opened, but before he could respond, she said, "Please don't."

He closed his mouth and turned his gaze back out toward the mountains. She removed her hand and at last, said, "Hear me out before you speak."

When he didn't reply, she continued. "For the record, we didn't do anything last night."

Puzzled, he cocked his head. "But . . ."

Shaking her head, she said, "Nothing happened. Well, maybe a little kissing and hugging, but that was it. I told you I wanted to prove we could be friends."

Eric was confused. The last thing he remembered was Nicole leading him into the bedroom.

"I'm not asking for anything, Eric."

Out of the corner of his eye, he caught her pausing to take a sip of coffee. "Let me rephrase that. I'm not asking for a commitment of any type. None. Zero. You don't owe me anything. You're free to go about your business as you please, and that includes seeing whoever you want whenever you want."

He turned to look at her, a puzzled look on his face. She placed her hand back on his arm and squeezed. "What I *am* asking for is that we remain friends. That's all I want."

"I don't know if—"

She silenced him by putting her finger up to his lips. "That didn't require a response, and I don't want one right now. We both must get to work. I'm leaving to go back to my house and you need to get ready. I'll see you at the lab."

She got up and walked into the kitchen. He heard her put the coffee cup in the sink, and minutes later, the sound of her car, leaving.

30

Two days later, Nicole awoke and took her temperature. She jotted down the results. Since her trip to LA, she had been dutifully recording her vitals daily. She knew that normal body temperature, although often quoted at 98.6°F, actually varied by as much as one and a half degrees, depending on the individual, time of day, and other mitigating factors. Clinically speaking, body temperature wasn't considered elevated until it was higher than 100°F. A fever lasting more than a couple of days was usually an indication of infection.

Scanning over her results since the infection, she concluded that everything looked good. Although she could probably discontinue the monitoring, she decided she would drop back to once a week just to make certain.

She looked at herself in the bathroom mirror and smiled, thinking about sleeping with Eric a few nights ago. They had done a little more than kissing and hugging. She reached down and touched herself as she thought about how hard he had gotten when she'd massaged him. He was hers for the taking, but she held out. She wanted to stoke his desire.

She closed her eyes and thought about the night they'd had sex. Her fingers started moving faster as she remembered how he had looked into her eyes as they made love. That was what she wanted. Her body shuddered as she climaxed.

She stood there a minute, enjoying the afterglow. Opening her eyes, she went to wash her hands, and noticed her nose was bleeding. *That's odd,* she thought. She grabbed a tissue, and went into the bedroom. She sat on the edge of her bed, pinched her nostrils together, and tilted her head slightly forward to stop the bleeding.

After a few minutes, she went back and looked into the mirror. Satisfied it had indeed quit bleeding, she took her shower. The only thing she could figure is that she blew her nose when first awakening. Maybe she had been more vigorous than she thought.

When she arrived at the lab, she got her coffee and went to her desk. She felt warm. She convinced herself she was coming down with a cold, the symptoms familiar. Her sinuses were beginning to clog, and her nose dripped.

Later in the morning, she went to the cafeteria and fixed her mom's classic cold remedy: hot tea, as hot as you could stand it, with lemon and honey. Although a scientist, Nicole was convinced some of the old-time cures like hot tea or chicken soup were indeed legitimate.

By early afternoon, she was feeling feverish.

"Are you okay?" Wally asked.

"I'm all right, just coming down with a cold."

"You look like shit," he said as he walked off. Good old Wally, ever the sensitive type. She couldn't think of a quick retort, so she returned her attention to work.

By five o'clock, she knew she was running a fever. She didn't have a thermometer at work and was hesitant to ask anyone for one. Tera Pharmagenics, especially in the lab, had a strict employee health safety policy. A fever got you sent home with additional monitoring and lots of paperwork.

She left work early and swung by Ingles to pick up some lemons and chicken soup. As soon as she got home, she went into the bathroom and took her temperature. 100.8°. Not enough to be alarming, but definitely a fever.

It was just a cold, she told herself. She took a couple of Tylenol, heated up some chicken soup, and made another cup of her grandmother's tea.

After her meager dinner, she wrapped herself in a blanket from head to toe. Like a mummy, she waddled to the living room, turned on the television, and surfed the channels. She found a National Geographic special about Hawaii, which she hoped would warm her.

In the dark, Nicole awoke, disoriented. The television was on, zebras running across the screen. Her blanket had been thrown aside, and she was sweating profusely, even though wearing nothing but a t-shirt. She glanced over at the mantle clock above the fireplace. A quarter after three.

She forced herself to get up and find the thermometer, although she knew she was running a high fever. Exhausted by the time she reached her bathroom and found it, she sat on the tile floor, leaning back against the cabinet below the sink. She stuck the instrument in her mouth and closed her eyes. When it beeped, she took it out and squinted to see the result.

103.2°F. *Not good,* she thought. For the first time, she started to panic. Something was wrong, bad wrong. She tried to think rationally about her symptoms and kept coming back to an inescapable conclusion: The Hapeville virus had returned and come back with a vengeance.

* * *

The next morning, Eric went up to the lab to find Nicole. She wasn't at her desk, so he walked over to Wally's office and stuck his head in the door. "Do you know where Nicole is?"

Wally shook his head. "No, I haven't seen her today. I figured she took the day off."

Puzzled, Eric said, "No, not that I know of. If you see her, would you ask her to call me?"

"Sure. Yesterday afternoon I did hear her say that she was coming down with a cold."

Eric shook his head as he walked back to his office. It was almost noon. Maybe she had an appointment outside the office.

She'd not mentioned anything about taking the day off. Although he gave both of his scientists free rein, they were good about clearing their schedules with him beforehand if it involved more than a few hours out of the office.

Back at his office, he checked with Carmen. She wasn't aware of Nicole being off and had not received any calls from her. *Odd,* he thought. He'd give her a call before he left if he hadn't heard from her by then.

At the end of the day, Carmen told him good evening as she prepared to leave. "Did you ever hear from Nicole?" she asked.

Eric looked up from the document he was working on. He'd been busy working on a presentation, and Nicole's whereabouts had slipped his mind. He shook his head and answered, "No, I didn't. Did you?"

Carmen shook her head. "No, sorry. You didn't bring it up again, so I figured you'd talked to her."

"I'll give her a call. Have a good evening."

"Thanks. You, too."

He called Nicole's cell phone. It rang several times and then went to voice mail. He disconnected and called Wally.

"Hey, boss. What's up?"

"Did you ever see Nicole or talk to her?"

"Nope. She was a no-show today."

"Thanks." He disconnected, not wanting to get into a discussion with Wally about it.

Now, he was worried. Nicole never disappeared for more than a few hours without letting him or Wally know.

He saved the presentation he was working on, stuffed a stack of papers into his backpack and headed out. He'd swing by Nicole's house on the way home and see if she needed anything.

As he pulled out of the parking lot, his phone vibrated. He looked at the screen and saw it was Nicole.

"Nicole, where are you?" he said when he answered. He heard an unintelligible sound on the other end of the line and asked, "Nicole? Is that you?"

It sounded like "Mmmmpf." Then, a crash.

"Nicole, talk to me." He looked at the phone and almost ran off the road. It seemed like the call was still connected, but he couldn't hear anything. "Damn cell phones."

He disconnected the call and redialed. It rang four or five times, then went to voice mail. He called again and got the same result.

When he got off I-40, he raced down Jonathan Creek Road and wheeled left onto Utah Mountain Road, almost sideswiping the truck sitting at the stop sign. Taking the narrow, twisty road as fast as he dared, he whipped into Nicole's gravel driveway near the top of the mountain and skidded to a stop.

Her VW was parked in its usual spot. He got out of the Jeep, ran to the side door of her house, and peeked inside.

Nicole was laying on the kitchen floor, a pool of blood next to her head. The door was unlocked, and he threw it open, stepping inside. "Nicole," he screamed as he knelt beside her.

She wasn't moving. He could see the slightest movement of her chest. She was breathing, but not responsive.

Staring at the puddle of blood under her face, he reached out and touched her carotid artery. Her pulse was weak. She was breathing, and her heart was pumping. Both good signs.

The blood appeared to have come from her nose. Up close, it didn't look as bad as it first did. Maybe she fell and hit her head, but he didn't want to risk moving her.

He dialed 911.

31

Fifteen minutes later, two paramedics from the volunteer fire department pulled up outside. They ran in, and Eric shared with them what he'd found and his initial assessment.

They gently turned her until she was on her back, one of the paramedics relaying vitals and other information over the radio, presumably to a doctor on the other end. Eric noticed there was no indication of a fall.

"What sort of work does she do?" the paramedic checking Nicole asked.

"She's a scientist who works for me at the Panther Cove lab," Eric said.

The paramedics glanced at each other, then the one talking on the radio said into the microphone, "She works at the Tera Pharmagenics lab."

The radio crackled with a few questions.

"Any sign of trauma?"

"Negative."

"History of fainting or seizures?"

The paramedics looked up at Eric, who shook his head. "Negative."

There was a pause, then the radio voice said, "We're sending a chopper. Meet you at the foot of Hemphill in the 276 median in fifteen minutes."

The paramedics loaded Nicole up into the ambulance and sped off, leaving Eric behind. He had wanted to follow them down the mountain, but they assured him there was nothing he could do. They were taking her to Mission Hospital in Asheville, and he could check with them on her status.

He put his hands on his hips and surveyed the kitchen. At least he could clean up the blood on the floor before he left. He looked in the pantry for a mop and bucket. Nothing. The best he could find was a stained, but clean towel, apparently one she'd used before for dirty work.

Eric walked back over to the table and started to kneel to wipe up the blood. The chair was askew, so he straightened up and pushed the chair under the table to get it out of his way.

He noticed a handwritten log of some sort on the tabletop. An oral thermometer lay next to it. Curious, he took a closer look at the document. It was a simple chart with headings for Date, Time, and Temp. The page was over half filled with entries, and he recognized Nicole's handwriting. The last entry, near the bottom of the page, was for today's date.

He looked at the time written down and then compared it to his watch. It was less than an hour ago. His eyes shifted over to the temperature. 103.2. That was an acute fever.

Eric stared at the page, trying to make sense of what he was seeing. *Nicole was apparently tracking her temperature, but why?*

He moved his finger up the page to the first entry where the temperatures were elevated. She recorded it yesterday afternoon. As he went down the page, checking the times, her temperature had steadily gone up. Whatever it was, it indicated a raging infection of some sort.

With a start, he realized why it all seemed familiar. The pattern was the same as the Hapeville patient he'd seen at Emory.

He grabbed his phone and pressed 911 for the second time that evening. He had to get in touch with the medivac team. Now.

Eric tried to get the dispatcher to re-route the helicopter to Atlanta. Unsuccessful, he hung up and called Terry Lumpkin at CDC. The call went to voice mail.

"Shit," he said aloud. He almost slammed the phone down on the table but realized at the last second he couldn't afford to break the phone. He punched the Disconnect button and stood there, his mind racing.

He looked at his watch. It was too late to try to catch them at the foot of the mountain. By the time he got there, the chopper would be on its way to Asheville. He guessed the flight would take fifteen minutes since Asheville was only twenty miles east. He had to stop that helicopter from landing at the hospital.

He called the main number for CDC.

"This is Dr. Eric Carter, with Tera Pharmagenics. I need to talk to Dr. Terry Lumpkin. It's an emergency. I called his cell phone, but it went to voice mail."

The operator transferred him to the duty officer. Eric repeated his request, even giving the person Terry's cell phone number to show this was legitimate.

The duty officer, apparently following some sort of checklist, started his interrogation, beginning with establishing Eric's credentials.

After the third question, Eric interrupted. "Look, there is a person infected with the Hapeville virus within minutes of landing at Mission Hospital in Asheville, North Carolina. I don't have time to play twenty questions right now. That person and the crew need to be quarantined immediately upon arrival. If you can't make that happen, then you need to transfer me to whoever can. If you don't, then you're going to be in the middle of a shit storm the likes of which you've never experienced. Do you understand?"

The voice took his number and said someone would call back shortly.

Eric hung up, not knowing if his threat was taken seriously or not. Four minutes later, his phone buzzed. It was Terry.

As concisely as Eric could, he explained the situation to Terry. "There are three of us, plus the helicopter crew, who have been exposed to Nicole. It's about to be a whole lot more if we don't get a handle on it immediately."

He looked at his watch and did a quick mental calculation. "I figure you've got maybe ten minutes before that chopper lands at Mission Hospital."

"Stay put. I'll call you back," Terry said. The line went dead.

Eric set his phone on the table. He looked down at the small pool of blood on the floor and realized that he was potentially looking at a reservoir seething with the Hapeville virus. He still had the ragged dish towel in his hand, which was now shaking.

* * *

Two days later, Eric sat in Terry's office. He had just been released from the isolation unit at Emory University Hospital, where he'd spent the last thirty-six hours. He had exhibited no symptoms, and tested negative for the Hapeville virus.

"How are you feeling?" Terry asked.

"Good. How are the paramedics?"

"They've been released as well. Negative for Hapeville."

"The helicopter crew?"

Terry shook his head. "The pilot and co-pilot are okay. The flight nurse tested positive twelve hours later. That stuff spreads fast."

"Jesus," Eric said, digesting the news. "If only—"

"If only what? There's nothing you could've done. As it was, you probably saved the others as well as countless potential victims at the hospital." Terry stared at him. "We were lucky, Eric. The nurse is responding to the Fluzenta. We expect her to recover fully."

"How's Nicole?" He thought he saw Terry shift uncomfortably in his chair at the mention of her name.

One of the questions Eric had been asked when they'd taken his history and physical upon admission was what other contact he'd had with Nicole in the prior week. He reluctantly stated that they had spent the night together two days earlier, but didn't have sexual relations.

"I need to ask you a few questions, Eric."

"Sure."

"You stated on admission that you had spent the night with Nicole two days prior, but didn't have sex."

Eric lowered his head and nodded. "That's correct."

"Were there other times, times when maybe something did happen?"

Eric bristled at the line of questioning. "What are you getting at, Terry? I'm not sure I like where this is going?"

Terry fixed him with a stare. "I'm just doing my job." He picked up a sheet of paper on his desk and held it up. "You repeatedly tested negative for the active Hapeville virus."

"Yes, I know, and I feel fine. So, what does that have to do with Nicole?"

"You tested positive for the H4 antibodies."

"What? That's impossible." To have antibodies meant that the person had contracted or been previously exposed to a virus.

Terry waved the sheet of paper. "Our lab re-tested you twice. All three times, H4 antibodies showed up. I'm wondering 'how?'"

How in the hell could he have H4 antibodies? Eric thought. He shook his head. "I honestly don't know, Terry." He took a deep breath. "Between me and you, I did sleep with Nicole—once—but that was several months ago. It was a stupid mistake and that was the only time. Maybe she had been exposed at some point, I don't know."

Terry nodded. "Maybe so. Thanks for sharing that information. I know it wasn't easy, but we needed to know. As far as Nicole, she's stable, but no improvement. She's still in a coma. We've upped the Fluzenta, but it doesn't seem to be working."

Eric wrinkled his brow. "I wonder why not?"

Terry shrugged. "Nothing is one hundred percent effective, you know that."

"Anything I can do? I'd like to get back to the lab if it's okay."

"You're a free man. Keep a close eye on things for a while. You know the drill; any fever, cough—"

"Unusual bleeding, etc. Yes, I know. I promise to be a good ex-patient."

Terry's face turned serious. "That was close, Eric. Too close."

Eric nodded. "I know. Thanks, Terry. For everything. Keep me posted on Nicole."

Terry nodded. "I will. Don't be a stranger."

Eric had to rent a car since the Emory transport team had brought him to Atlanta. There was an Enterprise Rent-A-Car on Cheshire Bridge Road, only a few miles away. Terry had arranged for a CDC employee to drop him off.

Eric walked down to the main lobby to meet the driver. He'd asked Terry who he was looking for and Terry told him the staffer would recognize him. Eric stood near the entrance, looking around, trying to spot the driver.

Someone tapped him on the shoulder, and he spun around to see Rae standing there.

"I heard you need a ride," she said, smiling. She held out her arms and Eric started to embrace her, then stopped, and backed away. She frowned and cocked her head.

"This might not be a good idea," he said, keeping his distance. "I don't want to put you in harm's way," he said, quickly explaining his actions.

She relaxed and stepped over to him. "If Emory University Hospital and the CDC pronounce you safe, then I'll take their word for it." She held her arms open, and this time, he reciprocated.

He buried his face in the crook of her neck, inhaling her scent, and feeling her body next to his. He realized he was shaking as he held her, and tears rolled down his cheeks.

This was one of those moments that he would never forget. If he lived to be a hundred and could no longer recall his name, he would remember Rae being there to greet him this day.

She held him for as long as he wanted, there in the middle of the lobby of the Centers for Disease Control.

When he finally released her from the extended hug, he held on to both of her hands and looked into her eyes. "I have never been so glad to see someone as I am to see you."

She smiled. "That's better. I was beginning to think I'd made a mistake."

He shook his head. "Just overwhelmed. Surprised. Scared."

"Well, I know you're anxious to get home. But, since it's late, I took the liberty of getting a room across the street. I figured we could stay here in Atlanta tonight and head out first thing in the morning. I know you're probably exhausted."

32

After breakfast, Rae had insisted on driving him home. She had booked a flight out of Asheville later that afternoon, and Eric was glad to get back to the lab.

After they left Atlanta, he kept thinking about his conversation with Terry. *How did he get the H4 antibodies?*

In the early years at the lab, Eric had been more hands-on. At that point, they were working with the H4N4 virus. He remembered no remarkable events, and no illness other than the occasional cold. But, H4N4 was avian, so there wouldn't have been any symptoms.

Then it dawned on him. He was focusing on the "how," but he was missing the point. Somehow, somewhere, he'd been exposed to H4. That was the only way to acquire the antibodies.

The important thing was that he had them. That was why he didn't get Hapeville. He'd touched Nicole, and probably come in contact with her blood. When he first arrived on the scene, he had no idea she had Hapeville, so he hadn't taken any precautions. The antibodies had protected him.

He picked up the phone, called Wally, and asked him to come to his office.

"Hey, boss, glad you're back. How're you feeling?" Wally said when he walked in.

"I feel good. I was lucky."

"How's Blondie?" Wally never relented, but the fact that he asked, showed he cared in his own way.

Eric shook his head. "Not good. She's still in a coma. They've upped the Fluzenta, but it doesn't seem to be effective."

He asked Wally if he'd done any more research on the comparison between Hapeville and H4.

Wally shook his head. "I was waiting for you to get back to me, then everything happened. Did you ever show it to Nicole?"

"No, I didn't." He told Wally about CDC finding H4 antibodies in his blood.

"No shit. That's weird. How the hell did that happen?"

Eric shook his head. "I don't know." He wasn't about to tell Wally that he'd slept with Nicole. "Maybe I was exposed to it back when we were working with it. The how is unimportant. All I know is it's there."

He told Wally about his idea. Being the analytical scientific type, Wally listened with interest.

"It makes sense," Wally said. "You didn't get Hapeville because you already had the antibodies."

Eric nodded. "H4N4 is avian. Humans don't get sick from it, only birds."

"Let me work on it."

"Get back to me as soon as you can."

Eric called Frank and explained what he wanted to do.

"Have you lost your mind?" Frank said. "You want to deliberately introduce a lethal pathogen to a sick Tera Pharmagenics employee. Listen to yourself, Eric. Do you realize what kind of liability we'd have?"

"It's not lethal to humans, Frank."

"Oh, really? I'm not a scientist, but aren't a lot of people contracting Hapeville? And isn't Hapeville H4?"

"It's not the same, Frank."

"No. Hell, no. We're not giving Nicole H4."

"She's going to die, Frank, if we do nothing."

"She's not going to die. Tell them to up the Fluzenta."

"They've tried that. She's already had six times the maximum dosage ever given in our studies. It's not working, Frank. Hear me on this. Fluzenta is not working. We've got to try something else."

There was a hesitation from Frank. "That doesn't make sense. It should be working."

"Nothing is one hundred percent successful, you know that. Fluzenta is no different than any other drug."

"What I mean is that it's worked for everyone else."

"It's not working with her."

"And your bright idea is to give her a known virus?"

"What have we got to lose?"

"What have we got to lose? Like the entire frigging company, Eric. Besides, she's already infected with the H4 virus."

"No, Hapeville is a variant. I think that the pure H4N4 strain will stamp out the mutated version because it's an inferior copy. There is still no evidence of human infection with unadulterated H4N4."

"Sorry, that's a risk I'm not willing to take."

"Frank, Nicole is going to die if we don't do something."

There was a pause on the line. "We have zero evidence that your theory is valid. If we try it and she dies, then guess who's going to be blamed for her death?" He let the words sink in and then continued in a softer tone. "It's a shot in the dark, and we can't afford to roll the dice."

Eric hung up the phone, turned, and stared out his office window. The scientist in him had to agree with Frank. But emotionally, he wasn't convinced. He'd gone over the scenario yet again and was even more convinced that the pure H4N4 was the answer.

He wandered up to the almost deserted lab, looking for Wally. Since Tera Pharmagenics had started the manufacturing process, most of the laboratory workers didn't keep the same crazy hours. Wally, of course, did.

As usual, he was on the computer. Eric looked at the office and shook his head. He was surprised it hadn't been condemned.

"What are you working on?" Eric asked, startling Wally.

"Damn," he said, turning around to face Eric. "I didn't hear you walk in. I was looking at some new data on the manufacturing process. I think we can safely eliminate a couple of steps and save us some time in the incubation phase."

"That's good."

"What are you doing up here?"

Eric shrugged. "Restless, I guess. Have you had a chance to take another look at the H4N4 data?"

Wally nodded. "I did. What data we have supports your theory. I think it's got merit and we should proceed with testing."

Eric looked at Wally. He didn't share his conversation with Frank. "How certain are you?"

Wally cocked his head, pondering the question. "Very. Why? What are you thinking?"

Eric shook his head. "I'd rather not say."

Wally thought, then said, "Is this one of those 'don't ask, don't tell' things?"

He nodded. "I trust your opinion, and I know you'd tell me if you thought there were any flaws."

Wally studied his boss, trying to discern what was going on. Finally, he said, "Let me phrase it another way. If I get Hapeville, then I want you to give me the H4N4. Don't bother with Fluzenta."

Eric was shocked by Wally's statement. He wondered if the brilliant scientist knew what he was considering. "That's pretty strong."

"I know. And, I mean it." Wally rose from his chair and stretched. "I'm low on doughnuts and Coke. Going to run down to the cafeteria to resupply. You want anything?"

Eric shook his head. "No, thanks anyway." He watched as Wally hurried down the hall. As he turned to leave, he stopped. Out of the corner of his eye, he saw a full package of white, powdered doughnuts on the edge of Wally's workspace. Next to them was a six-pack of Cokes, minus two.

Wally was guaranteeing his own plausible deniability. Eric hesitated and then walked over to Nicole's office.

As he walked in, he glanced around to see if any other employees were nearby. The closest person was halfway across the floor, hunched over a workbench, intent on some task that Eric couldn't see. A couple of other people were on the far side of the building. Other than that, the lab was empty.

He paused when he got to Nicole's desk. It looked like she'd just been there moments ago. She had a secure refrigerator against the wall, the same as Wally's.

Eric stepped over and entered his security code, the only other code authorized to access the unit. He knew there would be a record of his access, but there was no way to verify what was in there or what was taken. The security officer had recommended that all contents be tagged with radio-frequency identification labels, but that wouldn't be implemented until the first of the year.

Taking one more glance around to make sure no one was near, he opened the door and looked inside. Quickly, he rummaged through the contents of the shelves in the small box. When he got to the second shelf, he found what he was looking for. It was a box containing six test tubes, all labeled. He found the one he wanted, removed it, and stuck it in his shirt pocket.

He closed the door, which automatically locked, and stood. Turning his attention to Nicole's desk, he spied a sheet filled with numbers. A quick glance confirmed it was what he thought, so he picked it up and walked out.

He almost ran head-on into Monique, the employee who had been hunched over the lab table.

"Oh, excuse me, Dr. Carter," she said.

"No, no, excuse me." He held up the sheet he'd removed from Nicole's desk. "I was reading this while I was walking and didn't see you. Sorry."

"Did you find what you needed?"

He nodded. "Yes, thank you. Nicole had been working on this for me before she . . . before her illness and I just came by to pick it up."

About that time, Wally walked up. "Hey boss, did you find what you were looking for?" He was holding a Coke and a small package of powdered doughnuts.

"Uh, yes, thank you." He turned to Monique. "Again, sorry for almost running you down."

Eric walked toward the door of the lab, lightly patting his shirt pocket and feeling the test tube inside.

He went back to his office, gathered a few things off his desk and told Carmen he was going home early.

At the house, he carefully took the test tube out of his pocket and placed it in a small cooler that he'd filled with ice. He fed Felix, packed a few things for an overnight trip, and locked up the house. He pulled out of his driveway, convinced he was doing the right thing, and headed south toward Atlanta.

Three hours later, as he turned into the parking garage at Emory University Hospital, he called Terry. He'd originally planned to wait until morning, but figured that it might be easier to do what he wanted tonight.

"Hey, Terry. Eric. Listen, I think I'm on to something. I'm in Atlanta and wondering if you can give me temporary access to Nicole." He went on to explain that he was working on something using Nicole's blood and needed to get a fresh sample. As soon as he could get it, he'd be heading back to his lab in North Carolina.

"You should've called. I could've gotten it for you and had it delivered."

"I know, but it was one of those profound moments, so I drove down tonight. Time is of the essence." He hated being duplicitous with Terry, but it was the only ruse he could come up with to gain access to Nicole. "I've got everything I need. I'll be in and out in minutes."

"Give me ten minutes to talk with the charge nurse and I'll call you back."

"Thanks, Terry."

He parked the Jeep, got his kit out of the back seat and headed over the walkway to the hospital. By the time he got to the main building, his phone buzzed.

"I talked with Leila, the charge nurse this evening. She'll be waiting for you in the isolation unit. Do you remember how to get there?"

"Yes, thank you. I'll give you a call in the morning and fill you in."

"Let me know if you need anything else."

When he got to the isolation unit, they buzzed him in. He was met by a stocky woman with short gray hair, almost as tall as he.

"I'm Leila," she said, extending her hand. "I'm the charge nurse this evening."

"Dr. Carter," he said, intent on maintaining the pecking order, although Leila didn't impress him as particularly concerned about it. This was her unit, and she called the shots.

She looked down at his bag. "Dr. Lumpkin said you needed a blood draw?"

He nodded and smiled, trying to ingratiate her to the extent possible. He reached into his kit and pulled out two 5 ml Vacutainers. "This is all I need."

She eyed him and reached for the test tubes. "You came a long way for this. I'll have one of my nurses draw it for you."

He drew the empty vials back toward him. "No, I need to collect it myself."

She put her hands on her hips. "Well, it seems we have a problem, then."

Shit, Eric thought. He hadn't considered this. He assumed that after he'd talked to Terry, he would be able to go into the room and collect the specimen himself.

He tried to relax and softened his voice. "Leila, I respect that this is your turf and I won't intrude. I know you and your staff are more than capable of drawing this sample for me. I appreciate that and all you've done for her."

He leaned toward her and lowered his voice another notch. Leila had to lean toward him to hear. "The truth is that this may be the last time I get to see Nicole. We've worked side-by-side for the last eight years. As a close friend of hers and a fellow professional, I'm asking for a few minutes with her while I collect this."

The tears that formed in his eyes were real. He was speaking from the heart. Leila studied his face, her jaw set. After ten or fifteen seconds, her features relaxed and she gave him a slight nod.

"Full PPE. You know the drill."

His eyes glistened as he nodded, acknowledging her requirements for personal protective equipment. "Yes. Thank you, Leila."

He took the gear from the cart and stepped into the restroom where he dressed. He made sure the vial of H4N4 was in his pocket along with the two empty tubes and accessible while wearing the gown.

Leila was waiting for him when he stepped out. She checked his protective gear, and satisfied he was compliant, she told him to follow her. He wondered if she was going to have someone go in with him, but when they got to the door of the airlock leading to Nicole's room, she stopped.

"The two-way intercom is active in the room. If you need anything, let us know."

He smiled and nodded. "Thank you," he said softly.

When he got inside the room, he assessed where Nicole's intravenous lines were located. Nicole was on multiple IV drips, so he took a minute to evaluate what was running through her body.

He was careful to keep his body between the glass wall and Nicole so an observer wouldn't be able to see what he was doing.

Nicole was on her back, eyes closed. The soft beep-beep of the monitor echoed in his mind. Her color didn't look good. They had her intubated, which meant a machine was doing the breathing for her. Her chest rose and fell, and the hiss of the ventilator was rhythmic.

He drew the blood first, filling the vials, and holding each one up in plain view of the observation window in case someone was watching. He lay the dark red tubes on the side of her bed and put his hand on Nicole's arm. Even though he wore double gloves, he teared up as he rested his hand lightly on her arm.

He held the pre-filled syringe containing the H4N4 in his free hand. The port he was going to use to administer the virus was just above his hand on her arm. In a matter of seconds, he could inject the virus into her body and no one would know the difference.

"I miss you," he heard himself whisper. "I want you well, so we can go fishing again. I've still got a few secret spots to show you."

He looked at the syringe containing the virus. *Would it save her? Or would it kill her?* He thought it would be easy. Before he walked into her room, he was convinced it would save her. Now, a sliver of doubt gnawed at him.

The battle raged within. Doctors played God every day. He thought about Wally's comment. But that was Wally's decision, not hers. Who was Eric to self-anoint himself as Nicole's proxy? It would be simpler if she had given him prior approval, as Wally had implicitly done, but Nicole hadn't done so.

He realized that there was no easy answer, the true definition of a dilemma. He jumped when the voice came over the intercom, and he almost dropped the syringe.

"Dr. Carter? Are you okay?"

He turned his head and nodded, not trusting himself to speak. He swiveled back, his eyes settling on Nicole's face. He realized his hand was stroking her arm and he smiled. Willing her to give him a sign, he stared. The soft beep of the monitor next to the head of the bed sounded.

Her chest moved up and down with every soft click of the respirator.

Nothing. This would have to be his decision and his alone. Either way, he would carry this burden for the rest of his life.

"I'm sorry, Nicole." He leaned over and kissed her forehead through his surgical mask, hoping somehow, she would know and understand. He stared at the syringe, but couldn't do it.

He removed his hand from her arm and picked up the two vials of blood, transferring them to the hand containing the syringe. He palmed all three and placed them in his pocket. As he turned to leave, he could taste the salt in the tears rolling down his cheeks.

Traffic was light as he drove back to North Carolina. Eric was content to be wrapped in the darkness and silence of his Jeep, the sound of the tires on pavement the only noise. It was a fitting punishment for his choice. He continually looked over at the small cooler on the seat next to him, taunting him, a symbol of his cowardice.

He had made his decision, and he would have to live with it. He was logical enough to accept that, although he would always question whether or not he did the right thing. Now, all he could do was pray.

33

How's Nicole doing?" Wally asked the next morning. He was standing in the doorway of Eric's office, leaning against the frame.

Eric shook his head. "No change. Still comatose and in critical condition."

"So much for Fluzenta, huh?"

He shrugged. "I think it has something to do with the fact that Hapeville is a variant. I brought back two vials of her blood. Go through it with a fine-tooth comb, see what you can find. Maybe we can use her antibodies to build a vaccine or something."

"You couldn't talk her father into giving permission to use H4?"

Eric had told Wally that was his reason for going to Atlanta, to personally plead with Nicole's father to let him administer the H4 virus. He shook his head. "Nobody has the legal authority, not even her father. She had no Health Care Directive as far as anyone knows."

"That sucks. I still think that's the answer." Wally waited for Eric to comment.

Eric shrugged. "I agree, but we've got a protocol we have to follow."

"Okay," Wally said. He seemed disappointed. "I'm headed back upstairs. I'll get going on her blood analysis."

"Thanks, Wally."

Eric got ready for a staff meeting, and when he returned, Carmen handed him a message. "Dr. Lumpkin called. He wants you to call him as soon as possible."

At his desk, Eric dialed the number. Terry answered on the second ring.

"Hi, Eric. Thanks for getting back to me so soon."

"No problem. What's up?"

"Not to sound so melodramatic, but we may have a problem," Terry said. "If I send you some pictures, could you look at them? Immediately?"

Eric's curiosity was piqued. Anytime a Director at the CDC called and wanted him to look at something, it got his attention.

"Certainly. What have you got?"

"Not sure. Something unusual. I'd rather not say any more on the phone."

"That sounds ominous."

"I'm sending it to your email as we speak. Your eyes only. Call me on my cell when you're done."

Eric hung up the phone, his head spinning with questions. He clicked on his email, decrypted it, and read Terry's note before opening the attachments.

Eric opened the files to view them. It took a few seconds, since they were both high-resolution photos. There were two pictures of two very similar genes.

At first glance, Eric thought they were duplicates, even though one was labeled "Hapeville" and the other "H4N4." He squinted and looked closer at the areas Terry had mentioned. There seemed to be a misplaced gene on the Hapeville virus.

Eric pulled up Terry's notes on the left screen of his two-screen display and re-read them. He shifted his focus back to the right screen. The *KC1P4* gene was missing from the Hapeville virus.

This was the same thing that Wally had discovered. Now, CDC had picked up on it. He knew that it was only a matter of time before they reached the same conclusion as he and Wally had. Hapeville was probably man-made.

He got up to get a cup of coffee and go outside to think. The pavilion was deserted, for a change. He sat on the edge of the picnic table, feet on the seat. The forested hills portrayed a stunning palate of oranges, yellows, and reds. It was a beautiful sight to behold.

Wally had been right. That particular gene missing was unnatural. Certainly, it could have been a mutation. That happened regularly in nature. The puzzling part wasn't the missing gene, it was how the virus could have survived without it. In evolutionary terms, that would be like going from a dinosaur to a bird in a few hundred years instead of a few hundred million years. Nature didn't move that quickly.

As he finished his coffee, he realized the shit was about to hit the fan. The virus had been manipulated. Soon, the entire world would know. The questions now were "who" and "how."

He walked back into the building and immediately went up to the lab to find Wally.

"Hey, boss. I was looking for you."

"Good, I'm looking for you. Come with me down to my office. I want you to look at something."

When they got back downstairs, Eric went into his office and shut his door. "I want to show you something."

He led Wally around behind his desk and brought up the images he'd received from Terry. "I just received this from Dr. Lumpkin at CDC. It's what you said."

Wally leaned over and looked at the screen for no more than ten seconds before he snorted. "I know," he said. "That was why I was looking for you. That's the same virus that's in Nicole's blood."

Eric shook his head. "What?"

Wally pointed to the Hapeville virus on the screen and said, "That is the exact same Hapeville virus that is in Nicole's blood."

Eric was confused. Everyone knew Nicole had Hapeville, but assumed she had a natural variant from working with the H4N4 virus in the lab. "How could that be? There was no contact between Nicole and the other victims. She's an outlier."

"I don't know how, but all I can tell you is that Nicole's Hapeville is identical to the others."

Dumbfounded, Eric sat back in his chair. Not only was the virus man-made, but it was in Nicole's blood. His mind was straining to connect the dots. He looked up at Wally.

"Do you realize what we're saying?"

As always, Wally got straight to the point. "Yes, it's a man-made virus, and since it's present in Nicole's blood, the logical conclusion is that she created it. My guess is that she deliberately injected herself."

"But . . ."

Still on a roll, Wally continued. "Maybe she inhaled it, but either way, she deliberately contracted Hapeville so she could test the efficacy of Fluzenta. Pretty clever for a blonde chick."

For once, Eric didn't bother to correct him. "You've been reading too many conspiracy theories, Wally. Do you realize how diabolical that all sounds?"

Wally nodded. "And I also realize how plausible it sounds. You're in denial. Give me another explanation."

Eric racked his brain, but couldn't come up with anything that would come close to passing muster, even to himself. He looked at Wally, who had crossed his arms over his chest, a smug look on his face.

* * *

For the second time in as many days, Eric was driving to Atlanta. This time, Wally was seated next to him and the small cooler was in the back seat.

Eric had called Terry and told him that they were on their way. When they arrived at CDC four hours later, they were immediately escorted to Terry's office.

Thirty minutes later, Terry opened the door to his office and ushered him and Wally in. Eric was surprised to see a strange woman sitting at the conference table.

"Eric. Wally. I asked Eva to sit in. She's an expert on VHFs."

Eric shook his head, wondering what that had to do with Hapeville. Viral hemorrhagic fevers were some of the nastiest viruses known, with no cure or effective treatment. Ebola was a prime example.

"I know little about VHFs. It's not our area of expertise, you know that," Eric said.

Terry nodded and sat back in his chair. "I realize that, but I think there may be a link. Do you want to go first?"

Eric took a deep breath and nodded. He briefly explained what they'd found and asked Wally to elaborate.

When Wally had finished, Terry said, "That fills in a few gaps on our end. As you've surmised, Hapeville doesn't precisely match anything we've seen. The closest is an avian flu—H4N4. That's why I called you originally."

"It definitely has H4N4 origins, but with some interesting differences," Eric said. He looked at his notes and showed them the drawing, pointing out the unfamiliar variations in the virus structure.

Eva nodded. "That's the part I recognize. Consistent with most VHF viruses. It's as if an avian virus mated with a VHF and this is the evil spawn."

"What's the incubation period for H4N4?" Terry asked.

Eric shrugged. "Three days, give or take."

Terry looked over at Eva. "That explains why we weren't convinced that the subject in the Atlanta airport was the first. Nicole is the index case."

"How did Nicole get infected?" Eva asked.

Eric took a deep breath. "We suspect that Nicole created the virus and infected herself. So far, we can't prove anything, but it's the only thing that makes sense."

"Nicole was on the flight from Atlanta to Los Angeles the Saturday before the first cases were reported," Terry said. "The same flight as Phillip Brown. He was seated one row behind her."

Jesus Christ, Eric thought. *What has Nicole done?* But Nicole didn't give any signs of being infected. If she was infectious . . .

Wally spoke up. "I've been looking through her notes, but we haven't been able to hack her computer yet."

"Send it to us," Terry said.

Eric shook his head. "You obviously aren't aware of Wally's skills. I can assure you if anyone can hack it, it's the guy sitting next to me."

Terry shifted in his seat and looked at Wally. "Not to insult you, but we have access—"

Wally waved him off. "Yeah, and the FBI had all kinds of resources too, but they couldn't hack the San Bernardino iPhone. They had to pay hackers to do it for them."

He was referring to Syed Farook, the San Bernardino California terrorist that was responsible for fourteen deaths. "I happen to know one of the hackers very well," Wally said.

Eric swallowed hard and looked at Wally, who had a Cheshire grin. "You?"

"That's all I'm going to say on the subject," Wally said, folding his arms across his chest.

After a few moments of complete silence, Eric spoke. "We'll continue to try to hack her computer. In the meantime, we've put together a team to reverse engineer what she did. That will take longer."

"We're going to need to test everyone at the lab," Terry said. "Immediately." The tone didn't imply it was negotiable.

Eric nodded. "Of course. As soon as we're done, I'll call and set it up. You can test us today while we're here."

Eva asked, "Fluzenta isn't effective—long-term—against Hapeville?"

Reluctantly, Eric shook his head. "It appears not. Apparently, it offers short-term protection, which is why it took a while for the symptoms to manifest in Nicole."

"We think it is related to the missing gene," Wally said. "Without that gene, Hapeville is able to overcome Fluzenta. Since that's not a possibility we expected, we didn't consider it in the design of Fluzenta. The protection doesn't last."

Terry closed his eyes and mumbled a curse.

"We still believe Fluzenta is effective against the H5 strains," Eric said in defense of his drug. "It just doesn't work with Hapeville."

Terry shook his head and swore again. "So, all of the people we've been giving Fluzenta—"

"That brings me to the reason we wanted to talk to you," Eric said. "I think we have a solution." He pointed to the small cooler he'd brought with him. "I want to give Nicole the H4N4 virus."

Eva and Terry looked at him as if he'd stepped off a spaceship.

"Give us ten minutes to explain," Eric said.

He and Wally quickly launched into their spiel to convince the CDC. They had rehearsed it on the way to Atlanta, knowing it had to be convincing but short. Halfway through, Terry held up his hand.

"I need to get two other people in here." He stepped over to his desk and called his assistant. "Find Monica and Keith. Get them here, stat."

Ten minutes later, there was a knock on the door. Monica and Keith joined them. Terry quickly made introductions, and then asked Eric if he and Wally could start over.

Three hours later, and after a heated discussion, the group reached an agreement. Terry was going to personally speak with the ethics committee at the hospital to seek their approval to proceed with administering the H4N4 virus to Nicole.

"I'll call you as soon as it's official," Terry said, walking Eric and Wally to the elevator. "I'm hoping I can get in touch with everyone this evening." As soon as they pressed the button on the wall, the doors opened. Eric and Wally stepped inside and turned to face Terry.

"We're going to get a bite to eat," Eric said. "Then we'll be across the street in the lobby. Thanks, Terry."

Terry nodded as the elevator doors closed.

34

"What do you want to eat?" Eric asked Wally as they walked to the parking garage.

Wally looked at him and shrugged. "I don't care. As long as it's quick. I'm starving."

Eric knew there was a Mellow Mushroom nearby. It was convenient, and he didn't want to be away from the hospital for too long. He felt like they had convinced Terry, but he wondered if Terry would be able to secure the approval of the ethics committee in time to save Nicole.

They drove the short distance, parked, and went inside.

"Good call. I can always eat pizza," Wally said.

"It's quick and it's good. Terry and I used to eat at the original place downtown. Still the best pie around."

As soon as they were seated, they ordered a couple of beers and pizza, not bothering to look at a menu.

"Do you think they'll do it?" Wally asked.

Eric shrugged. "I think Terry and his staff bought in. But when you get committees involved, who knows?"

"What's this going to do to Tera Pharmagenics?" Wally asked after taking a deep drink from the frosted mug.

Eric shook his head. "I'm not sure. Haven't even thought about it, to tell you the truth." He took a drink and considered Wally's question. "Obviously, Fluzenta is dead."

"Maybe not. As you said, it's still effective for the other strains. Plus, maybe we can come up with an H4-based vaccine?" Wally said.

"Possible. But I'm not sure Tera Pharmagenics has any credibility left in the marketplace. First, we have to prove that the pure H4 virus works in stopping Hapeville."

Over pizza and another beer, they discussed what steps needed to be taken. They also talked about getting access to Nicole's computer.

"I hate taking you away from that, but I felt like you needed to be here for this," Eric said.

Wally shrugged. "I've got a couple of people working on it. Right now, there's not a lot I can do. They're just babysitting some software that's running. Anything comes up, I can handle it remotely until we get back. It would be a lot easier if you could figure out her password."

Eric nodded. "I know. I keep racking my brain, trying to figure out what it could be or where she might have written it, but she was pretty careful."

Halfway through the large pizza, Eric's phone buzzed. It was Terry. He took a deep breath. A quick verdict was not necessarily in their favor.

"Done already?" Eric said as soon as he answered.

"We lucked out. Half of them were in another meeting and I was able to reach the others by phone."

Terry's hesitation made Eric think the decision was not favorable.

"We've got the green light," Terry said. "God help us if it's the wrong move."

Eric exhaled. "It's the right call, Terry. We're heading back over. We'll meet you in her room." He hung up and nodded, looking around for their server. He motioned him over, and fished three twenties out of his wallet.

He handed the young guy the money. "This should cover it. We need to run. Thanks."

The student mumbled his thanks and walked away. Wally finished his beer and they drove back over to Emory.

When they got to the floor, there was a delay before they got buzzed in. A crowd had gathered outside Nicole's door.

"What the hell?" Eric said.

"This doesn't look good," Wally replied. As soon as he said it, Eric realized what was going on. The staff was in the middle of responding to a code or a medical emergency.

Terry was standing at the edge of the door, looking inside. Eric, with Wally on his heels, sidled up next to him. "Terry, what's happening?" he said in a hushed voice.

Terry, shaking his head, turned to face him. "She's not responding. I heard the page on the way up. Nicole coded."

Five minutes later, the attending physician called it, a euphemism that meant there was nothing more to be done for the patient. It was an official event and the time of death recorded for the medical record.

Staring at the floor, Eric, Wally, and Terry walked back to Terry's office in complete silence. Eric couldn't believe that Nicole was dead.

He should've given her the H4 when he had the chance.

"I'm sorry," Terry said to them. "We did everything we could. I'm sorry it wasn't enough."

I could've done something, Eric wanted to scream at him. Instead of dicking around waiting for a fucking committee to approve giving her the H4 virus that could've saved her.

"What now?" Wally said.

Eric looked at him, then at Terry.

"I'm not sure," Terry said. "She was the only Hapeville patient here. The others are in different facilities."

Eric was processing and raised his head. "I still think H4 is the solution."

Terry nodded. "I understand. But we can't give it to the previous patients if they appear to be doing well. We'll have to go through different channels to get it approved for another patient somewhere else." He cleared his throat. "I've talked with the FDA. They're sending out an emergency order rescinding the approval of Fluzenta until further study."

Eric stared at him. He knew it was coming, but still, the news was hard. They were back to where they started.

Even worse, since Hapeville was now loose and spreading. Terry didn't say it out loud, but Eric's credibility was in question. Eric needed to get back to Panther Cove. He looked at Terry.

"We're going back tonight. Nothing we can do here."

Wally sat up straight. "Tonight?"

Eric nodded. "That way we can get an early start at the lab in the morning."

"I understand, Eric," Terry said. "Again, I'm sorry. For everything."

"Me, too."

The ride home was quiet. Even Wally seemed subdued. Eric didn't know whether it was because they were exhausted or because of Nicole's death. It was probably a combination of both.

They stopped at a convenience store in Clayton, Georgia for gas and a restroom break. Inside, they bought coffee and Wally added a bag of powdered sugar doughnuts.

Outside, Wally said, "I'll drive. You get some sleep." He held up the bag of doughnuts and his coffee. "I'll be fine."

For once, Eric didn't argue. He was drained. Normally, he wasn't a good passenger, but tonight, he welcomed the opportunity to shut his eyes for a few minutes. As Wally pulled out on the highway, Eric reclined the seat, closed his eyes, and was asleep in minutes, his coffee untouched in the console.

Later, he awoke and looked outside. It was still dark. He squinted, trying to figure out where they were.

"We're almost to Waynesville, boss," Wally said.

Eric shook his head and yawned, trying to clear the cobwebs. "Damn, I guess I fell asleep."

Wally chuckled. "Based on your snoring, I'd agree."

"Sorry. I hope I didn't talk in my sleep." He took a sip of his coffee, which was cold, and spit it out. Once a few more synapses connected, he turned to Wally. "I was dreaming about fly fishing with Nicole."

He shared the story of the first time he took her fishing on Jonathan Creek. By the end, they were both laughing at the image of a somewhat prissy California girl trying to cast a dry fly on a waterway in North Carolina.

"I'm going to miss her," Wally said.

Eric looked at him, waiting for the punch line that never came. It was one of the few times he'd seen Wally so serious on a personal level.

When they got to the lab, Wally pulled up next to his Gremlin.

"Go home and get some rest," Eric said. Sensing that Wally was about to argue, he added, "Get out of here. I'll see you later this morning."

Wally got out and into his car. Eric waited to see if it started. The Gremlin fired up and Wally drove away.

Eric pulled out of the parking lot and headed toward home. There was almost no traffic this late. As he exited I-40 and headed south, something in the back of his mind troubled him but he couldn't put his finger on it.

He turned on Hemphill Road, then soon crossed Jonathan Creek. He smiled at the memories, thinking about the story of Nicole's first fly fishing trip that he shared with Wally.

After he had crossed the little bridge, he slammed on brakes and pulled off on the shoulder.

Nicole told him once that her most prized possession was the Orvis vest that Eric bought for her birthday. *If my house was on fire, the only thing I'd grab would be that vest.* Her words. He needed to get her vest.

He made a quick U-turn and returned to US 276, where he turned right, traveling the short distance to Utah Road. He wound his way up the mountain, turned into Nicole's driveway and parked behind her Volkswagen.

He fumbled around and found his flashlight underneath his seat, then switched the Jeep off. The engine made a ticking noise as it cooled, the only sound other than a dog barking some distance away. *It was dark up here,* he thought. The only light came from a security light out by the driveway.

He knew she kept a spare key under the flower pot on the back porch. When he got out of the Jeep, he glanced around, quickly shining the flashlight toward the back deck. Following the beam, he went up the steps and stopped. There were six large flower pots. One on each side of the back door, one on each side of the steps he'd just climbed, and one in each of the far corners of the deck.

He thought for a minute, trying to get inside of Nicole's head and figure out which would be the most likely candidate.

The back door made sense. He walked over and lifted the first one, tilting it on edge with one hand and shining the light underneath. Nothing. Quickly, he did the same with the one on the other side of the door. Again, nothing.

He swore as he let the heavy pot down. Four more to go and the way his luck was going, it would be the last one.

Furtively, he glanced around. He decided it would make more sense to put it under one next to the steps. That would be more convenient. He lifted the one on the left side and smiled. The key was underneath.

Inserting the key in the lock on the back door, he turned it and felt the deadbolt retract. He opened the door and quietly closed it behind him as he stepped into the kitchen.

It felt odd being inside Nicole's house alone, knowing she was gone forever. He looked around the kitchen, then spied the keys hanging from a rack near the door. He grabbed the VW key fob and went back outside.

He looked inside the car and didn't see what he came for. Unlocking the trunk, he opened it and smiled. Her fly-fishing gear was right there where he suspected.

He picked up her vest and rifled the pockets. The first three held fly boxes, snips, and various other equipment. In the fourth pocket, he found a small wallet containing her North Carolina fishing license.

He removed it and found a piece of folded paper stuck behind it.

"Mind if I ask who you are and what you're doing?" The deep male voice startled him.

Eric had not heard or seen anyone come up. He started to turn around and the voice said, "Don't move.

Put your hands up where I can see them, then turn around very slowly."

He didn't know whether to drop the vest or not. He decided on slowly holding it up so the man could see it and his hand. He transferred the piece of paper to his hand holding the vest and held up both hands as he slowly turned around.

An older man wearing coveralls was pointing a shotgun at him. Eric forced himself to look at the man and try not to look at the gun.

The man was about his height, weighing a few pounds more and with less hair. He looked to be well into his seventies, but his eyes looked focused, and the gun was steady. Eric was betting he knew how to use it, too.

"I'm Eric Carter, Nicole's boss at the Panther Cove lab. My driver's license is in my wallet in my back right pocket. I can give you a number to call to verify what I just told you."

"Real slowly, why don't you get it out of your pocket and throw it over to me."

Eric did as he was told. Still pointing the shotgun at Eric, the man knelt and picked up the wallet at his feet. He opened it and found the license. He glanced at it and grunted.

"What are you doing in her house and going through her car?"

Eric debated on what to tell the man. It probably wasn't wise to play too loosely with the truth when the man was holding what looked to be a 12-gauge shotgun pointed in his direction. Hard to miss from that range and Eric was well aware of the damage a 12-gauge could do.

"She's in Atlanta and asked me to get something out of her fishing vest."

"Really?" The man spat to his side. "You might want to try that one more time before the sheriff gets here."

Shit, Eric thought. This guy knows more than I realized. He took a deep breath and started over.

"Nicole was in a coma at Emory University Hospital in Atlanta. She passed away earlier this evening. I was there. She was working on a project at the lab and we desperately need the password to her computer. You can call the main number at the lab and ask them to confirm my identity, or you can call the main number at the Centers for Disease Control in Atlanta and ask for Dr. Terrance Lumpkin. He can vouch for me."

The man nodded. "Why didn't you just get the sheriff to come out and help you get it?"

"Because it would take too long." He started to add that surely the man understood that, but he didn't want to come across as a smart-ass outsider. "I just drove back this evening. It's really very urgent."

"Did you find it?"

Eric thought about how to answer. If he was truthful, then maybe they could work something out. If he lied and wasn't successful, then he'd be leaving in the back of a deputy's car.

"I found a piece of paper next to her fishing license. It has what I think is the password. It's in my left hand, next to her fishing vest."

The man studied his face, then said, "Show me."

Very carefully, with his free hand, Eric took the paper out and held it up for the man to see.

"That's all I want, I swear. You can keep my license, and you've seen my vehicle and tag number. You're welcome to check my car and my pockets. I knew to look under the flower pot for her key—I've been over here before. And she's been over to my house."

"Where might that be?"

Eric nodded west. "I live up Hemphill Road. Next door to Harlan and Gertrude Burgess. She's my aunt."

The old man broke into a grin. "So, Gertrude's your aunt? And you live next door to them, huh? I've known them since I was a young'un."

Eric breathed a sigh of relief. He wished he'd thought of that earlier.

About that time, a Haywood County Sheriff's car pulled up behind his Jeep. *Shit.* Now things were about to get even more complicated.

The deputy, a younger man, was putting his hat on as he got out of the vehicle. He rested his hand on the butt of his pistol and stood next to the car behind the door. "Everything okay, Luther?"

The old man lowered the shotgun and nodded. "Yeah, Mike. I didn't realize this young fella was a comin over to Miss Nicole's house, so I came to check it out. He's okay, just fixin to leave. Sorry to bother y'all."

The deputy relaxed and walked over to Luther, keeping an eye on Eric. "You got any ID?" he asked Eric.

Before he could answer, Luther, his new buddy, said, "Aw, Mike, he's alright. He's a local. Lives over off Hemphill next to Harlan and Gertrude."

Eric finally relaxed. He'd just gotten the Haywood County stamp of approval.

* * *

When he got back to 276, he called Wally. "Where are you?"

"I'm at home, just like you ordered me."

"I'm on my way to the lab. I'll meet you there."

"Damn, Eric, I just started playing Warcraft. Can't it wait—"

"I've got Nicole's password."

There was a hesitation on the line, then Wally said, "I'm on my way."

Eric parked at the lab, and before he could get inside, Wally drove up. Eric fidgeted at the main entrance waiting for Wally to park and make his way to the lobby. As they walked up to the second floor, Eric explained what had transpired.

They went to Wally's office, where Eric handed Wally the piece of paper he'd found in Nicole's fishing vest.

Switching screens, Wally brought up the login screen to Nicole's computer and typed the password in. The computer hesitated, then displayed Nicole's home screen—a picture Eric recognized. It was Nicole with her first trout she'd caught fly-fishing. Eric had taken the picture on Jonathan Creek.

"Where'd you find it?" Wally asked.

"In her fishing vest. I should've known to look there to start with."

Wally exhaled. "This makes things a lot easier. Give me a while to go through her directories and find the docs related to Hapeville. I'll call you as soon as I have them."

"Thanks." Eric turned and went back downstairs to his office.

Now they could access Nicole's notes on how she modified the H4 virus.

35

Eric and Wally spent the next forty-eight hours going through Nicole's notes. Not surprising to Eric, she had documented everything meticulously, including her physical history after inhaling the modified H4 virus now known as Hapeville.

Each of them had reviewed her notes independently. Now, they were sitting at the conference table in Eric's office to discuss their thoughts on a solution to stop the spread of the deadly man-made virus.

"You first," Eric said.

Wally shifted in his chair and exhaled. "If I had to decide today?"

Eric moved his head up, then down, waiting for Wally to proceed.

Eric saw two options for a vaccine. One was based on the pure H4N4 virus and the other was based on the antibodies in Nicole's blood. They had ruled out a vaccine based on antibodies in Eric's blood, reasoning that Nicole's antibodies would be more effective since they were formed based on the Hapeville virus.

If Wally was having trouble choosing, it meant that neither was a clear favorite to the chief scientist. This wasn't going to be an easy choice. "Time's up," Eric said.

Wally shook his head and paused. "The upside is better with—"

Eric held up his hand. "Tell me your choice first, then defend it."

Wally snorted, familiar with Eric's process. "It's Morton's fork," Wally said. "You know that."

Eric smiled at the reference. Morton's fork referred to a dilemma where both choices are undesirable. It was named after John Morton, one of Henry VII principal advisors. It was an appropriate description of their situation. He folded his arms and waited.

Wally stalled as long as he dared. "Nicole's antibodies."

"Why?"

"Less risk. The dangers of giving millions of people H4N4 are unknown. We might be creating a new monster."

"Nicole's antibodies didn't save her," Eric said. The implication was that no one knew if it would work for sure.

Wally bristled. "She was too far along. Plus, I think that Fluzenta may have interfered in some way. But, we don't have time to do the necessary testing. Besides, H4N4 hasn't saved anyone either."

"True. So, you're betting the farm on Nicole's antibodies?"

"Given your artificially constructed parameters—yes."

Eric relaxed. "If it makes you feel any better, that's my choice, too. I agree with what you're saying. My gut tells me that we're running out of time. We're going to be asked that question very soon."

It came sooner than he realized.

His phone buzzed. It was Harlan and Gertrude's number, their only one. They were one of the few people Eric knew who had a landline. They'd tried a cell phone a couple of years ago, but when it wouldn't work reliably in the mountains, Harlan returned it and swore he wanted a real phone line. "At least I always get a dial tone when I pick up the receiver," he'd said on more than one occasion.

"Hello?" Eric said after he pressed Answer.

"Eric?"

"Hey, Harlan. Is everything okay?" Gertrude occasionally called, but Eric couldn't remember the last time he'd spoken to Harlan on a telephone. He wasn't sure he ever had.

"I don't think so." There was a catch in Harlan's voice. "Gertrude . . ."

"What's the matter, Harlan?" Eric's antennae went on full alert.

"She's burning up, Eric. I've tried giving her aspirin, but it doesn't seem to be helping."

Eric asked a few more questions, then told Harlan he was on his way. "I'll be there in thirty minutes."

"Do I need to call 911?" Harlan asked

"No. Let me get there first. I'm on my way."

He disconnected the call and looked at Wally. "How much longer before you have antibodies?"

Wally shrugged. "Two, maybe three days."

Eric swore, then shook his head. "We don't have time." He stood. "Gertrude's sick. I think she's got Hapeville."

Wally followed him up to the lab. "How the hell could she have contracted it?"

"Maybe she somehow got it from Nicole. I don't know, but right now, that's not the issue."

"What are you doing?" Wally asked, struggling to keep up with Eric's long strides.

"Don't ask. And when we get to the lab, I want you to go to your office."

Wally managed to insert himself between Eric and the retina scanner. "I'm going with you."

Eric shook his head. "No, Wally. This is my decision. Besides, if my aunt does have Hapeville, it would be dangerous for you."

"And this is my decision. You don't have to let me ride with you, but you can't keep me from going there."

"Wally, don't be stupid. I'm immunized. Harlan's already exposed. You've seen what that virus can do."

"You need help, and I'm going."

Eric pushed past him and keyed the scanner. The door unlocked. Eric walked in and shut the door in Wally's face. Inside the lab, he took three steps, then heard the door click. Wally strode in and caught up with him.

Eric stopped in his tracks and pointed a finger at Wally's face. "Get out. You're fired."

Wally shrugged. "Then you'll have to call security because I'm not leaving."

Eric pulled out his cell phone, aware that several employees nearby were watching and listening. "I will, I swear."

Wally folded his arms and smirked. "Go ahead. I don't give a rat's ass."

Eric leaned toward Wally and hissed, "Has it occurred to you that you may be risking your life? This is not something to—"

"I don't care. I'll take precautions, but you need help."

Eric stared at him and saw nothing but rugged determination. It was clear that Wally wasn't going to budge. "Fine. Do what the hell you want." He wheeled and walked toward Nicole's office to get the pre-loaded syringes, filled with the pure H4N4 virus.

When he stepped outside of the lab entrance, Wally was standing there waiting for him, holding a large box.

"Protective gear. Gloves and masks," Wally said.

Eric shook his head. "That may not be enough."

Wally shrugged. "It's airborne. We'll be fine. Besides, we don't have time to get her to an isolation unit."

"You are one stubborn son of a bitch," Eric said.

Wally grinned. "I wonder where I got it from. That *is* your fault."

When they got to Gertrude's, Harlan came out on the porch to meet them. At a safe distance, Eric explained that Gertrude might have a serious infection. He and Wally were going to don protective gear as a safety precaution before going inside.

"I'd feel better if you would wear it, too," Eric said.

Harlan shook his head. "I've been by that woman's side for all these years. If I've got whatever she has, so be it."

Eric and Wally slipped into their gear, and Harlan led them inside.

"I'm worried, Eric," Harlan said as he led them into the small bedroom. "She's never been this sick."

Eric reached out and placed his gloved hand on Harlan's shoulder. "We're going to take good care of her."

When they walked into the bedroom, Gertrude was lying on her back, her eyes closed. She reminded Eric of Nicole, and he tried to push that thought out of his mind.

At the bedside, he withdrew an antiseptic wipe and a syringe out of his pocket, explaining every step to Harlan so he would know what was happening.

After he had withdrawn the blood, he placed a bandage over the puncture and stood there for a moment, his hand resting on his aunt's arm. Although he knew what was wrong, he had to confirm it before calling it in.

He gave Gertrude a light squeeze, then walked over to the bathroom sink where Wally waited with the test strip they'd retrieved from Nicole's office. As Wally held it, Eric discharged a tiny drop of blood on it, then dropped the syringe in the red biohazard container that Wally had set on the counter.

The strip began to turn blue, just as Eric had expected. Gertrude had Hapeville flu.

They turned around and walked over to Harlan, standing at Gertrude's side, his hand on hers.

"Harlan," Eric began. "Gertrude has a dangerous type of flu, a new strain that right now has no vaccine. It's called Hapeville, for a small town near Atlanta where it was first discovered." He let the words sink in, wanting Harlan to fully understand the gravity of the situation.

"I'd like to test you, too, just so we know."

Harlan nodded.

Eric tested Harlan, but to his surprise, Harlan was negative. Eric explained that, and once again, asked Harlan if he'd be willing to wear protective gear. This time, Harlan agreed.

On the drive up to the house, Eric had considered how to approach Harlan. He knew the direct approach was best, but with no medical background, Harlan might not grasp the magnitude of what Eric was proposing.

They went back to the living room where Eric focused on his uncle.

"We're working on a vaccine, but it won't be ready in time for Gertrude." He cleared his throat. This was difficult, even more so since it was his aunt lying in the next room.

Eric held up the preloaded syringe. "This is another virus, let's call it Canton." Canton was the name of a small town in the area, just east of Waynesville. Eric was trying to explain in language that would resonate with the elder man standing in front of him.

Wally started to speak, but Eric put his hand out to silence him.

"What I'd like to do is inject the Canton virus into Gertrude. I know that might sound strange, but I'm betting that the Canton virus is powerful enough to choke out the Hapeville."

Harlan stared at him, his eyes searching Eric's. "Kinda like putting a panther in a box with a coyote to get rid of the coyote."

Eric smiled and nodded. "Exactly."

"So then, what do you do about the panther after he's killed the coyote?"

He was relieved that the old man understood the dilemma. He hoped Harlan could take the next step, which required a tremendous leap of faith. "I have reason to believe that we have a solution, but it's extremely tough to explain."

Harlan studied Eric's face again, then a thin smile crossed his lips. "You've never put a panther in a box with a coyote before, so you don't really know what's going to happen."

Harlan understood. In his simplistic way, he comprehended the entire situation much better than Eric had been able to articulate it.

Eric nodded. "That's right, I don't. What I do know is that if we don't do something, the coyote is most likely going to kill her."

Harlan glanced at Wally, then looked back at Eric. "I don't need to hear anything else. I'd trust you with my life, and I'm trusting you with Gertrude's. There ain't no guarantees in this world, and I understand that. If you're telling me that's the best chance she's got, then you need to get on with it."

After Eric had given Gertrude the first injection, he and Wally went outside and sat in the rocking chairs on the front porch. Harlan was still inside, sitting in a chair next to Gertrude. "It's where I belong," he told them.

They quietly watched the light of day dim as the sun was setting behind the mountains. Eric took a sip of the clear liquid out of the Mason jar in his hand, wiped his mouth on his sleeve, and then passed it over to Wally. "This is sippin whiskey, Wally, so be careful."

Wally held the jar up and considered it. He shrugged and took a big mouthful. His eyes opened wide as he swallowed and then coughed. "Jesus. That's like jet fuel. Good thing there's no open flame around."

Eric chuckled. "I told you."

They sat there in silence for another couple of well-spaced sips. A Plott hound barked in the distance, and they watched as a mamma bear and her two cubs walked along the tree line not fifty yards away.

"I need to call this in to CDC," Eric said.

Wally took another drink, then set the jar down on the table. "No, no you don't. He told you nobody was taking her out of this house. And I believe him."

"But they are in a much better position—"

"Bullshit. You're starting to sound like every other doctor I know. You do stuff because you can." An owl hooted in the woods off to their right, behind the barn. "She's old, and she's probably not going to survive this." He held up his hand. "Not because of the H4. I told you before, I'd rather have it than anything else, and I stand by that."

Wally looked around and lowered his voice. "The older you get, the harder it is to cheat the grim reaper. Even a common cold can do it at this point in the game. You know that."

Wally held out his hands toward the horizon. "If they're happy here, then let it be. I know if it were me, I'd rather die here than in some hospital plugged up to a bunch of machines. Let it be their decision."

Eric looked at Wally, surprised at his level of compassion and understanding. It was a side of Wally he'd seldom seen. He nodded. "Maybe you're right. It's probably too late now anyway." He picked up the Mason jar and took a swig. "Is this stuff getting smoother or am I getting drunk?"

Wally laughed. "I don't know, but neither of us is going to be driving tonight, so what does it matter?"

36

Eric awoke the next morning in the spare bedroom, the smell of coffee wafting through the air. It was daylight, but barely. He and Wally had taken turns through the night, monitoring Gertrude.

Around four a.m., he'd given her another injection. If anything her condition had worsened. Wally took over, and Eric went to bed to catch a little well-needed sleep before morning.

He stopped by the bathroom to relieve himself and splash a little cold water on his face. As he padded into the kitchen toward the coffee pot, he heard voices out on the front porch. He found a mug, poured a cup, and went outside.

"Morning," Harlan said.

"Morning." He wanted to ask Wally, who was seated next to Harlan, if there was any change in Gertrude. Instead, he cautiously decided to sit and ease into the conversation first.

Harlan turned his attention back to Wally and continued with the story he'd been telling.

Eric listened politely and realized it was a story about a younger Harlan and Gertrude before they were married.

It related to Harlan asking Gertrude's father for permission to marry his daughter.

It was a touching, but funny story, well-honed after many years of telling, and they all laughed when Harlan got to the punch line.

"He looked me right in the eye and said, 'She's yours. There ain't no bringing her back.'" Harlan paused and gathered his thoughts as the laughter faded. "We've had our ups and downs, like most, but I never wanted to give her back. Ever."

Eric swallowed, and he felt his eyes moisten. That was the kind of love he wanted, the kind that lasts forever. He looked over at Wally, who shook his head just enough to signal that things had not improved.

Harlan started to rise. "I got some grits, eggs, and country ham I can cook for breakfast. Sorry, I can't do no biscuits—that's Gertrude, not me."

Eric started to get up, but Harlan fixed him with a stare. "You boys sit here and enjoy your coffee. Least I can do is fix y'all somethin to eat."

Eric eased back into his chair as Harlan walked inside, letting the screen door shut behind him. "Any change?" he whispered to Wally.

Wally shook his head. "Temp and respiration are about the same."

"Shit," he said, under his breath. "We need to get her to the hospital." He leaned forward in his chair, about to stand.

Wally eyed him with something resembling contempt. "I thought we already had this conversation."

He started to protest, then thought back to their discussion last night. Wally was right. This is what Gertrude and Harlan wanted. He needed to step back and see it from their perspective.

Relaxing back in his seat, he nodded. "We did. And you're right."

By the time they finished their coffee, Harlan had appeared at the door. "Chow's on. No guarantees. As I always say, make sure they're good and hungry first."

They stepped inside and over to the table where Eric had enjoyed many delicious meals. It was odd to see Gertrude's place, closest to the kitchen, vacant. Harlan stuck out his hands and Eric followed suit, linking his hand with Harlan's. Wally hesitated, then figured out the protocol. Once he'd linked hands with Eric and Harlan, the elder man bowed his head and said grace.

The food was good. Maybe it was what Harlan said about making sure the guests were hungry, or maybe it was just that a home-cooked comfort meal was what they all needed. When they finished, Eric ordered Harlan to go to Gertrude's side while he and Wally cleaned up. This time, Harlan complied without arguing.

"Man, that was good eats," Wally said as he stood next to Eric at the sink. Eric washed dishes and Wally dried.

"Nothing like fresh, home-raised food," he said, handing Wally another plate.

Wally looked at him quizzically, and Eric laughed. "You need to walk around behind the barn. See where your breakfast came from."

His friend glanced toward the door and shook his head. "Maybe they're some things I'm better off not knowing. Remember, I'm a city boy. All my food came from the deli or in a package from the market."

When they were done with the dishes, they walked back to Gertrude, stopping to politely knock on the door jamb before entering. Eric took her temperature and pulse, calling out the numbers for Wally to record. There was no change.

"I'm going to walk outside and see if I can get a better signal." Seeing the dirty look from Wally, he added, "I'm just going to call Rae."

"I'll stay here," Wally said, his posture relaxing.

Eric had discovered on previous visits that if he walked out toward the eastern edge of the clearing around the house, he could usually get a more reliable signal to place calls.

Rae answered on the second ring. "Where have you been? I've been worried sick. No one knows where you are, not even Carmen."

"I'm sorry, she's next on my list. It's been kind of hectic the last forty-eight hours." He gave her the condensed version of what happened.

"Don't you think she should be in the hospital?" Her tone was not accusatory nor condemning, but gentle and supportive.

"No." He shared the discussion that he and Wally had regarding that subject. "It's out of my hands," he said. "It's what Gertrude would want. And I know it's what Harlan wants."

"I understand. For what it's worth, I agree. I feel for you, though, and wish I was there with."

He smiled. "I know, I do too."

He promised to call back later and disconnected. Talking with Rae made him feel better along with her agreement on what he was doing. He clicked on Carmen's number next.

"It's about time," she said testily. "Not like you to go AWOL on me."

"I'm sorry Carmen. I didn't want to put you in an awkward position." He gave her a more abridged version of events but included the fact that Wally was with him.

"I'm sorry to hear about your aunt. Frank is looking for you, and so is Dr. Lumpkin. I know they think I'm covering for you, which I would do, but this time I didn't have a clue." Her voice sounded hurt.

"Again, I apologize. I know it wasn't fair, but I wanted you to be able to truthfully say you didn't know where I was."

"I forgive you—this time. But what do I tell everyone?"

"The truth, or at least a part of it. My aunt who raised me is dying, and I want to be with her without interruption. I don't think it will be long. I don't want to be bothered and I'll be in touch with you. That's it."

"I'm so sorry Eric. Is there anything else I can do?"

"Just keep the wolves away."

That afternoon, Gertrude's vitals started showing minor improvement. Eric was cautiously optimistic, but he didn't want to give Harlan false hopes. All he would tell his uncle is that she seemed to be stable and not getting worse.

Later, he and Wally went outside for a break to get some fresh air. The chickens roaming loose in the yard reminded Eric of his Aunt Ida's place where he grew up.

"Real free-range chickens, huh?" Wally said. "Is that where our eggs came from?"

Eric laughed. "Yep. And if you ever have fried chicken here . . ."

Wally grimaced as he realized what Eric was saying.

"Too much information. Gertrude's getting better, isn't she?" Wally said.

Eric nodded. "I think so. I want to see how she does tonight before we encourage Harlan too much. It could be temporary."

"If it works, does that change your thoughts on the vaccine?"

Eric shrugged. "Not sure. I haven't thought about it. I just want Gertrude to get well." He looked at Wally. "I've never heard you talk about your family."

"Mom and Dad are gone. I've got one brother, older. He's a cop in Boston. I've got a few aunts, uncles, and cousins there, too."

"That's good. Other than Ali, Gertrude's the only family I've got left." They walked a few minutes in silence, then he added, "I know she's getting up in years and the day is coming, but I'm not ready to lose her yet."

"We never are."

37

That night, Eric volunteered to take the first shift while Wally slept. They had moved Harlan's recliner to the room and placed it next to Gertrude's side of the bed. Eric tried to get Harlan to go to bed and get some much-needed rest, but he refused to leave her side.

Eric sat in a rocking chair in the corner of the room, reading. He had brought a Michael Connelly novel and was halfway done. The only sound was the ticking of the grandfather clock in the hallway. That, and Harlan's snoring. Eric was glad he didn't have to sleep with that on a regular basis.

Near midnight, he took Gertrude's temperature. It was down to 101.2, which was better than before and getting closer to normal. He noticed beads of sweat on her forehead. The fever was breaking. He took the stethoscope and listened to her chest. Her heartbeat sounded stronger.

He sat back in his chair and allowed himself a smile. Gertrude was healing. He wished he could witness the epic battle he pictured being fought inside her body. The H4 virus was forcing her body to attack the Hapeville virus and winning. Gertrude's immune system, now with a powerful ally, was mustering forces to repel the unnatural invader.

The remaining question was yet to be answered. Once the Hapeville virus had been conquered, would the H4 virus go dormant as Eric predicted? Or would it mutate and attack the host? Eric hoped he was right.

He got comfortable in the chair and opened the book to the place he'd marked, trying to keep his eyes open for another hour before waking Wally to relieve him.

He awoke with a start, the book folded across his lap. He thought he heard something. Straining to hear, he looked at his watch. 2:34. He didn't know how long he'd been asleep.

"Harlan." There. Again. The raspy voice. *What the hell?* Disoriented, he looked around the room. His gaze landed on Gertrude. Her eyes were open, and her head was turned toward her husband.

"Harlan," she said, this time a little stronger and a little louder.

Oh my God, it was Gertrude. She was calling Harlan. Before Eric could rise, Harlan's eyes flickered, then settled on Gertrude. His look of astonishment mirrored Eric's.

"Gertrude?" Harlan whispered.

She smiled. "Who else did you think it was, old man?"

* * *

Gertrude thought she'd been asleep. When Harlan told her she'd been out for 48 hours, Eric and Wally had to confirm it before she'd believe him. Other than being thirsty and hungry, she claimed she felt fine. When Wally took her temperature, it was elevated less than a degree above normal.

Although Harlan offered to cook her breakfast, Eric suggested that she start with a glass of water and then some grits. “Let’s start you with something bland at first and see how that sits on your stomach. Wally and I can do that.”

In the kitchen, Wally whispered, “What now, boss?” as Eric filled a small pot with water.

Eric shook his head. “I don’t know. I hadn’t got that far.” He put the pot on the stove and turned it on High. “I’ve got to call Terry.”

Wally watched as Eric measured out a cup of grits. “What exactly are those?”

Eric looked at him. “Grits? You don’t know what grits are?”

“Not really.”

He laughed. “Ground corn. Growing up in Boston, I know you’ve had polenta, right? Same thing.”

Wally’s eyes opened wide. “No. Really?”

“Really. Italians may put different things in it than we do in the South, but the base is ground corn either way. Call it what you will.”

Wally shook his head. “Well, I’ll be damned. I’ve been eating grits all along and never knew it.” He stared at the ground cornmeal for a moment before looking up at Eric. “What are you going to tell Dr. Lumpkin?”

“The truth. I don’t care about the consequences. Gertrude’s back, and that’s what counts.”

When the grits were ready, Eric spooned a generous portion into a bowl, added salt and butter. “Voila,” he said, handing the bowl to Wally. "Grits. Take this to Harlan for Gertrude and I'll dish us up some."

After they had eaten, Eric excused himself and walked outside to call Terry Lumpkin.

"It's about damn time you called," Terry said. "I thought I was going to have to suit up and come get your ass." Terry rarely cursed or raised his voice. The combination spoke volumes.

"What the fuck is going on?" Terry said.

Eric winced and held the phone away from his ear. "I think—"

"At the moment, I'm not interested in what you think, *Doctor* Carter. Let me lay it out for you."

Eric was wise enough to shut up, relieved he wasn't in Terry's physical presence.

"We need to examine your aunt thoroughly," Terry said. "I want my team to examine the four of you at the house, first, to make sure none of you pose a threat. Once that's complete, we'll fly the four of you here for more tests."

"Yes sir, I understand." Eric wasn't about to press any more of Terry's buttons. He figured it'd be easier to argue with Harlan than Terry.

"I think—" Eric caught himself and corrected before Terry could say anything, "I mean, I will get her and her husband to Atlanta."

"You're damn right you will." The line disconnected without Terry giving any more instructions.

Harlan wasn't a problem. He was so glad to have Gertrude back, he would've been willing to do most anything that Eric asked. Gertrude, however, wasn't keen on flying. Eric assured her it would be safe and comfortable, not to mention considerably quicker.

He explained the process to the group. First, a small advance team from CDC would meet them at the house. The CDC group would be in spacesuits as a precautionary measure. Gertrude, Harlan, Eric, and Wally would be tested onsite to make sure they were not infectious.

Once that was complete and the results verified, they would be flown to the CDC in Atlanta for further tests.

"How long do we have to stay in Atlanta?" Gertrude asked.

Eric shook his head. "I don't know. They will want to make sure we're all safe before they let us come back, but I don't think it will be long."

"Do we have to go?" Harlan asked.

As he pictured an irate Terry Lumpkin, Eric nodded and opened his eyes wide. He didn't say it, but this group was going to Atlanta one way or the other. "There's a lot to be learned from how Gertrude survived it and why you didn't contract it. This is valuable information that will help others."

Gertrude reflected. "I've never flown before. I have to admit, I'm nervous about that part. But, if we can help others, then we'll do whatever you say."

"How did you and Wally avoid getting it?" Harlan asked.

"I don't know." Eric had checked his and Wally's blood every day with the test strips, and each time, it was negative. Eric knew he had the H4 antibodies, but didn't know how to explain that to his Uncle. He didn't understand it himself.

"Maybe it was because we were careful about our exposure," Eric said, "or, maybe it was luck. I'm sure that's something that CDC is very interested in as well."

"Maybe it was an angel," Gertrude said.

"Maybe . . ." Eric's voice faded. He had started to disagree, but then realized he didn't know. Who was he to say with certainty that there wasn't divine intervention?

Maybe Gertrude was right.

38

Eric went outside and called Kate, steeling himself for the inescapable tongue-lashing. He was surprised when Kate answered the phone and the first words out of her mouth were "Are you okay?"

"How—"

"Carmen called me. She told me what she could and that you would fill me in as soon as you were able. What's going on, Eric?"

Thank God for Carmen, he thought. Once again, she'd saved his ass. "Have you got a few minutes to talk?"

"I've got all evening, just tell me what's happening."

He started with Nicole's death, leaving out the part about him going to Emory to give her the H4 virus. He told her about Gertrude falling ill with Hapeville. "She was dying, Kate. With Harlan's permission, I gave her a very experimental treatment."

"Oh my God. How is she?"

"Well, she's up and about. Still weak, but getting stronger. A team from the CDC is on their way here to check us all out, then we're going to Atlanta to verify that everything is fine."

"How did you and Wally avoid getting it?"

He smiled. "I honestly don't know. Gertrude says it was an angel."

Kate laughed. "She's doing well, I can tell. Please tell her I asked about her."

"I will. How's Ali?"

"Curious. I tried to tell her as little as possible so that she wouldn't be worried, but you know how perceptive she is. If you're done with me, I'll put her on the phone."

"That would be nice. I know I've been neglectful, but I'd like to see her this weekend."

There was an awkward pause, and Eric anticipated Kate's concern. "If CDC gives me a clean bill. You know I'd never do anything to jeopardize our daughter's health."

Kate laughed nervously. "I wasn't implying—"

"I know. And if I were you, I'd be concerned, too. No offense taken. I'll call you tomorrow and let you know."

"Thanks. Take care of you, Eric. I'll go get Ali."

"Where are you, Daddy?" Ali's voice brought tears to his eyes.

"I'm at Gramma's house. She's been sick, so Uncle Wally and I have been taking care of her."

"Is she okay?"

"She's fine. I'll let you talk to her when we're done, if you'd like."

"I miss you, Daddy."

"I miss you, too, Ali. Hopefully, I'll get to see you this weekend. I've already talked to your mom about it."

Ali squealed. "Yes, and we can have supper with Gramma."

He started to say that Gertrude might not be up to it, but he knew that a team of horses wouldn't be able to keep her from cooking for Ali. "I'm sure she'd like that."

They chatted for several more minutes, then he put Gertrude on the phone. He heard her promise to cook whatever Ali wanted and shook his head. After another few minutes, he held his hand out for the phone.

Beaming, she said her goodbyes and gave the phone back to Eric.

"I love you, Ali," he said.

"I love you, too, Daddy. Call me tomorrow."

"I will." Eric disconnected the call and stood there, looking out over the valley below. The light was starting to fade and the temperature was going down also. The last few days were a blur. He had to stop and think about what day it was. So much had happened.

The phone in his pocket vibrated. He pulled it out and looked. Frank. *Might as well get it over with,* he thought.

"Hello."

"Well, it's about goddamn time. Were you planning on letting me know what the hell was going on anytime this year?"

"It's been kinda hectic, Frank."

"Oh, really? Care to enlighten me?"

He told Frank essentially the same story that he told Kate.

"Wait a minute. Did you give your aunt the H4 virus? And it worked?"

Eric could hear the tumblers falling into place in Frank's head. "It's one person, and it appeared to work. That's what CDC wants to confirm."

"I'm coming up there."

Eric chuckled. "I don't think so, Frank. We've been quarantined. You won't be able to get here."

"Quarantined? That's bullshit."

"Afraid not. Terry's serious. And trust me, you don't want to cross him. There's one road in, and the Haywood County Sheriff's Office has it blocked, based on strict orders from CDC."

"We'll see about that."

Eric heard a click and Frank was gone. He shrugged and called Rae.

"Hey, stranger. Have I told that you I miss you?" she said when she answered the phone.

Eric grinned. "Not lately." He told Rae what the plan was. "It looks like I'm off limits for another twenty-four hours. After that, you can have your way with me."

Rae laughed. "I intend to. Get a good night's rest, because you're going to need it."

"Where are you?"

She laughed. "Next door. I'm at your house. Somebody had to take care of Felix."

"Shit. I'd forgotten—"

"It's alright. You've had a lot on your mind. I've been here since the day after you got there.. Believe me, he hasn't starved."

Now it was his turn to laugh. "We're going to have company this weekend."

"Really? Who?"

"My daughter."

There was a slight pause, then in a quieter voice, Rae asked, "Are you sure? I mean, I did meet her that other weekend, but . . ."

"I'm sure. The two of you got along well. I think it's time she knows about us."

"How's Gertrude?" Rae asked.

"Amazing. She'd already promised to cook supper for us Saturday night, thanks to Ali."

"And how are you?"

"Better, now. I'm ready for a vacation."

After he had hung up with Rae, he walked back to the house. Gertrude and Wally were sitting at the table. Harlan was in the kitchen standing at the stove.

"Have y'all got Harlan cooking?" Eric asked as he walked into the kitchen.

"If you call warming up some frozen vegetable soup cooking, then I'm guilty," Harlan said, laughing as he stirred the pot.

"I tried to fix supper," Gertrude said from the table. "But that stubborn old man made me come sit down."

Harlan leaned over and whispered to Eric. "You and I both know that Gertrude does what she wants. I ain't never made her do much of anything in fifty years and tonight's no different. I can tell you there ain't nothing wrong with her."

Eric helped Harlan dish up the soup into bowls, and they took them to the dining room table. This time, when Harlan sat, Wally was quick to extend his hands and bow his head, much to Gertrude's delight.

"Eric, why don't you say grace, please," Gertrude asked.

Eric gulped. It had been years since he'd said any kind of a blessing and he wasn't sure he remembered how.

He grabbed Wally's hand and Gertrude's and held on tight, as if holding on to them would help him find the words.

"Lord, we thank you for the many blessings you've given us, especially the recovery of my Aunt Gertrude." He felt her squeeze his hand in encouragement. "Bless this food you've provided and use it to nourish our bodies." He tried to think of anything he'd missed, and coming up blank, he concluded with "Amen."

There was an echo around the table as he heard Gertrude and Harlan say, "Amen." Eric could've sworn he also heard Wally say it. When he looked over at his scientist, Wally grinned, and gave him a little shrug.

39

The next morning, the CDC team showed up promptly at daybreak. As advertised, they were in spacesuits. They poked, prodded, and took blood samples. One of the team also took air samples. Once they were done, they retreated to the relative safety of their vehicle parked forty yards away from the house.

Eric occasionally peeked out the windows, looking for any signs. Finally, the one who'd identified himself as the team leader exited the van and started peeling off his protective gear. He walked over to Eric, who sat on the front porch.

"Dr. Carter," the man said. "None of you showed any indication of the active Hapeville virus. We didn't find it in the air samples, either. You and Ms. Burgess have the H4 antibodies present. We're cleared to fly to Atlanta as soon as you're ready."

"Thank you. I'll tell the others." He turned to walk inside, and the spokesman continued. "Oh, Dr. Carter? I wanted to tell you that a Frank Liles showed up at the checkpoint last evening. Apparently, he was none too happy about the fact that he wasn't allowed to proceed."

Eric laughed. "Thanks. He's just my boss. He'll get over it."

He rounded up Gertrude, Harlan, and Wally. They quickly finished packing, and the four of them rode down the mountain in the CDC van to the waiting helicopter. Eric recognized Tigger, the pilot who'd flown him to Atlanta the first trip.

"Dr. Carter. Good to see you again, especially after what I've heard."

Eric laughed. "Yes, it's good to be here, I must say." He introduced Gertrude and Harlan. "This is the first time they've ever flown."

Before starting the chopper, Tigger took the time to turn around and introduce himself. "It's a beautiful day for going to Atlanta. Sit back and enjoy the ride." He had them buckle their seatbelts and put on their headphones.

"Just talk normally. Everyone on the aircraft can hear you, so if you have any questions, just ask."

Eric saw Gertrude reach out for Harlan's hand as the co-pilot started the engine.

The crew completed their checklist as the turbine warmed up. Satisfied everything was good, Tigger looked at the co-pilot, who gave him a thumbs up. Tigger increased the throttle, and after the engine spooled up, he deftly manipulated the collective to get the helicopter off the ground.

Gertrude was grinning from ear to ear as the aircraft slowly lifted off, then tilted forward and gained altitude. Harlan looked stoically ahead. As they turned south, the co-pilot said, "We're looking at a flying time of fifty-nine minutes to base."

After a few minutes, the couple started to relax and gaze out the window, pointing out familiar landmarks to each other and marveling at the wonders of flight.

They arrived at the Centers for Disease Control helipad right on schedule as Tigger eased the craft down on the surface with only a slight bump. The co-pilot shut the aircraft down, and as soon as the rotor stopped turning, Tigger turned around and looked at Gertrude. "Well? What did you think?"

Still grinning, Gertrude flashed him a thumbs-up. "This beats Harlan's driving."

Inside the building, they were ushered into Terry's office. He walked over and hugged Gertrude. "You probably don't remember me," he said.

Giving him a sharp look, she nodded. "Oh yes, I do, Terry. I remember you and Eric coming up to see us. Your last trip, Harlan showed y'all how to clean a chicken, and we had it for Sunday dinner. Chicken and dumplings, as I recall."

Terry laughed and shook his head. "Aunt Gertrude, your memory is better than mine. And those are still the best chicken and dumplings I've ever had."

"Well, you just need to come on back, and I'll fix them for you again. This time, I'll even clean the chicken."

"You've got a deal," he said. He invited them into the conference room next door, where a small group awaited their arrival.

Wally looked at Eric and shook his head. Eric thought he looked a little pale.

They spent the first couple of hours debriefing, with questions coming from all areas. After lunch, the group disbursed for testing with the plan to get back together late in the afternoon for a wrap-up. Terry had decided the four would stay overnight before heading back to North Carolina the next day if all of the tests were negative.

Gertrude was subject to the most intensive testing since she was the only one of the four that had contracted Hapeville. When Eric finished, he was escorted back to Terry's office alone.

Terry leaned back in his chair, shaking his head and sighing. "It was good to see Gertrude and Harlan. She looks like she's doing well. She's still sharp as a tack."

Eric laughed. "Yes, she is. I'm keeping my fingers crossed."

"From everything we've gathered, your theory about H4 has considerable merit."

Eric allowed himself a smile, but Terry continued. "Of course, so did Fluzenta."

Eric's smile disappeared. "Fluzenta works, just not for Hapeville. For what it's worth, Wally and I both agree that the best option is a vaccine based on Nicole's antibodies. H4 is too risky."

He looked at Terry, trying to discern what he was thinking. "I know you're unhappy with what I did, but I was desperate. Gertrude was dying, and it was the only option I had under the circumstances. I'm relieved it worked, but I can't recommend it."

Terry nodded. "How close are you to the vaccine?"

"I think we'll have something soon, hopefully in time for those who contracted Hapeville. Having Nicole's notes gave us a huge head start."

"Tera Pharmagenics has no credibility left in the market, you know that."

Eric nodded. "Anything we come up with will be made immediately available to all manufacturers."

Terry cocked his head. "Frank Liles agreed to that?"

Eric smiled. "Not yet, but he doesn't have a choice, does he?"

Terry stared at him. "I'm sorry, Eric. I know you were counting on a windfall from Fluzenta."

"I still think Fluzenta has value and is effective for some strains, just under a different banner. Obviously, Tera Pharmagenics is done. What's important is that we find a cure for Hapeville, since it was Tera Pharmagenics that unleashed this plague on the world. I just hope we haven't done something that we can't fix."

Terry turned serious. "We finished testing all of your employees at Panther Cove."

"And?"

"No one tested positive for Hapeville."

Eric exhaled. "That's a relief."

"No one tested positive for the H4 antibodies, either. You were the only one."

Eric furrowed his brow. He wondered where his friend was going with this.

Terry leaned forward over his desk. "I'll be honest with you, Eric. Some people are saying this looks suspicious."

"Suspicious? What are you saying?"

"Step back and look at it. Outside of the patients that contracted Hapeville, you are the only one with the H4 antibodies. You find Nicole's password that unlocks the secret. She created the Hapeville virus, tested it on herself, and then disbursed it on a flight from Atlanta to Los Angeles. That explains all of the cases except your aunt's. Nicole is dead and can't comment. How did you get the antibodies and how did your aunt get Hapeville?"

Eric opened his mouth to respond, then stopped, understanding where Terry was going. He considered Terry's theory, then shook his head. He tried to keep his voice even.

"Are you suggesting I had something to do with this?"

Terry held his hands out, palms up. "I'm not accusing you, Eric. But think about how this looks from where I sit."

Eric stared at Terry. "Do you think that I would create and release a virus, just to get Fluzenta to market?"

Terry shook his head. "No, I don't. But a billion dollars is a lot of money, and I do believe there are people who would." He sat back in his chair. "A lot of people want an investigation. I'm not sure how much of this will ever be made public, but it may be out of my hands."

Eric nodded. "I understand."

"What are you going to do?"

"To be honest, I haven't thought about it. Again, my focus is a cure for Hapeville."

Terry stood and extended his hand. "Let me know if I can help."

"Thanks, Terry. For everything. We'll talk soon."

*   *   *

The next afternoon, after the last debriefing, Terry escorted them back to the helipad for their flight home. Dusk was fast approaching, and the lights of Atlanta were beginning to twinkle in anticipation of evening. Once again, Tigger was the pilot.

"I'm glad to see you're flying with me again," he said to Gertrude with a wink. "It must not have been too bad."

"I'd fly with you anytime," she said. She buckled her seatbelt and placed the headset over her ears like a pro.

This time, Tigger flew straight to the Panther Cove lab, where they had a lighted pad and more room without tying up traffic on US 276. Eric had called Carmen en route, and she would be there with a company vehicle waiting for them.

As Tigger circled the helipad lining up his approach, Eric saw a van emblazoned with the Tera Pharmagenics logo. Carmen stood out front, her arms folded. Standing beside her were Rae, Kate, and Ali.

Parked next to the van was a black Town Car with tinted windows. Frank Liles stood with his hips up against the hood, smoking a cigarette.

Eric hadn't expected a welcoming committee. He was glad to see Rae and Ali, even Kate, but he had mixed feelings at the sight of Frank. Since Carmen hadn't mentioned it, he assumed that Frank's appearance was a surprise to everyone.

They touched down, and with rotors still spinning, the co-pilot escorted all of them safely to the side of the helipad. Eric gave Tigger a wave, which he acknowledged with a nod, and then the copter took flight as quickly and as smoothly as it had arrived.

Ali ran to her Dad's outstretched arms. "I want to go for a ride," she shrieked, as she tightly hugged his neck.

"Not today, but one day. I promise," he told her.

Kate and Rae hugged Gertrude and Harlan while Carmen hugged Wally.

Ali smothered her dad with kisses as if she knew what he'd been through. Still holding her, he held out an arm toward Rae, who stepped over to hug him and managed to get a brief peck next to Ali's face.

"I'm glad to see you," he said.

She smiled and nodded, kissing him once more and then taking a small step backward. She nodded toward Kate, inviting her forward. Kate hesitated, then moved to him. No air kiss this time. Kate hugged him, kissed his cheek, and put her hand on his face. She whispered, "I'm glad you're safe."

Eric blushed. That was the most intimacy Kate had displayed since before their divorce. "Me, too. Thanks for coming and for bringing Ali." He looked over at Rae, and she was still smiling. She gave him a slight nod, indicating her approval.

He motioned Carmen over, and when she was within reach, he gave her a huge embrace, surprising her with his enthusiasm. "This is your doing, I presume?"

She wrinkled her brow, shook her head, and then looked over at Rae. Carmen leaned forward and whispered in his ear, "She's a keeper. Don't screw this one up."

Out of the corner of his eye, he saw Frank, waiting for the welcome home wave to subside. Still holding Ali, Eric told the group gathered around him, "One minute. I'll be right back, and then we're going to the house."

He walked over to Frank with Ali's arms still draped protectively around his neck.

"Welcome back," Frank said, stubbing his cigarette out on the asphalt.

"Thanks. I'm glad to be back."

Frank looked around, ill at ease. "I was hoping we might have a few minutes to chat. It won't take long, I promise."

Eric looked at him and slowly shook his head. "Not going to happen this afternoon or evening."

Frank started to say something and Eric held up his free hand. "Call me in the morning for breakfast—if you're still in town." He turned and walked back to his family, leaving Frank standing there speechless.

40

Eric was driving down Hemphill, headed into town for breakfast with Frank. Frank had phoned first thing this morning, but Eric didn't return the call until he was walking out the door.

Last night had been one of those evenings Eric wished he could have somehow captured and preserved, to store it away and occasionally take out a spoonful to remove the bitter tastes of reality.

He was amazed at how well Rae and Kate had gotten along. Under different circumstances, they could've been good friends despite their differences. While graciously accepting Rae, Gertrude and Harlan were also glad to see Kate.

Ali had warmed up to Rae even more, no doubt because of her mother's acceptance. Kate had left Ali for the weekend.

When he left this morning, Ali was still asleep, having stayed up way past her usual bedtime. Eric was hoping he'd be home before she awoke, but he wanted to meet with Frank face-to-face. He expected it to be a short meeting.

He'd told Frank to meet him at the Panacea Coffee House, next door to Frog Level Brewing in Waynesville. The coffee was excellent as well as the food, but more importantly, they could sit outside next to the creek for privacy.

Eric turned onto Commerce Street, and was surprised to see the black Town Car parked out front. Frank was always late. Eric could count on one hand the number of times Frank had been on time for anything, including his own wedding.

He parked across the street and walked into the coffee house, looking for Frank. The waitress walked over and told him that his party was probably the man sitting outside. She took his order for a cup of the French roast. Eric thanked her and walked on through, where he saw Frank sitting at a table alone, nursing a cup of steaming coffee.

"Nice place," Frank said as Eric sat opposite him. "Good coffee, too."

The waitress brought Eric's coffee and asked if they were ready to order.

"What's the quiche today?" Eric asked.

"Rosemary, tomato, and bacon."

"Sounds good, I'll take that." Eric looked at his watch. "I've not got a lot of time this morning, Frank."

Frank nodded. "That's fine. I've got to leave soon myself." He looked up at the young girl. "I'll take the lox and bagel plate."

After she had walked away, Frank said, "I think we've got a good chance to recover and get back on track if we can get a Hapeville vaccine out quickly."

Eric took a sip of his coffee and stared at Frank. He shook his head. "What happened, Frank? To us?"

Frank had a puzzled look. "What do you mean?"

"Where did we go wrong? Starting out, we wanted to save the world. We worked insane hours, remember? Living off pizza and beer."

Frank smiled and nodded. "Yeah, those were crazy times. But now we've got a chance to hit it big. We can turn this around."

Eric snorted. "Bullshit. We lost our way."

"No," Frank said defiantly, "No, we haven't. We've still got—"

Eric slammed his fist on the table, sloshing coffee out of both cups. "You put Nicole up to it, didn't you?"

Frank hesitated. "What do you mean? I didn't put her up to anything."

"You're a liar, Frank. Nicole kept a very detailed journal. It's all there." Frank studied his face, looking for deception and finding none.

Eric pressed. "The only people who've read it are Wally and me—so far."

"What are you saying?"

"We'll have a Hapeville vaccine out, within a month."

Frank appeared to relax and take a breath. "That's great news, really good. I knew you'd come through, Eric. You always do."

"Bearant's going to be making it as well as others." Eric grinned as he let the words sink in. The look of confusion returned to Frank's face.

"Bearant . . . they're going to license it?"

Eric nodded. "Oh, yes."

"That's—how did that happen? I just talked with Lewis Griffin yesterday. He didn't mention it."

"You're going to *give* them the license. Them, and anyone else on the planet that wants to manufacture the vaccine."

A look of horror crept across Frank's face as he tried to comprehend what Eric was saying. "What do you mean, 'Give?' We can't do that. That's insane. Why would we give it away? It's worth a fortune."

Eric leaned over the table. "Because it's the right thing to do."

Frank's face flushed with anger. "You've lost your fucking mind. There's no way we're giving—"

The server brought their food and refilled their coffee cups as the two men sat back and eyed each other.

As soon as she walked away, Eric leaned over and said, "You've got two options and only two: One, you give it away and you don't go to jail. Two, the contents of Nicole's journal go to the HHS Inspector General's office, the CDC, and to every major news organization in this country."

Eric sat back and started eating, waiting for Frank's reaction.

Frank stared at him, eyes narrowed. He hadn't touched his food. "You don't understand. I can't tell Chip that we're giving the license away." He snorted. "It doesn't work that way."

Eric looked Frank in the eye. "That might be preferable to telling him that he's the focus of a national *criminal* investigation."

A thin smile crossed Frank's face. "You're bluffing," he said, but the words didn't seem to have the same conviction as before.

"Try me." Eric paused to let the threat sink in.

Frank's smile faded. "You're playing a dangerous game. If I go down, you go down with me." He pointed at Eric. "You were responsible for the lab, and she reported to you."

Now it was Eric's turn to smile. "Nicole's files clearly implicate you. It's all there, every call, every text, notes from every meeting. You're the CEO, so the spotlight will be on you."

Frank crossed his arms. "You're lying."

Eric took another bite, then pushed his plate to the middle of the small table, and stood, glaring down at Frank.

"You've known me for a long time, Frank. Are you sure you want to take that chance? You've got twenty-four hours to give Dr. Terrance Lumpkin at CDC a letter stating that Tera Pharmagenics will grant a license at no charge to any pharmaceutical firm that wants it to manufacture and stockpile an adequate supply of the Hapeville vaccine."

As he turned to leave, he said, "Breakfast is on me. I'll pay the check on the way out."

Back home, he found Rae out on the deck with a cup of coffee. Another mug, empty, was upside down on the table next to the carafe. "Ali still asleep?" He sat and poured himself a cup of coffee.

She nodded. "How did your meeting go?"

Eric had previously told Rae everything, including what he was going to do this morning.

"Okay, I think. We'll soon find out." He told her about his conversation with Frank.

"What do you think he's going to do?" she asked.

Eric shrugged. "I don't know. I thought I knew him, but after I found out about him and Nicole . . ."

"Hopefully, he'll do the right thing. For the wrong reasons, maybe, but the motivation doesn't matter."

He smiled. "True. Either way, I'm out of a job, and you realize that probably means you are, too."

She reached out her hand, which he took and squeezed. "As long as you're in my life, I don't care. We can find other jobs."

Before he could reply, the door opened. In her pajamas, Ali padded out and over to Eric. She crawled up into his lap and put her arms around his neck.

She whispered in a loud voice, "I asked Rae to go to London with us to see the Queen." She turned and smiled at Rae.

A look of trepidation crossed Rae's face as she heard Ali's comment. She shook her head slightly. Clearly, she hadn't been expecting Ali to say anything.

Eric couldn't help but grin. "It's okay," he mouthed silently to Rae so she would relax. He turned and whispered back to Ali in a voice loud enough for Rae to hear, "I think that's a great idea. What did she say?"

Still beaming, Ali said, "She said I had to ask you."

Eric and Ali both looked directly at Rae. "We'd love for you to come with us to London for Christmas. Will you?" Eric asked.

"Please," Ali added.

Rae's eyes glistened as she nodded. "Of course. I'd love to come with you two."

Ali's yelp echoed in the silence.

"Now that we settled that, who wants breakfast?" Eric asked.

Simultaneously, both Ali and Rae answered, "I do."

Ali poked her finger into Eric's chest. "You cook, Daddy."

Epilogue

Six months later.

Eric clicked the touchpad on his computer, closing the teleconference window that was displayed on the large wall screen in his office. It was replaced by Eric's screensaver, a picture of Ali, Rae, and him in front of Buckingham Palace at Christmas.

"That's an awesome pic," Wally said. "London is a fun place, especially at that time of year."

Eric smiled. "Thanks. We had a great time. We even got to see the Queen, waving to the crowd from her balcony. I have to admit, it was pretty exciting."

They had just finished a conference call with Lewis Griffin, Eric's boss, and two other Bearant managers.

"That's great news about Fluzenta—damn, I meant Fenzastin," Wally said. "I've got to stop doing that. Everything turned out okay, didn't it, boss?"

Eric nodded. As soon as the vaccine work was done, Tera Pharmagenics filed for bankruptcy. Bearant acquired the assets, including licenses, for pennies on the dollar. They renamed Fluzenta and submitted a new application, which the FDA had approved. Eric and the entire staff at Panther Creek now worked for Bearant.

Wally looked at his watch. "How 'bout a beer to celebrate—I'll even buy."

Eric smiled and shook his head. "Sorry, not this afternoon. Clark and Jenny are coming over for dinner, so I need to get home on time. Rae wanted me to stop and pick up some wine on my way."

Wally nodded. "Tell everyone I said, 'Hello.' Tell the Princess that I have the new Harry Potter game for her. No more stuffed animals."

Eric laughed. Since she would be moving to Orlando in June, Ali had been spending almost every weekend with him and Rae. Kate had also agreed that Ali could spend summers with Eric in North Carolina.

Wally gathered his files and started to leave. "I'll probably drive down and have a couple."

"Maryann must be working," Eric said. Wally seemed to be spending more time at Frog Level, but only when she was working. Rae had picked up on the chemistry from the beginning. Eric had thought it unlikely, but finally had to agree when he saw the couple holding hands on the street.

Wally blushed. "Have a nice weekend," he said, turned, and walked out.

Eric looked out the window at the same view he'd enjoyed the last ten years. Even though the sign out front now said Bearant Pharmaceutical, the office and the furnishings were the same.

Bearant had taken the lead role in championing the Hapeville vaccine, dubbed Peters Vaccine, after Nicole

Peters and narrowly averted a worldwide epidemic. Eight different pharmaceutical firms produced the vaccine and sold it at cost so that it was affordable for everyone.

Eric, like the handful of people who knew the ugly truth, had mixed feelings about Nicole being portrayed as a heroine. It had been Terry's idea, in deference to Nicole's parents, who had no knowledge of what had really happened.

He looked at the stack of work on the corner of his desk. At his request, Carmen had put it there before she left. It was his "weekend" work, but seemed to be smaller than it once was. He suspected that Carmen was deliberately trimming the pile to protect him. He shook his head, and stuffed it into his backpack.

In the parking lot, he saw that Wally's truck was already gone. The Gremlin had finally died, and Wally now drove a shiny, new pickup truck.

Some things had changed, Eric thought, as he made his way over to the faded red Jeep. Rae, Carmen, and even Wally had been after him to buy a new Jeep, but Eric had decided he would keep it. With new tires, battery, and a top, it was as good as new. It kept him grounded, and that was good.

He opened the passenger door to put his backpack in, and noticed a sheet of paper in the seat. Curious, he picked it up and turned it over.

It was a copy of an article from *The Mercury News,* the daily newspaper published in San Jose, California.

CEO of Pharmaceutical Firm Drowns

Avalon, California – The search for Frank Liles, the former head of now-defunct Tera Pharmagenics, has been suspended this morning, the LA County Sheriff's Office announced.

Liles apparently fell overboard Sunday night while anchored near Catalina Island. When his wife awoke the next morning, he was missing. After the guests and crew searched the boat and were unable to find him, the Coast Guard was notified.

Local authorities investigated the incident and concluded that while the circumstances were suspicious, they had no choice but to classify it as an accidental drowning.

His body has not been recovered.

Holding the article in his hand, Eric looked around the parking lot, wondering who had left this. No cars were parked nearby, and he saw no one.

He turned around to look behind him, and fifteen yards away stood a man, staring at him. He was standing by the open door of a nondescript silver sedan.

Something about him seemed familiar, but Eric couldn't place him.

The man was medium height with short brown hair, and appeared to be in his thirties. He seemed to be in fit physical condition with a military-like posture. As Eric studied his face, the man smiled and waved.

The gesture completed the connection, and a chill ran down Eric's spine. That was the man Eric had seen at his house, when he and Ali were out on the deck.

Eric started toward him, but the man got in the car and drove off.

Clutching the article, Eric walked back to the Jeep, where he stood and reread it. When he finished, he shook his head and looked out at the mountains. He was sorry to hear about Frank.

He had not talked to him since that morning in the coffee house. The day after, Frank had sent a letter to Terry as requested, granting unrestricted licensing rights to the Hapeville vaccine.

Frank had previously told Eric that West Coast Capital had liquidated their holdings in LeConte Pet Products, which was true. What Eric didn't know at the time was that Chip Miller also owned a sizeable personal interest in Bearant. Miller was now on the board of Bearant. Whether Frank knew or not, no one would ever know.

Eric crumpled the article, threw it in the trashcan, and got into his Jeep.

Message received and understood. As far as he was concerned, the departed would rest in peace.

Acknowledgments

I am forever indebted to countless others for their help and generosity in my writing journey.

Clark Williams and Frog Level Brewing are real. I encourage you to visit if you're in Waynesville, NC. I am honored to call Clark a friend, and deeply appreciate his years of service, his friendship, and his willingness to share his memories with me.

Special thanks to the following people for taking the time to read my manuscript and offer much-needed advice: Otis Scarbary, Mary Jo Burkhalter Persons, Jay Holmes, Cindy Deane, Clara Blanquet, Fred Blanquet, Barry McIntosh, and Donna Jennings. You guys are the best.

I am fortunate to have Heather Whitaker as an editor and good friend. She continues to help me grow as a writer.

Thanks to Kieran Sultan, M.D. for help with pathology questions. I appreciate Karl Steele and Scott Cherry for answering my questions on law enforcement.

Carl Graves did it again—another amazing cover. Thanks to Phil & Kristen Photography for the picture on the back.

As always, any mistakes that remain are mine.

Last, thanks to my wife, June, for supporting me and having faith in my writing. I couldn't do it without you.

27484587R00224

Made in the USA
Lexington, KY
05 January 2019